Reality Prism: A Raven Novel

by

Paul E. Vallely Major General, US Army (Ret)

and

John D. Trudel

Praise For This Book

"Reality Prism: A Raven Thriller is a must read for Americans and for all who love freedom. The President of Egypt, General El-Sisi, asked General Vallely why the US cut off military aid to Egypt after the second Revolution. Why did America make its national decisions looking through a 'Political Prism,' versus seeking solutions by looking through a 'Reality Prism?'

"Indeed. We have witnessed destructive actions by our political and military leaders and suffered the tragic consequences. We are a nation in deep decline.

"Orwell was right. Communication and media have massive influence in an age of Mind War, Biowarfare, Big Tech censorship, Cancel Culture, and false flag deceptions. We face external and internal threats that drive to dismantle America as we have known it. We are less free than we were before 1776. Some 30–40% of our population are virtual zombies, locked down, isolated, and fearful. Those who dare speak out are dehumanized. "We the People" are divided as never before.

"Reality Prism is a memoir, a predictive thriller, a recent history of events, a tour through 21st Century geopolitics, and an **Endgame**. It overviews the ripping apart of our Constitutional Republic by a pack of enemies, traitors, and deep state officials (both parties) who now serve themselves, not those who elected them. It highlights the 'Awakening of America,' The Global Shadow Government, and how we must stand united.

"Chapters are **actionable**. They suggest what we can and must do to regain our **freedom, prosperity**, and **safety**. To take America back: **Read this book!**"

THOMAS G MCINERNEY, LT. GEN. USAF RET.

FORMER ASST VICE CHIEF OF STAFF, USAF. COAUTHOR OF ENDGAME, THE BLUEPRINT FOR THE WAR ON TERROR, AND NUMEROUS OP EDS IN WASH POST, NY TIMES, WSJ, WASH TIMES, AS WELL AS FOX NEWS, AND NUMEROUS RADIO SHOWS NATIONALLY.

***

"One of the tactics an enemy of freedom deploys is to persuade free people that 'nothing can be done about it.' Whatever the assault upon our freedoms might be, if we can be made to succumb to fear, doubt, and hatred, we can be controlled and ultimately vanquished. The truth, though, is that something **can** always be done about it—**if** one can squarely face the **truth** of the situation, no matter how frightening, implausible, and threatening it may seem.

"*Reality Prism: A Raven Thriller* provides us the opportunity to see current global events as they are, not as the 'mind magicians' would have us believe. The authors' life experiences and courage to face off with evil in the real world have given them a unique ability to help us see today's threats through a different prism.

"Providing more than a shift in perspective, this book offers workable ideas and actions we can take to save and secure this great Republic. This is an important book for all freedom-loving Americans."

Lee Kessler, Actress,
Author of *White King and The Seat at the Table*

***

"Reality Prism: A Raven Thriller is a kaleidoscope of verifiable facts presented with certainty as well as woven into the deep shadowy fictional world of Raven operations. Ultimately, each reader must choose to be actionable for Liberty or to become a victim of the coming chaos.

"Looking forward to the book, and then having you and Paul on the program."

Tom Niewulis, **Samuel Adams Returns**,
http://samueladamsreturns.net

***

"The genesis of the *Reality Prism* is outlined in the preface of the book. There was an epiphany during MG Vallely's delegation trip to Egypt. The President of Egypt, General El-Sisi, posed a question to General Vallely as to why the US cut off military aide to Egypt after the second Revolution. He could not understand why America always seemed to make its national decisions looking through a 'Political Prism' versus looking and seeking solutions by looking through a 'Reality Prism.'

"Reality Prism is a memoir, a predictive thriller, a recent history of events, a tour of 21st Century geopolitics, and an **Endgame**. It overviews the ripping apart of America's Constitutional Republic by a pack of enemies, traitors, and deep state officials (both parties) who serve themselves, not those who elected them. The authors showcase the 'Awakening of America,' The Global Shadow Government, and how citizens must stand united. *Ca été un réel plaisir de vous lire mon Général."*

Thierry Laurent Pellet, French Entrepreneur

"**Reality Prism** is a memoir, a predictive thriller, and a history of recent events. It provides a tour through 21st Century geopolitics. In a fascinating discussion, **Reality Prism** overviews the ripping apart of our constitutional Republic by enemies foreign and domestic.

"The Global Shadow Government is exposed. The authors demonstrate the nexus of Global antagonists challenging nation states throughout the world, while amassing great wealth. The problem that global elitists pose to national sovereignty is revealed, while simultaneously addressing the Global Shadow Government and how we must respond to the challenge.

"The danger posed by Deep State operatives is assessed. The authors provide multiple strategies to rid the administrative state of the burden of internal enemies sequestered within the government structure. The traitors within the GOP who betrayed President Trump throughout his tenure in office are identified.

"Multiple strategies to isolate and remove the threats are presented. The authors show the way to achieve a united stand for a national strategy that includes an Endgame that draws upon the latent strengths of our rich heritage and our diverse society. Finally, the authors highlight the 'Awakening of America.' It is a riveting read that shows the way to a more workable national strategy that can achieve greater prosperity and security in the Twenty-first Century."

Colonel Andrew P. O'Meara, Jr., US Army (Ret.)

"**Reality Prism** is a next-level Raven spy thriller. I didn't think a John D. Trudel novel could get any more 'real,' but the combo of the consummate storyteller and General Paul Vallely's own experiences is breathtaking. It's a thrill-ride!"

Victoria Taft, Host of the Adult in the Room Podcast; writer, PJ Media; Radio Host.

Contents

DEDICATION

I dedicate this book, the *Reality Prism* to my family: my always loyal and loving wife, Muffin, my precious daughter and son-in-law, Dana and Eric Covington, our dearest son, Scott Paul Vallely (deceased) and wonderful, talented, grandson, Caleb and my cherished sister, Jewell Willis.

Paul E. Vallely

I dedicate *Reality Prism* to my supportive, honest wife, Pat. She is kind, loving, and without her, this book would not have happened. And to Captain Langford C. Metzger, USAF (deceased), a loyal friend and skilled warrior.

John D. Trudel

A Road Map for Readers
Reality Prism, the book.

Despite a Revolution, a Civil War, a Great Depression, Two World Wars, and a Cold War with nukes, America has never faced the level of threat, chaos, propaganda, and fear we've suffered recently. The techniques used include those Hitler used to collapse the Weimar Republic into Nazi Germany (National Socialists), commit mass genocide, and almost take over the world.

We now suffer **Mind War, Biowarfare,** and other stresses to reduce our population, cripple our military, and destroy our ability to think and function. Robert Malone MD explains **Mass Formation Psychosis**, and how we, as a society, can possibly get out of it.

https://media.gab.com/system/media_attachments/files/094/657/077/origina l/9e187db6670bb47b.mp4

Reality Prism discusses what is happening to destroy our Western Civilization, who is doing it, and what **We the People** can do to prevent a new **Dark Age**. We use a mix of predictive fiction and non-fiction to get the message across. Here is a key to make it easier for readers:

Chapters without a key are for your general reading, the normal narrative.

Threat These chapters discuss the **threats** we face. Comprehensive and terrifying, but nonetheless true. The end of life as we know it. **The New World Order. The Great Reset.** Fake News hides such threats.

In an age of **Mind War**, coming horrors are being dismissed as conspiracy theories. You are being kept in fear and diverted by other threats. When you understand what is intended, and from leaders you have trusted, it can be upsetting. A typical comment, "It was so extreme, depressing, and true...."

Action These chapters are **actionable**. They suggest what we can and must do to regain our **freedom, prosperity**, and **safety**. To take America back.

Heroic Fiction These chapters are **heroic fiction** of the type that is now being erased and censored, along with our culture. The Western Hero's Journey is as old as **Beowulf** and as new as **Star Wars**. From 1776 to the days of Tom Clancy, it was a huge category of fiction. No longer. Such tales are now censored.

Amazon admits to Chinese agents inside the company approving books. It is brutal in Hollywood, with remakes of major movies like *Red Dawn* and *Top Gun* canceled. Some seek to make normal Americans the threat. Every mechanism of government is being weaponized against political opponents.

"White supremacist terrorism is the deadliest threat to the United States."

President Joe Biden

For more see https://blog.johntrudel.com/burning-books-in-cyberspace-orwell-lives/

Preface

by

Major General Paul E. Vallely

US Army (Ret)

Egypt has always inspired me with its history. The pyramids, the sphinxes, its vast deserts, and biblical references are overwhelming. Over the years, Egypt has been a close ally of the United States, militarily and economically. On September 11, 2001, Bin Laden and Al Qaeda terrorists attacked America by suicide airplane attacks on the Twin Towers in New York, the Pentagon, and Shanksville, Pennsylvania, that changed the world. One should also remember a second attack that took place on 9/11, in 2012 on the other side of the world in Benghazi, Libya, where we lost four brave Americans. This was followed by the Arab Spring that continued to destabilize the Middle East region. President George W. Bush ordered American Forces to invade Iraq in March 2003 based on the threat of WMD (weapons of mass destruction) possessed by Iraq. None were found as they were shipped (assisted by Russian Spetsnaz) to storage fields in Syria prior to the invasion. Reported terrorists' training centers were the other reason President Bush used for attacking Iraq. In fact, Iraq was never a threat to the United States and was an unnecessary war. This action set the Middle East on fire!

A tidal wave of consequences hit Egypt in February 2011, when President Hosni Mubarak was removed in what was called "the First Revolution." In the chaos, the Muslim Brotherhood, led by Mohamed Morsi, took power. Morsi's plan was to move Egypt to an Islamic State because it was primarily a Muslim nation. In fact, Egypt had been a tolerant nation of other religions. Mubarak was a despot and dictator, and Morsi was even worse—a despot, zealot, and radical Islamist. Much of the younger and older generations in Egypt turned their backs on Morsi and the "Brotherhood."

There were seven months of protests against Morsi and the Muslim Brotherhood in 2013, now termed "the biggest mass protests in Egypt's history." Complaints included authoritarianism and the radical Islamist agenda that ignored secular opposition and the rule of law. Specifically, Morsi took over the state's judicial system and "temporarily" suspended the Constitution.

Protests peaked in June 2013, and Morsi was removed from office on July 3, 2013. This was called "the Second Revolution." Some call it a coup. **It was not a coup**! It was an angry and distrustful population rising up and demanding justice, which then was supported by the rank and file of the Egyptian Military.

An interim government was appointed, followed by continuing violent clashes between Morsi supporters and security forces, culminating in the Rabaa massacre. The Obama administration, Congress, and "Fake News" sided with Morsi, to the point where military and other foreign aid to Egypt was suspended. In early 2014, General El-Sisi, Egypt's Minister of Defense, retired from his military career, and announced he would run as a candidate for president. He won with 97 percent of the vote. This series of events touched my life in an incredibly positive way.

***

It was late September, an early fall in Montana in 2013. I received a call to inquire if I would co-chair a non-government (NGO) delegation to Cairo, Egypt. The purpose was to meet the head of the Egyptian Armed

Forces and other groups involved with the protests and removal of the Muslim Brotherhood and President Morsi (the Second Revolution). After serious thought, I accepted and was then briefed in detail on the mission of the delegation. We rendezvoused in Washington, DC, with the delegation team and departed for Cairo on October 5, 2013.

The Obama government was supporting Morsi and his Muslim Brotherhood. It rejected the military control of the Egyptian government and the removing and jailing of Morsi. Our Congress passed legislation to block foreign and military aid to the newly formed government. This upset the Egyptian government and the military generals, who were dealing with almost insurmountable challenges to restore order and recover a devastated economy. The leadership threatened to align itself (again) with the Russians for the aid that was being denied by the US government.

These events brought to Egypt a leader named Fattah Saeed Hussein Khalil El-Sisi. First Egyptian Revolution (2011), Mohamed Morsi, was elected to the Egyptian presidency. El-Sisi was appointed Minister of Defense by President Morsi on August 12, 2012.

In October 2013, I co-chaired a US delegation to meet with General El-Sisi, the Commander-in-Chief of the Armed Forces, who later became President of Egypt. The delegation mission was to assure General El-Sisi that the American people solidly supported the removal of the Muslim Brotherhood and President Morsi after this second revolution. A vast majority (young and old) of the Egyptian people supported the removal of Morsi by El-Sisi.

Our US delegates were welcomed by El-Sisi and his staff of twelve generals. I had the respect of the Egyptian high staff, as many were fellow graduates of the Army War College in Carlisle, Pennsylvania. I was a bit apprehensive as I thought that I might be held in disdain and perceived as a supporter of US actions against Egypt. (The thought went through my mind: *Maybe they believed I was an Obama apostle and one of his generals?* Not the case!) General El-Sisi and I bonded, as I did with his staff. There was mutual respect as fellow graduates of the Army War College.

As our meeting progressed, it was apparent that the staff generals were terribly angry. They were incensed that after forty-five years of being good allies, the US Congress would stop aid to Egypt. I tried my best to explain that while Obama supported the Muslim Brotherhood and Morsi, most Americans did not support Obama's action. It was widely known that Obama was sympathetic to Islam and the Brotherhood's reign. Obama famously said in his book that he would "Stand with the Muslims."

After a lengthy discussion, General El-Sisi turned to me and asked, "Why does America always seem to make its decisions looking through a *Political Prism* rather than through a *Reality Prism?*" Suddenly, I had an epiphany! I related to the history of Egypt, the pyramids as a symbol, and how they appeared as a prism as seen on our dollar bills.

It seems apparent that US politicians, post-Cold War and World War II, have rarely looked through a *Reality Prism*. They skewed their analysis and perceptions to gain personal political advantage. El-Sisi knew from his military experience that the important decisions must be made based on the reality of the enemies' intentions, capabilities, and the happenings on the battlefield.

The political battlefield is much the same in its analysis. As we view the refraction of light through a prism, we visualize the distortion of reality into facets of deceit and deception, **OR** into facets of truth and survival.

The US Dollar Bill

The all-seeing eye over the unfinished pyramid on

the dollar bill is supposed to portray the United States as a land continuously growing and far from finished, although some believe it indicates a connection to the Illuminati secret society.

7

Hidden Symbolism of the Dollar

There are clear **masonic symbols (like the pyramids)** hidden within the dollar bill. Together they tell of the creation of a New World Order based on the slavery of the peoples with the power elite at the control.

Annuit Coeptis

"Providence favors our undertakings"
Could our undertakings be "truth," "reality," or false premises or promises?

***

General El-Sisi went on to explain why he and his fellow staff generals (listening intently) had to make decisions regarding Egypt and the Middle East by looking through a *Reality Prism*. The room was filled with tension between our delegation and his generals, who felt betrayed.

El-Sisi elaborated and stated his responsibility was to secure, stabilize, and protect Egypt and its citizens. His mission required the control and security of the Sinai Desert, the Suez Canal, and Egyptian borders with a troubled and dangerous Libya to the west and Sudan to the south, too. He stated emotionally and emphatically that he must deal daily with *reality* and that making politically convenient decisions would be the destruction of Egypt. My takeaway from that discussion with El-Sisi was that senior responsible leaders must analyze issues based on the *real* facts and situations, not the ambiguity of political analysis.

In times of impending major crisis, the gap between reality and politics can become enormous. Contrast, for example, the distance between Neville Chamberlain and Winston Churchill in early 1940 with Hitler ascendent. Ponder the consequences, had Chamberlain's "peace in our time" viewpoint prevailed. One will often come to vastly different conclusions when looking through a *Reality Prism* of issues and situations, versus a prism of political analysis. I started to connect in a philosophical way with the comparisons of the pyramids and the prisms!

After our extended meetings and briefings with the Egyptian Joint Staff, we were scheduled to meet with other key groups. Over the next three days, we were introduced to and briefed by members of the youth movement, the labor unions, a major women's group regarding women's rights in Egypt, the Egyptian Chamber of Commerce, and a round of tours to the pyramids, Giza, and a special meeting with the Pope of the Coptic Church at his Giza desert compound.

It was enlightening to visit with the Pope to discuss and understand the persecution of the Copts under the Muslim Brotherhood. Due to misunderstandings regarding their theology and political allegiances, Coptic Christians have been persecuted for centuries. Here is what you need to know about this religious minority: The Coptic Orthodox Church split away from the broader Christian community in AD 451 due to differing beliefs about the nature of Christ.

Egyptian Coptic ancestry maintains a discrete ethnic identity from Muslim Egyptians, commonly renouncing an Arab identity. Genetically, Copts are a distinct population, though more nearly related to the Muslims of Egypt than to any other people. Like other Egyptians, Copts are a diverse community, with noteworthy genetic, ethnic, and cultural differences continuing between Copts from Lower and Upper Egypt.

Coptic Church

Meeting with Coptic Pope Tawadros II

I learned that over one hundred Coptic churches had been burned and destroyed by the fanatics of the Muslim Brotherhood. General El-Sisi, a Muslim himself, helped restore order to the Copts and authorized finances to rebuild churches. Mine was a spiritual visit with the Pope, but one that gave me a better understanding of the religious dynamics existing in Egypt.

Our second evening included a dinner with General El-Sisi and his staff at the exclusive, regal Egyptian Officers Club in Cairo. We had cemented mutual trust and friendship. We were able to hold on to hope that the American people in the end would be with the Egyptian people, despite Obama's personal religious and political views.

Over the next two days, we met with a group of some fifteen members of the youth movement. They explained their distaste for the Muslim Brotherhood, Morsi, and how Islam had controlled the lives of Egyptian people under Islamic law and traditions. I was impressed with their passion for freedom and democracy. The same held true for a meeting at the downtown Marriott Hotel with members of several women's groups. They were delighted to meet with our delegation and discuss the future of women in the Egyptian society from academics to business.

The next morning was filled with briefings from the head of Egyptian Intelligence Services and other members of the new cabinet. The briefings focused on regional threats to Egypt, from the Sanai to Egypt's western border with Libya and the southern border with Sudan. The Muslim Brotherhood still had serious and dangerous groups scattered throughout the country.

We had a ceremonial farewell from General El-Sisi and his staff at his headquarters. Many thanks were extended to our hosts. An epiphany of *Reality*!

End

INTERLUDE

The Great Reset, planned for decades, has arrived. Civilization and the world are under more stress than at any time since the fall of Rome. Freedom in America is the lynchpin, the last bastion. We are under attack from Mind War, bioweapons, and most of our centers of power are compromised.

"Fear is the mind killer." Americans are more fearful than we were during WW II and the Cold War. As Mark Levin said, "We are now less free than we were before the American Revolution."

This book, by a recognized military expert and an award-winning thriller novelist, attempts to speak to this in a form that will appeal to readers, a mix of fiction and non-fiction. Our goal is to inform, to cut through the noise, and to inspire action.

From *Beowulf* to *Star Wars*, the hero's journey has been a key part of Western Culture. Tales of George Washington and his ragtag army standing firm against the greatest military in the world inspire us. So do the tales of Churchill and the Britain that stood firm against Hitler, Lincoln freeing the slaves, and thousands of tales of heroes defending freedom from tyranny against the odds.

We thought that if we framed key parts of our message as a novel—an interesting tale of good vs. evil, with Raven and his small team trying to sort things out and survive, with readers wanting them to prevail, some good things might happen:

- Greater potential readership.

- More appealing to the common American, severely burned out by mind-numbing arguments and counter arguments while locked in his house, losing free speech, and the right to assemble.
- The more the radical left raged and censored, the more attention our book would get.
- The vast numbers opposed to us, and their lists of credentials, would be less relevant.
- Some on our side could defend our novel as a great read, without going down into the weeds with their own arguments.
- And, by being engaged, our readers could respond to false attacks while rooting for Raven.

Raven lives. **So does America**.

***

The deliberations of the Constitutional Convention of 1787 were held in strict secrecy. Consequently, anxious citizens gathered outside Independence Hall when the proceedings ended to learn what had been produced behind closed doors. The answer was provided immediately. A **Mrs. Powel** of Philadelphia asked **Benjamin Franklin, "Well, Doctor, what have we got, a republic or a monarchy?"** With no hesitation whatsoever, Franklin responded, **"A republic, if you can keep it."**

Book One – Non-Fiction
Chapter One — The Awakening

A wakening is the act of starting to understand something, usually something major, that leads to a new and better understanding of events. In 1776, Americans awoke to the fact that to stay free and prosper, they must separate their fortunes from England.

In the 21st century, America slept as Marxism (disguised as Progressive Socialism), Globalism, the rise of unaccountable ruling elites, and an ascendant Communist China were dismantling our great country, not by direct warfare, but from within. It was like a beautiful building being destroyed from within by destructive armies of termites. There was no Pearl Harbor, no major issue that divided us like the Civil War, and no major foreign war or power that openly threatened us militarily. China's **3 Warfares Doctrine** underpins the Chinese Communist Party's (CCP) plan to instead conquer the free world without firing a shot. [So far, it is working.]

From the time our Constitution was framed, Americans argued intensely, but honestly. It was one of our strengths. Quite often, conflicting groups would agree on better solutions than what either side advocated. Coming together through honest discussion was the American way.

No, it did not always work. We had a Civil War in **1860** that almost destroyed us. The Democrats made it all about race. They still do, even after the **1964 Civil Rights Act,** which the Democrats, the Civil War's slave owners, opposed. The issues that led to that war were broader. True, slavery was a major issue, and most slaves in the South were Black, but race did not spark the war.

Democrats **owned** slaves and Republicans **freed** them, but even Lincoln (R) did not free the slaves in the South until 1863. Lyndon Johnson's Great Society (D), also known as the "War on Poverty," made Black people dependent, destroyed Black families, and trapped them in crime-ridden, filthy cities with failed schools. This is the new form of slavery: "**The Great Reset**" plans to take it worldwide.

As one researcher noted, "1619 may be more insidious than instructive." The 1619 "from-this-point-forward" and "in-this-place" narrative arc silences the memory of the more than **500,000** African men, women, and children who had **already crossed** the Atlantic.

The 1619 narrative being used to indoctrinate our children has little to do with **America**. It denotes when 20–30 enslaved **Africans** captured by the **English** privateer ship *White Lion* from the **Spanish** slave ship *San Juan Bautista* were dropped off (traded for supplies) in Virginia. They were the first recorded Africans to arrive in England's mainland American colonies.

Honest debate is today being replaced by demonization. Radical left professors are requiring students to turn in recordings (for grades!) of them silencing opponents by accusing them of racism (or worse). Federal Agencies are now targeting (as terrorists!) soccer moms who protest Critical Race Theory at local school board meetings.

Perhaps the most frightening thing is that the radical left plans to make the **Fake** January 6th "insurrection" into their lifeline for the 2022 elections. With their falling polls and disastrous policies, the Democrats' best hope for keeping power is to somehow disqualify their political opponents from being legitimate candidates. This is discussed in a later chapter.

For now, it is sufficient to mention the **National Terrorism Advisory System Bulletin** that was issued with little notice on February 07, 2020. Unmentioned in Fake News is that the **main** "Key Factor" contributing to the **"current heightened threat environment"** is **free speech itself**. The exercise of our sacred First Amendment rights is now an act of terrorism.

Key factor #1 of the bulletin lists as its **first** sub-item: *"The proliferation of false or misleading narratives which sow discord or undermine trust in US Government intuitions."* **In short, if you criticize or disagree with the government (or Big Tech social media, or Fake News) you are officially a domestic terrorist.** This is right out of Stalin's Russia and the NKVD, best known for "The Great Purge." Effectively, our government agencies are now weaponized against political opponents.

https://www.dhs.gov/ntas/advisory/national-terrorism-advisory-system-bulletin-february-07-2022

Also, discrimination, long illegal in America, is now **advocated** **if it is discrimination against Whites**. A parent complained at a school board meeting about his daughter being raped in the girls' restroom by a sexual deviant. The parent was arrested. The pervert student was not charged. He was instead transferred to another school, where he became a repeat offender. At present, the announced criteria for filling a vacant seat on the Supreme Court seems to be a Black vagina, with support from both parties.

Such cases signal a shift from "equal justice" to "social justice." They move America from exceptionalism to brutal tribalism. From being a proud First World Country to being a squalid banana republic.

Such policies are far removed from America's traditional "equality under the law," and "innocent until proven guilty." America was always multiethnic, but of a common culture. Our own unique culture. The motto **E Pluribus Unum**, "Out of Many, One," the literal Latin proposed by the First Continental Congress in 1782, summed it up perfectly.

There were countless benefits: equality under the law, freedom of religion, strong families, a striving for exceptionalism, freedom, and the pursuit of happiness. We were safe. We were prosperous. Life was good. We were living "The American Dream," and the entire world knew it.

Unfortunately, we had powerful enemies who knew our strengths and weaknesses. Mostly forgotten now is the Cold War (1945–1990), a time when two generations lived in fear, a time of fallout shelters, hoarding food, and **Doctor Strangelove**.

Some military leaders (e.g., Patton and MacArthur), seeing Communism as the enemy and deeming America more powerful, wanted to end the threat. That was something that America's public and political leadership would not accept. Neither side wanted to start a war that might go nuclear. Geopolitical policy became MAD, Mutually Assured Destruction. It sounded mad indeed, but it worked for a time.

It worked only because we had seasoned leadership and a bi-polar world. Both sides knew the Russians would never risk their steady gains by overstepping. Proxy wars were tolerated, but both sides worked to avoid direct confrontation and restrain allies. With a few exceptions (USS Pueblo, U2) both kept an unwritten agreement to not kill spies or interfere with mutual surveillance.

During the Korean War, especially after China escalated, both sides pretended the UN could prevent or end conflicts. It never has, of course, so, after Cuba, a Red Telephone hotline was added between the White House and the Kremlin to avoid mistakes.

Eisenhower was a seasoned, trusted, wartime leader, but even he warned us strongly of a dangerous "Military Industrial Complex." People around the world were terrified. What would happen when ambitious, inexperienced politicians inevitably took over? One mistake could turn the world into a cinder.

Along came John Kennedy, who wanted "softer" options. His policy was "Measured Response." If Communists attacked, we would respond with the same level of force and hold the stalemate. The Russians, expert chess players, liked that. So did China. Hence, Vietnam, a land war in Asia.

Kennedy was backing away from that policy before he was assassinated, but the die was cast. No more "Cold War," but instead a period of "pretend peace," constant limited war, insurgency, and bloodshed.

In America, we suffered leftist incited rioting, burning, and spitting on our soldiers sent to fight America's far-off enemies. Bill Ayers, a mentor to Obama, bombed the Pentagon, and later bragged about it. John Kerry, as a serving Navy Reserve officer, met with the North Vietnamese in Paris during the Vietnam "Peace Talks." Neither was ever held accountable.

Secretary of Defense McNamara, an accountant, kept a tally of body counts on the nightly news to prove we were winning. Communists could not care less. Life was cheap. The Tet Offensive was a military disaster for N. Vietnam (massive casualties and no regional capitols held), but, thanks to Walter Cronkite (then highly trusted) who told the public we had lost badly, it was a major media victory for the left.

Three years **after** the Vietnam peace treaty was signed ending the war, Democrats (including Joe Biden) in Congress broke it by cutting off military aid. America abandoned South Vietnam, the embassy fell, and "the Killing Fields" followed. Over a million people died.

Much later, Reagan finally ended the Cold War, the Berlin Wall came down, and we won. The USSR dissolved. As one intel official put it, the military mission shifted from slaying dragons, something we had mastered, to killing nests of snakes, foreign and domestic. A new threat. One that is close and deadly.

And so it is that our enemies, foreign and domestic, now work to destroy America by exploiting our freedom and tolerance, by dividing us into polarized groups. They have worked at this not for years, but for decades. Even China, now our greatest foreign threat, meticulously avoids nuclear threats. It is winning by a mix of biowarfare and 4th Generation Mind War, with China's bioweapons funded by US taxpayers.

When the masks went on for COVID-19, they came off for the planned destruction of America. Now, after a stolen election, we get to choose between **Freedom and Tyranny**. Some in power, including Democrats, Fake News, Big Tech, Big Pharma, the Washington Swamp, unaccountable bureaucracies, the FBI, and the CIA, may prefer Tyranny. *Total control may keep them in power.*

Minor changes can have massive impact. Most think the Department of Education has been around forever. No. The story of the DOE started in 1867 under Andrew Johnson, but only to collect statistics on education. These were excellent, until 1979, when Jimmy Carter made a federal takeover of education. The Department of Education is now a cabinet position, and our schools are failing.

K-12 education has slipped to where one can no longer find credible US government data. According to a **Business Insider** report in 2018, the United States ranked 38th in math scores and 24th in science, falling from top excellence, to not even being in the top twenty. Some states (e.g., Oregon) no longer require proficiency in math, reading, or science for high school graduation.

Home schooling and charter schools, fiercely resisted by bureaucrats and teachers' unions, are in demand. Black people trapped in the inner cities are desperate for better schools and more law enforcement but are getting the reverse. Seventy percent of Black people favor vouchers for education.

Worse yet is that schools, including universities, have shifted from teaching "how to learn" to "what to learn," which includes indoctrination about "Critical Race Theory" and revisionist history, like "The 1619 Project."

Parents who dare object (at local school board meetings!) are threatened with being targeted by the FBI as **terrorists** under **the Patriot Act**. Marxists, well-funded and now in power, say children belong to the State [Hillary's "It takes a village to raise a child."]. Parents are enraged.

Free speech is banned on college campuses. That is now spreading to all schools and other venues. Who dares walk through a large city wearing a MAGA hat? It is deemed a "hate crime."

Beyond that, the DC bureaucracies have grown exponentially, and are now fully unaccountable. They develop more pages of rules every year than does Congress. You cannot fire them and the rules they pass have the power of law. *Biden's damaging "vaccine mandate" was justified by a **press release**!*

You can go to prison for breaking some "law" that was never passed by any elected, accountable official. In cases like Biden's "Vaccine Mandate" (which does not even exist), a press release was deemed sufficient to justify mass firings, and even an odd speech by Biden himself that demonized healthy, law-abiding Americans (including health care workers and the military) who declined to take problematic experimental vaccines. He even accused them of destroying the health care system and selfishly taking up hospital space.

Such a situation would have been unimaginable to America's founders. There are many other examples.

**

The Democratic Party (and key Republicans) decided to move swiftly to the left long before the 2020 election brought about the ousting of their enemy, Donald J. Trump, and the election of Joe Biden as America's new leader. They hated Trump, who was demonized, dehumanized, and attacked 24/7, basically for no reason, and despite his producing excellent results for America. *"Orange Man bad!"*

The Peoples' Republic of China (PRC) made a declaration of Peoples' War against the USA in retaliation for Trump's policies that embarrassed the PRC and revealed their dishonest trade policy. The declaration was followed by biological warfare attacks employing the COVID-19 virus. These aggressive operations were accompanied by Psyops and cyber-warfare to steal the 2020 elections. The CCP bribed the Biden family, effectively making the POTUS himself an agent of the CCP. Biden and others then collaborated with Communist China to harness American policy and operations to PRC interests, which explains the surrender of Afghanistan.

We have learned from email traffic released by whistleblowers that the Democrats collaborated with the CCP to develop the Wuhan virus, or COVID-19. It is the same virus that has been used by the CCP to wage biological warfare against the USA. The attacks have inflicted great harm and constitute a genocidal war crime that has morphed into a worldwide pandemic.

Evidence obtained by Project Veritas exposed the Biden administration's use of the COVID-19 pandemic for domestic political purposes, which has since been admitted publicly. The messages below reveal evidence of the use of the COVID-19 virus to advance the domestic policy of the Democrats. There is hard evidence that has exposed the conspiracy to use the pandemic for political purposes. Connecting the dots with the Project Veritas evidence, we see the logic that drives the Biden COVID-19 narrative.

- The winning strategy for defeating Trump in the 2020 election hinged on stealing the vote using mail-in ballots, rigged voting machines, Zuckerbucks, and various criminal acts.
- Massive absentee balloting was essential in amassing sufficient fraudulent ballots to overturn the Trump landslide that resulted in 74,000,000 votes for Trump.
- The pandemic supplied the justification for massive mail-in voting.
- The Democrats must maintain the pandemic conditions that produced the flood of mail-in and absentee ballots to deliver Democrat victories in subsequent elections.
- The pandemic lockdowns must continue through November 2022, if not November 2024, to allow the Democrats to flood the ballot boxes with millions of fraudulent ballots.
- Forensic audits of Trump's 2020 election, or future elections, must not be allowed to change the results.
- Continued use of easily tampered voting machines (e.g., Dominion) must continue.

The continuation of the pandemic scare demands a continued high death rate. Thus, therapeutics are forbidden to treat the virus. HCQ and Ivermectin are not allowed. The use of the experimental vaccines that have taken the lives of thousands of Americans are necessary to preserve the fiction that the Biden administration is doing all in its power to control the pandemic. Thus, shocking news about the harmful effects of the vaccines must be concealed by not reporting the actual cause of death. Death <u>with</u> COVID-19 is **different from** death <u>from</u> COVID-19. Gunshot victims or those hit by trucks are **not** COVID-19 deaths.

Recent data shows vaccines may be **increasing** the rate of infections as vaccine effectiveness collapses. This, coupled with intense campaigns to demonize "vaccine resistance" and force compliance, have moved America into an age of tyranny. It has also raised concerns about the population control (formerly called eugenics) long advocated by Bill Gates and others. Biden, with vaccine mandates, had many more COVID-19 deaths in 2021 than Trump did without vaccines in 2020.

Other than some legendary disasters (e.g., the Tuskegee Experiment that injected Black people with syphilis for decades), taking medication in America has always been a private matter between individuals and their doctors. "We've abandoned free choice to bureaucratic control." *Mark Levin recently said we are now less free than we were before the American Revolution.*

The following Democrat strategy to justify COVID-19 lockdown and win the elections has emerged:

- Conceal the harmful effects of the vaccines and show the success of Biden's strategy using vaccine mandates.
- Deny the use of therapeutics (Ivermectin and HCQ) that save lives and reduce the severity of the virus.

- Deny the true cause of death to present the optics of the worst possible pandemic scare.
- Maintain the highest COVID-19 death rate sustainable.
- Demand the continued use of masks and social distancing, as well as the vaccine mandate and lockdowns.
- Deny voters the right to vote in person to justify the mail-in voting requirement.
- Maintain the pandemic lockdown through the elections. [Or forever, for control.]
- Maintain control of the print and broadcast media. Replace news with propaganda.
- Censor free speech on social media.

The Communist Manifesto outlines the beliefs of the Communists and the program of the Communist League, a worker's party. The Communists were concerned about social and political inequality—conditions that still exist today—and via the manifesto, share their concerns and proposed solutions. This is the focus of the Democrats now in power.

Outcomes are now set by race, gender, or political whim. This polarizing policy has divided America and resulted in violent criminals being released and police departments being defunded, driving an upward spike in murder rates, and ignoring groups like Antifa and Black Lives Matter burning cities and looting businesses. **Anarcho-tyranny** must replace America's traditional equal opportunity and equal justice under the law.

America's original focus on faith and logic was tied to our greatness, as the foundation of a rational God became core for a linear society, seeking fairness and prosperity. But now liberals embrace every variety of contradiction, neuro-sickness, and hypocrisy.

The rise of the West was based on four primary victories of reason. The first was the development of faith in progress within Christian theology. The second victory was the way that faith in progress translated into technical and organizational innovations, many of them fostered by monastic estates. The third was that, thanks to Christian theology, reason informed both political philosophy and practice to the extent that responsive states, sustaining a substantial degree of personal freedom, appeared in medieval Europe. The final victory involved the application of reason to commerce, resulting in the development of capitalism within the safe havens provided by responsive states. These were the victories by which the West won.

Joe Biden's thirteen leftist contradictions:

1. Claims conquering COVID-19 is America's goal and demanding massive vaccine campaigns, while regularly allowing millions of untested and sick illegals into America.
2. That any individual or group actions to stop Trump were legal, by definition, and those involved will not be held accountable, no matter how legally or factually mistaken.
3. Anti-White racism is allowed. Whites are innate, biased racists who deserve any setbacks they receive.
4. Stating illegal Haitians shall not be "strapped" because they are precious while casually abandoning Americans and allies to torture and death in Afghanistan.
5. Stating fighting Global Warming is reason to shut down US oil production while then begging other countries to ramp up their oil production to help the United States.
6. Ran on unity message while defying GOP on every issue, refusing any consensus.

7. Implying only Anti-Trump is righteous, yet displaying incompetence on all policy changes.
8. Biden boasted he created the vaccine. A lie, but the troubled vaccine was Joe's only poll win.
9. Supports Milley, after the General officially undermined Trump by contacting China.
10. Claims Afghanistan exit a "Spectacular Success," though rated our worst foreign US mistake.
11. Enriched by son Hunter's foreign graft while pretending he was not involved with corruption.
12. He constantly lies and confabulates about every controversial issue.
13. Pretends competence while not answering any questions, claiming, "They won't let me."

Is this why "whiteness" is now considered a crime? It is a Biden policy. The Critical Race Theory and revisionist history (like The 1619 Project) being massively funded and inflicted on students in "public" (= government) schools signals hating America in general and Whites specifically. A more ominous signal is that Biden's AG has ordered the FBI to use the Patriot Act to treat parents protesting at local school board meetings as terrorists. PANORAMA EDUCATION, owned by AG Merrick Garland's son-in-law, is the main force promoting CRT. Panorama has contracted with 23,000 public schools and raised $76 million dollars from investors (as of October 2021) to promote Critical Race Theory, which is blatant anti-White racism.

Communist advocacy presumes simultaneous attacks on the political, military, arts, judicial, science, education, and religious components of society. By seeding crazy ideas into policies, across the board—the left creates a Potemkin Village sense of unreality. Specifically, if leaders can create a unified impression of maniacal decision-making, the elites can therefore foster a miasma of doom and powerlessness in the face of bizarre standards. The Democrats must either destroy a society or project that the society is undermined and therefore insolvent. Either way, a socialist imperative will be imposed.

For the Democrats to purposely build a national program from contradictions and lies while pretending their actions are above criticism is certifiable madness. Leftism demands its followers sacrifice honesty in the battle for world socialism. Specifically, Biden's pathological lying is typical of several mental health disorders, or it might be confabulation as the result of lost cognition. Or, according to Christian tradition, lying itself is the hallmark of Satan, indicating deep spiritual sickness.

Certainly, Marxism's radioactive cynicism presupposes lying as a hallowed tactic. One can describe criminal insanity as living in a perpetual state of dishonesty. In all events, perpetual dissembling cannot be sustained unless the entire populace becomes debased, cynical, and inured to deceit. As this transition is occurring in America, we are simultaneously devolving toward being just another third-world failure. Please pray for the USA, and God help us.

An *Epoch Times* article dated February 28, 2022, by Jeffrey A. Tucker *"Now is the Time for Mass Resignation from within the Ruling Class,"* clearly outlined why the elitist political leaders needed to be replaced. The *Freedom Convoy* movement in Canada visibly reflected the failures of the global elitists and their overreaching of authority and demands on the respective countries and populations. People across the globe have been awakened by the demands of masking, and forced and mandated vaccines and boosters. It is reminiscent of the movie, *Network,* in 1976 by Sidney Lumet, starring Peter Finch as newsman Howard Beale, screaming, "I'm mad as hell, and I'm not going to take this anymore."

This is one of the most well-known quotes in film history. It was a "Call to Action."

That **cry from the heart** crystalized the anger and powerlessness felt by the individual who has no recourse, option, or plan. It was anger without a clear target—just general rage at the disappointing state of modern life. Today there is a clear target for justifiable anger: **the disappointing leadership of political leaders worldwide,** who often serve as puppets of a Global Shadow Government. Simple to identify, but hard to fix!

The "Russian Hoax," the "Russian Collusion," and the massive plot to overthrow sitting President Donald J. Trump were evidence of the tricksters and traitors. We witnessed in early 2022 the Special Counsel Durham's releases of the Hillary Clinton paid-for fraud cybersecurity attack of the President's servers in Trump Tower and the White House itself. This brazen action was much more callous and illegal than the Watergate scandal against President Nixon. **The agencies responsible for securing the networks were hacking the networks.** And, of course, we witnessed the false flag actions of President Biden regarding the Russian-Ukraine conflict.

And so it is that our enemies, foreign and domestic, now work to destroy America by exploiting our freedom and tolerance, by dividing us into polarized groups.

When the masks went on for COVID-19, they came off for the planned destruction of America. Now, after a fraudulent 2020 election, we must choose between Freedom and Tyranny. Some in power, including Democrats, Fake News, Big Tech, Big Pharma, the Washington Swamp, unaccountable bureaucracies, the FBI, and the CIA prefer Tyranny. *Total control may keep them in power.*

Minor changes can have massive impact. Most think the Department of Education has been around forever. No. The story of DOE started in 1867 under Andrew Johnson, but only to collect statistics on education. These were excellent, until 1979, when Jimmy Carter made a federal takeover of education. The Department of Education is now a cabinet position, and our schools are failing. Carter also set up the SES, the "Senior Executive Service," which now prevents the majority of Swamp Bureaucrats from being fired.

Since then, K-12 education has slipped to where one can no longer find credible US government data. According to a **Business Insider** report in 2018, the US ranked 38th in math scores and 24th in science, falling from top excellence, to not even being in the top twenty. Some states (e.g., Oregon) no longer require proficiency in math, reading, or science for high school graduation. Home schooling and charter schools, fiercely resisted by bureaucrats and teachers' unions, are in demand. Black people trapped in the inner cities are desperate for better schools and more law enforcement but are getting the reverse. Worse yet is that schools, including universities, have shifted from teaching "how to learn" to "what to learn," which includes indoctrination about "Critical Race Theory" and revisionist history, like "The 1619 Project." Parents who dare object at schoolboard meetings are now threatened with being targeted by the FBI as **terrorists** under the Patriot Act. Marxists, well-funded and now in power, say children belong to the State [Hillary's "It takes a village to raise a child."]. Parents are enraged.

Whatever happened to the limits on power? The individuals who built our system of government led to the most prosperous society in the history of the world. They knew that restricting government was the key to a stable social order and a growing economy. At some point in the past century, the ruling class and elitists figured out what we call workarounds to government restrictions. The bureaucracy, as we used to call it, morphed into the "Deep State." What has been created is a toxic combination of big media, Big Tech, big government, global financial elitists, and designated puppets to conduct their "Global Reset."

One extremely easy and most obvious corrective path to take is for the ruling class to admit error, repeal all mandates, and allow for common freedom as outlined in our Constitution. As easy as that may seem, this solution hits a hard wall when faced with the arrogance of the elitists and their reluctance to admit past errors.

Try to imagine Joe Biden and Kamala Harris admitting to any errors of judgment (the border, lockdowns, inflation, Afghanistan). You can't. *That will never happen!*

People in America and around the world are fed up with the phony politicians and are saying, "No More." The obvious answer, of course, is removals, mass ousting, and resignations across the board in government, media, high-tech, and their senior military leaders. This needs to happen today, but it will not!

Americans have been the most privileged citizens on earth. Period! Regardless of whether one gained their citizenship by birth or naturalization—if you are an American, you are one of the most, if not most, privileged people on the face of this earth. Yet that is not what we are told by our so-called "ruling class," the self-anointed "elites" who call themselves progressive. They don't serve us, they exploit us. Some serve socialism and the New World Order.

If our leaders viewed all these occurrences and issues through a "Reality Prism," they would awaken to the true and real world. Please understand that our politicians (our elected leaders, our representatives) continue to enact legislation based on politics and getting reelected, rather than trying to solve problems within our society by looking at the real world as it is! Some plunder and exploit, instead of serving.

Our elected officials and bureaucrats often serve themselves, not those who elected them. They sometimes even serve our enemies, including cartels, China, Soros, and the New World Order. America, once "The Shining City on the Hill," is coming to resemble a corrupt third-world banana republic.

Our blueprint for saving America contains seven (7) critical strategies for defeating leftist ideologues and restoring our country to the principles and values that made it great:

- Achieve an American spiritual revival. **Preserve the Constitution and Bill of Rights.**
- Return to the **Rule of Law**. **Equal justice**, with officials accountable to "We the People."
- Reject historical revisionism and refute the big lies of the secular left.
- Preserve capitalism and reject socialism.
- Restore patriotism and love of country.
- Overcome specific **domestic** threats to America's Endgame.
- Overcome specific **foreign** threats to America's Endgame.

You have begun by reading the *Reality Prism*.

Please consider loaning or giving a copy of this book to a friend.

Speak out and speak up! Exercise your First Amendment rights while we still have them.

If we all do what we can, God will do the rest. **God Bless America.**

INTERLUDE

There is a danger in waking up to reality. You may crash into the "Woke Mob." They are a nasty bunch. The radical left weaponizes words, changes their meanings, makes personal attacks, inflicts violence, and erases history.

"A nation that forgets its past has no future."

Winston Churchill

"I am so old I remember when there were White couples in television commercials."

Ben Garrison Cartoons

Steve Bannon ✔
@SteveBannon

Robespierre, Lenin, Stalin, Hitler, and Mao all came for the kids, and through them the family. It's always the same playbook. Now Biden, Soros, and the 'Woke Inc.' have their turn at bat. They MUST be stopped dead in their tracks.

"Leftoids love supporting the censorship of "hate speech" and "racism" until they find out that 90% of it online is aimed at White people by anti-White racists."

Andrew Torba, CEO of Gab

"The deadliest thing about COVID is that it has destroyed science, logic and common sense."

William Hall, posted on Gab

Even Harry Potter figured it out! The radical left is insane!
"War is Peace.
Freedom is Slavery.
Ignorance is Strength.
The Penised Individual Who Raped You Is a Woman."

J.K. Rowling, Liberal Author.

"The woke mob is everywhere. Wokeness, as we think of it today, has its roots in decades of critical theory coming from universities. Today, it's intertwined with Cancel Culture, critical race theory and progressive activism—and it's everywhere you look."

Victor Davis Hanson

Chapter Two: The Global Shadow Government

The Right Major Crisis is Here

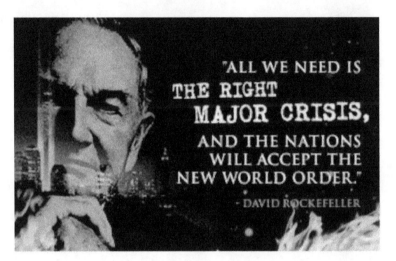

"ALL WE NEED IS THE RIGHT MAJOR CRISIS, AND THE NATIONS WILL ACCEPT THE NEW WORLD ORDER."
– DAVID ROCKEFELLER

H iding in the background of this global push is a new revolution now taking place, a revolution so far-reaching as to rethink all of society on this planet . . . a **Fourth Industrial Revolution**. Civilization has undergone three previous revolutions. The First Industrial Revolution was harnessing steam power. The Second Industrial Revolution was producing electricity, mass production, and nuclear power. The Third was in the development of the digital age. We now find ourselves enduring a Fourth Industrial Revolution. A revolution that makes all the others seem elementary. It is evil, anti-God in its concept and formulation. It will be government by technocracy—no democracy, no capitalism—a system of dictates, total control. It will be a world run by technicians, scientists, and intellectual elites. A government run by legions of Dr. Faucis and bankers, overseen by a bunch of Zuckerberg and Bill Gates type atheistic dictators, complete with genetic "computer bugs" to disable segments of our society with mandates. We already see this worldwide.

The *Fourth Industrial Revolution is AI*. It will involve designing and engineering the world around us, not merely using, or harnessing the atoms and molecules they are made of but hacking their digital code. If you think of our world as having molecules and atoms being arranged in a code, science today is on its way to hacking the digital code . . . changing our reality or creating, as my physics professor would say, stuff . . . stuff that does not exist in nature. They are talking robotics, growing people in laboratories, downloading our brains onto computers, artificial intelligence, and even redefining what it means to be human. We are already seeing gene editing, hacking biology by reprogramming DNA, and using new "vaccines" to domesticate and control the masses.

Hitler used "Yellow Stars" to denote undesirables. Biden did the same. He made the **unvaxed** a dangerous subclass, a step beyond Hillary's "deplorable" label, as is classifying parents who protest at school boards as "domestic terrorists." The **unvaxed** have been metaphorically bestowed the "Yellow Star of David," just as the Jews were in WWII. We already have "January 6 Gulags" and travel restrictions in America. Many expect vaccine passports and confinement to homes are in our future. It's already happening elsewhere.

We are also seeing the creation of synthetic food and artificial genders. But the real revolution will be found in cyberspace, the dipping in and out of a fifth dimension at will. A place where Big Tech, not nations, rule. "Build Back Better" really stands for "Destroy every sovereign free nation then build back as a one-world globalist dictatorship."

The New World Order is a way for the elite billionaires, and the powerful, to fully develop this new Fourth Industrial Revolution . . . become gods.

35

They say it will be a great future, but most of the world's population will **not** be invited. Climate change and COVID-19 are excuses, the catalyst for this transition. They have concluded that the world's population is much too large; that the planet will only need a fraction of the labor and human reproduction in the future. In any case, to them, too many people are "useless eaters," as they put it. So, a New World Order must be developed with a way to rid the earth of the excess population. Are we in the genesis of a planned depopulation?

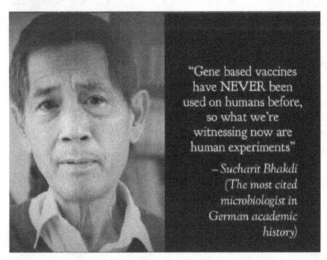

"Gene based vaccines have NEVER been used on humans before, so what we're witnessing now are human experiments"

— Sucharit Bhakdi
(The most cited microbiologist in German academic history)

Many scientists, physicians, religious leaders (except the Pope who is all in), and advocates like Robert Kennedy, Jr. are breaking their silence. They see this new world as being evil, with no attachments to religion, culture, nationality, morality, or basic human rights. They see an extremely dangerous future where right and wrong are blurred even more than they are now. Who is to say what is right and wrong if we terminate God and adopt a government concept of morality according to the ruling class's values and desires? Who dares speak the truth?

The right major crisis is indeed here. It is being used to accomplish what was impossible just a few years ago. Once again, America holds the future of the free world in its hands, depending on what it chooses to do about this threat.

So, this group of greedy, power-hungry, psychotic elites wants to change the world, put the remaining population into a modern feudal system, in their image, with almost unlimited technocratic power and without God. What could go wrong?

The Late David Rockefeller 1915–2017

From David Rockefeller's book, *'Memoirs'*, page 405:

"The super-national sovereignty of an intellectual elite and world bankers is surely preferable to the national auto-determination [self-determination] practiced in past centuries."

In that memoir, David Rockefeller also said that over forty years, he'd been thankful to the directors of *The Washington Post* and *The New York Times*, as well as *Time* Magazine and other excellent media, who attended meetings and kept promises of confidentiality.

Who is ruling the world and how do they do it? The New World Order.

They are responsible for the global epidemic, COVID-19 (and now, its endless variants), with multiple ineffective booster shots (jabs), lockdowns, vaccine passports, homeless camps, open borders, and the masking of the world. They imposed a level of totalitarian control not seen since Stalin's Russia and Hitler's Germany. They are dehumanizing those who fail to comply, like Hitler did to the Jews. They are behind the NWO, UN Agenda 2030, and The Great Reset.

Do powerful globalist ruling elites really run things? Is there a Global Shadow Government? Have elections been rigged and biased? We do know President Biden is a puppet and his puppeteer is Obama. We also know that Obama is a puppet of the Global Elites (the Shadow Government).

One of the recent major moves by the Globalists was the establishment of "the Schengen Area" in Europe. The Schengen Area is a group of twenty-six European countries that have agreed to abolish all passport and other forms of border control at their common borders. The region primarily serves as a single authority for international travel, with a unified visa policy. The area is named after the Schengen Agreement, which was signed in Luxembourg in 1985. Twenty-two of the EU's twenty-seven member nations are part of the Schengen Area. Four of the five EU states that are not members of the Schengen Area—Bulgaria, Croatia, Cyprus, and Romania—are legally obligated to join in the future; Ireland, on the other hand, maintains an opt-out and has its own visa regime. Iceland, Liechtenstein, Norway, and Switzerland are members of the European Free Trade Association (EFTA), but not the EU, and have signed agreements in conjunction with the Schengen Agreement. Three European microstates—Monaco, San Marino, and the Vatican City—are de facto part of the Schengen Area. The four EFTA member states, Iceland, Liechtenstein, Norway, and Switzerland are not members of the EU, but have signed agreements in association with the Schengen Agreement. De facto, the Schengen Area also includes three European microstates—Monaco, San Marino, and the Vatican City

Well, who are these Globalists? Bill Gates, Jeff Bezos, Warren Buffett, and George Soros, just to name a few. Let us examine the founding organization that spawned the "Global Shadow Government"—the Bilderberg Group. Many of the past members are now deceased. New bankers, new oligarchs, tech czars, and senior politicians make up the new Shadow Government.

The Bilderberg Group normally meets once every year. They skipped doing that under Trump.

One of the last meetings, before Biden, was held in June 2016 at the Taschenbergpalais hotel that is in Dresden. Up to 150 of the world's wealthiest and most powerful political leaders attend the annual event. The attendees include royalty, presidents, prime ministers, chief executives of major international conglomerates, media, the Council on Foreign Relations, and the Trilateral Commission. Just like the Bilderberg Group, the extent and reach of the powerful members of the Council on Foreign Relations and the Trilateral Commission have influenced the globe for decades. The current members of these groups and the earlier ones make it easy to see how powerful they are and what influence they have on global changes. Yes. *"The Great Reset."* We have identified eighty-eight current members.

It makes truly a minor difference who is the President in the White House because these power brokers are the ones really in charge. President Trump was the only one that knew well the "Globalists" and challenged them. Trump was never a part of the plan of these elitists. He turned the tables on them, and because of that, they ensured he would not be elected for his second term in 2020. In most cases, without their approval and support, there is no way to get elected.

President Trump challenged these Globalists in 2016. He delayed their *Great Reset* and their global agenda. They plotted, planned, and cheated to ensure that Trump would be defeated in 2020, and to ensure he is not elected in 2024. It worked. The United States got a puppet in Joe Biden with a handler named Barack Obama.

The first Bilderberg meeting was held in 1954. The organization was founded with the intent to create powerful connections between European countries and North Americans. The meeting is a secretive, informal discussion about global trends with open communication between the elite members of the world who have massive influence on world affairs.

No statements of any kind are allowed to be made to the press regarding the proceedings or what is talked about at the meeting. There are no meeting minutes taken and no reports of the discussions or official statement about the discussions is produced or made. Anything learned at the meeting can be freely used by any of the members; however, no one is permitted to talk about it.

More than four hundred heavily armed guards protect the attendees. The event space is hardened with physical barricades and elevated levels of security. It is this level of high security combined with the extreme secrecy that makes the conspiracy theorists go wild with speculation about what they do at the Bilderberg meetings.

The co-founders of the Bilderberg Group were two historical figures with checkered backgrounds. They were Prince Bernhard from the Netherlands and Józef Retinger, who was a political adviser, originally from Poland, who worked with the Vatican.

Throughout his later adult life, up until his death in 1984, Prince Bernhard claimed he was never a Nazi. A historian, Annejet van der Zijl, found documents at the Humboldt University in Berlin, which prove Prince Bernhard was indeed a Nazi Party member until 1934 when he left school to work for the huge German chemical company named IG Farben. IG Farben did atrocious things in support of the Nazis, including making the poisonous gas used to kill people in the German death camps.

Józef Retinger was a secret spy for the Vatican. He was expelled from allied countries for his activities in association with the Jesuits. He later went on to create the Council of Europe during 1949, which became part of a foundational movement, one which eventually led to the formation of the European Union.

1- Agustina Kämpfer
2- Amado Boudou
3- Sharon Johnston
4- David Johnston
5- Sjeikha Moza bint Nasser al Misned of Qatar
6- Prince Albert II
7- Princess Ariane of the Netherlands
8- Princess Alexia of the Netherlands
9- Princess Catharina Amalia of the Netherlands
10- Princess Lalla Salma of Morocco
11- Crown Prince Naruhito of Japan
12- Crown Princess Masako of Japan
13- Kofi Annan
14- Maria Anna
15- Geertrui Van Rompuy
16- President of the European Council Herman Van Rompuy
17- Crown Princess Mary of Denmark
18- Crown Prince Frederik of Denmark
19- Camilla, Duchess of Cornwall
20- Prince Charles, Prince of Wales
21- King Willem Alexander
22- Queen Maxima of the Netherlands
23- Maha Chakri Sirindhorn of Thailand
24- Prince Maha Vajiralongkorn of Thailandt

25- Princess Sarah of Brunei
26- Crown Prince Al-Muhtadee Billah
27- Maria Sousa Uva
28- President of the European Commission Jose Manuel Barroso
29- Princess Mathilde of Belgium
30- Prince Philippe of Belgium
31- Princess Sophie of Liechtenstein
32- Hereditary Prince Alois of Liechtenstein
33- Princess Stephanie of Luxembourg
34- Prince Guillaume of Luxembourg
35- Prince Daniel of Sweden
36- Princess Victoria of Sweden
37- Prince Felipe of Spain
38- Princess Letizia of Spain
39- Crown Prince Salman bin Hamad al Khalifa of Bahrain
40- Haitham bin Tariq al Said of Oman
41- Sheikh Hamed bin Zayed al Nahyan
42- Crown Prince Haakon
43- Crown Princess Mette-Marit of Norway
44- Prince El Hassan bin Talal of Jordan
45- Princess Sarvath El Hassan of Jordan
46- Helen Clark
47- Admiral James G. Stavridis
48- Fay Hartog-Levin v

Past members of the Bilderberger Group were some of the richest, most powerful, and most famous people in the world. Attendees from past Bilderberg meetings include:

Angela Merkel, Beatrix of the Netherlands, Bill Clinton, Bill Gates, Carl Bildt, Charles, Prince of Wales, Charlie Rose, Colin Powell, Condoleezza Rice, David Cameron, Dora Bakoyannis, Enoch Powell, Fouad Ajami, Frank McKenna, Fredrik Reinfeldt, Geir Haarde, George P. Shultz, George Soros, George Stephanopoulos, Georgios Alogoskoufis, Gerald Ford, Gordon Brown, Gordon Campbell, Guido Westerwelle, Haakon, Crown Prince of Norway, Harald V of Norway, Henry Kissinger, Jeff Bezos, John Edwards, John Kerr, John Kerry, Jon Huntsman, Jr., José Manuel Barroso, Juan Carlos I of Spain, Kathleen Sebelius, Lawrence Summers, Lester B. Pearson, Margaret Thatcher, Mario, Draghi, Mark Sanford, Paul Volcker, Peter Mandelson, Peter Sutherland, Prince Philip, Duke of Edinburgh, Queen Sofía of Spain, Rick Perry, Robert Zoellick, Ruud Lubbers, Sandy Berger, Timothy Geithner, Tom Daschle and William F. Buckley, Jr.

The **elites** are a more diverse class than are Globalists, entertainers, Wall Street types, bankers, corporate leaders, and others who have immense influence and power over society. It's about self-interest. They typically use their influence for anti-individualistic, immoral, and corrupted ends. The ruling classes express their power through laws, regulations, and petty enforcements. Intense speculation about the "ruling elite" many believe is running the world from behind the scenes can lead to the presumption that it is all-powerful and infallible. But is it? Identifying the human foibles and underlying desires of those who may be planning centralized domination could lead to a greater chance to offset their agendas.

However, if all that the most extreme speculation achieves is to help prevent such a grim outcome from reaching full fruition, then it will have served a useful purpose. It is also worth noting that a ray of optimism could change the dialogue.

An often-valid criticism of conspiracy theorists, or "truth-seekers," is that their fevered investigations into humankind's worst nightmares can leave some listeners feeling *more* fearful, and risks driving them into a state of disempowered paralysis, putting down the shutters when what is needed is engagement. Yet the unavoidable truth is that looking a potentially tough situation in the eye does mean facing up to disturbing realities that may have been swept under the carpet, for they might require urgent action.

Lifting the blindfold even just a little means that we might not run into the approaching wall at such a great velocity. If the idea of a secretive but all-pervading cabal running the world leaves some feeling shocked, the act of simply contemplating such an idea may spark a new awakening of consciousness.

The Pandora Papers: A Massive Leak Reveals the Offshore Dealings of Thirty-five International Leaders.

The "Pandora Papers," a leak of offshore financial data, was published by major news sites, revealing the secret holdings and agreements of some of the world's wealthiest and most influential leaders. According to *The Guardian*, the leak comprised roughly 12 million papers from firms that were engaged to set up offshore accounts in countries such as Panama, Dubai, Monaco, Switzerland, and the Cayman Islands. It was reported that the names identified in the papers include 35 world leaders, 300 other public officials, and more than 100 millionaires, according to the newspaper. Among those identified are current and former presidents, prime ministers, judges, mayors, military generals, and other prominent figures.

It was originally provided to the International Consortium of Investigative Journalists (ICIJ) in Washington, DC, which published the information. It subsequently disseminated the Information to publications such as *The Guardian, BBC Panorama, Le Monde,* and *The Washington Post,* among others. Since then, more than 600 journalists have researched the contents of the files in what has been dubbed the "biggest data breach in history in terms of financial data volume," according to the British newspaper *The Guardian.*

Offshore financial operations that allow some of the world's wealthiest people to escape taxes are revealed in the papers, according to *The Guardian,* which described them as "rare windows into the clandestine operations."

Despite the fact that not everyone mentioned in the papers was accused of any wrongdoing, several of the revelations made by the papers could have major consequences for the approaching elections.

According to *The Guardian's* reporting on the papers, Czech Prime Minister Andrej Babiš declined to comment on why he utilized an offshore investment corporation to purchase a $22 million château in the south of France.

Others listed in the files included Jordan's King Abdullah II, who owned $100 million worth of properties around the world and insisted he had done nothing wrong by holding those assets through offshore corporations, according to *The Guardian.*

They also reveal how a Russian woman purchased an apartment in Monaco for millions of dollars and amassed huge money after having a child at a time when she was apparently in a secret connection with Russian President Vladimir Putin.

Meanwhile, Ukrainian President Volodymyr Zelensky is reported to have transferred a 25 percent ownership in an offshore corporation to a friend who has since become a prominent adviser. According to *The Guardian,* the move occurred amid a campaign in which he pledged to reform the corrupt nature of his country's economic structure.

While offshore holdings are not illegal and can even serve legitimate security-related needs, their secrecy has been exploited in the past to facilitate criminal activities and money laundering through the employment of shell companies. It is another humiliation for Vice President Biden, who campaigned on the promise of greater transparency in overseas financial transactions. The United States is described as a "leading tax shelter" by the media.

The Elite and its Motivations

Something that is far too often overlooked in all of the conspiracy speculation is the realization that, even if we are under the control of a powerful cabal attempting to manipulate the world to its own ends, we are still essentially dealing with fellow human beings (putting aside ET/reptilian bloodline theories for the time being, of course).

They must have physical, social, and emotional needs, just like everyone else on the planet, even if the latter faculties are too easily neglected in the kind of mind that would plot events like 9/11 (an event widely suspected to have been staged by Western sources as part of a march toward the 'New World Order'). The personalities engaged must have their own families and friends, and they must be experiencing thoughts, feelings, and concerns in at least some of the directions. They, like the majority of people in our lives, may believe they are doing the right thing, despite the fact that we may believe their plans are foolish.

This is a really important point. Everyone has reasons for what they do, and they can often defend their behavior to themselves when faced with major problems from the outside. The motivations of those who believe that wiping out their own people would be a positive move, or who believe that planning wars and economic breakdowns to affect the creation of a unifying world government is an acceptable strategy, may be difficult to comprehend. However, many well-intentioned visionaries throughout history have voiced the need for such strategies. Of course, this does not imply that they are correct, but there is clearly a sizable, if small, segment of humanity who believes that the larger picture should take precedence over the interests of the masses. Many of those who have voiced support for eugenics and depopulation techniques, for example, are motivated by deep-seated environmental concerns or the conviction that we have lost our balance with nature and must prioritize the future of the earth over the needs of the general public.

Wells was a well-known and highly regarded writer who thought strongly that the only solution to world strife would be the establishment of the eponymous hierarchical structure, which he proposed explicitly in his 1940 book, *The New World Order*. This is a concept that is definitely out of date. Its origins can be traced back far deeper than Wells' idealized vision of the world. Some believe that both World Wars were purposefully planned, or at the very least utilized, in order to establish a mandate for world authority. Several years before the Civil War, in his book *The New Freedom* (1913), President Woodrow Wilson said unequivocally that a powerful force was already underpinning the commercial and political foundation of the United States:

"Some of the biggest men in the US, in the field of commerce and manufacturing, are afraid of somebody, are afraid of something. They know that there is a power somewhere so organized, so subtle, so watchful, so interlocked, so complete, so pervasive, that they had better not speak above their breath when they speak in condemnation of it."

But what stands out most in H.G. Wells' writings is his sense of joy and passion for the idea of a ruling collective that would put everything right and prevent "the disastrous extinction of Mankind." A Malthusian dislike for humanity is not discernible, nor is there any sense of malice in the characters' actions. Wells, on the other hand, was a proponent of eugenics at the same time. Many people find this concept completely repugnant, but here is the paradox: the very types of people truth-seekers tend to single out as the enemies of humanity are the very types of people who believe they are the saviors of humanity. It all comes down to one's point of view and where one decides to draw the line in terms of morality.

One world government founded on rigorous scientific values, as predicted by the philosopher Bertrand Russell, was inevitable, and Russell was shockingly candid about the civilization that would follow as a result. In his 1953 book *The Impact of Science on Society*, he writes, **"Diet, injections, and injunctions will combine, from an exceedingly early age, to produce the sort of character and the sort of beliefs that the authorities consider desirable, and any serious criticism of the authorities will become psychologically impossible..."**

Slowly but steadily, via selective breeding, the congenital disparities between rulers and ruled will expand to the point where they are nearly distinct species. A coordinated insurrection of sheep against the practice of eating mutton would become as unimaginable as a revolution of the plebs against the government.

Russell's beliefs appear to encourage rather than condemn such a world, and such thinking appears to be ridiculous, even if it does come near to describing the very philosophy that is now actively molding our society, as Russell claims. Even though it may be difficult, if not downright uncomfortable, for some to ponder, there is one important point to consider: What if such a way of thinking was conclusively proven to be correct? What if the notion of greater control, rather than less, is essential to the existence of humankind? Was it ever proved that the choice was between disaster caused by overpopulation, pollution, and overstretched resources, or a selectively bred, well-watched planet that governed itself and survived? What if it were possible to demonstrate that an anarchy-ridden post-Biden apocalypse society had no actual chance of surviving, whereas a carefully regulated disciplinarian civilization had a good chance?

However, when considering the world's present pressing situations, it is possible to discern, at least to a limited extent, how arguments could be made in these directions when seen from a particular point of view. As is always the case, the problem stems from the enormous question of who gets to make the final decision. Those who live in good circumstances and look down from a high vantage point must necessarily perceive things differently from those who are scraping by on the lower rungs of the social ladder; those who are at their mercy.

We currently have the ability to manipulate genetic information in our hands, and it will not be long before we will be able to routinely pick and create infants to have the features we desire. Also, as life expectancies continue to rise, and our understanding of tissue and brain cell regeneration continues to advance year after year, how long do you think it will be before life can be preserved indefinitely? As a result, if limitless access to such power is permitted (that is, provided the vast majority of people is allowed to survive in the first place—depopulation conspiracy theories are prevalent), the population crisis will unquestionably explode. In a world of immortals, not only would there be stagnation, but there would also be dominance from those who were the first to achieve immortality. From that point forward, they would effectively pick who would be offered the gift. Finally, such authorities would very likely have control over the genetic pool because the new eugenics had infiltrated society through the back door.

These challenges are already a part of everyday life, rather than the stuff of dystopian fiction. By harnessing the power of genetic engineering, which is currently changing our food supply—including both animal and vegetable products—and thus our entire ecosystem as spliced and altered genes make their way into nature through pollination and cross-breeding, humankind has already taken control of our planet's evolutionary destiny, and there is no turning back. Is it possible that people in control lack the moral compass necessary to shoulder such a monumental responsibility? How well will they perform in their role as the gods they have elevated themselves to be?

It is possible that a charter of strict regulation, constant surveillance, and genetic population control could be implemented with compassion and the broad support of a common consensus in an angelic society? But we are far from reaching that point of being. It appears unlikely that the kinds of objectives that many people believe the ruling class is enacting could be anything other than a plain attack on the majority of humanity in light of the fact that the motivations of those in power are so clearly in question. Any attempt to manage the world through compulsion and draconian means remains unethical in the absence of widespread agreement, regardless of the good intentions that may be lurking somewhere in the background of the plans.

What, on the other hand, is it that psychologically motivates this elite? What kind of brains are we dealing with here, exactly? How can we make an attempt to comprehend them in order to develop clearer answers and tactics for dealing with their behaviors in the future?

Inherent Deception

When it comes to global cover-ups, the problem is that they begin and grow—as deceit does so frequently for all of us—out of a lack of candor spurred by a fear of what people may say or do if they were to see the genuine vulnerability that exists within us. The elite is just as afraid of us and our emotions as we are of them—otherwise, they would not need to manipulate and control us in the first place. Many deceptive activities are the result of inner insanity, or a lack of faith in one's ability to communicate effectively with others. Our leaders appear to have been so accustomed to playing deceptive games that they are unable to employ any other tactic at this point. Everything, from the banking system to the administration of the House of Commons, appears to be founded on deceit. Right now, it is evident that people in charge of our life do not have our best interests at heart, and as a result, we do not trust them.

Not that some of the elites would even be remotely bothered about what any of us thinks of their actions. For those of us who may feel that provisos to explain such motivation is too generous to people who maim, kill, and deceive to get their way, for whatever reason, it should be noted that there do also appear to be those pulling the strings who simply seek power for power's sake. Based on historical precedent, we may conclude that selfishness, greed, even exhilarated bloodlust cannot be ruled out as primary motivators in some situations. If it turns out that this highly exclusive club was created by an extra-terrestrial gene that was seeded thousands of years ago (as some believe, based on ancient myths) and is currently being exploited and/or activated by celestial visitors, it may help to explain why concern for the needs of humanity appears to be as low on the list of its priorities as our general concern for the well-being of the planet.

The global elite can be divided into two categories: those who are well-intentioned and those who aren't. We're talking about high-ranking politicians, academics, intellectuals (as in the case of Wells and Russell), monarchies, and extraordinarily wealthy and influential families—all of whom are influenced by a complex mix of political, religious, and occult undercurrents. All of the obvious candidates. As a result, there is minimal need to go into detail here because there are numerous books and websites that do so. It is unclear how much of the grand plan each of them is aware of, and whether there are pyramids-within-pyramids among even the most powerful of the power structures at the very top.

Factions within Factions

The assumption is frequently made that the very existence of a ruling elite implies that those engaged must be all-powerful and of one mind, accurately orchestrating domino events to hit the required place every time, all in the service of a preset objective, which is not always the case. However, this may give them an unjustified sense of infallibility.

Several pieces of evidence indicate that there are divisions and disagreements among individuals in positions of power who have great impact over our lives. The world is a vast and complicated place. Even if there is broad consensus on how to proceed, the pressures of regional demands and personal prejudices will almost certainly cause the clarity of aim to be obscured from time to time. According to the information that has leaked out of Bilderberg meetings and other similar gatherings, it appears that there are as many disagreements, compromises, and negotiations there as there are in any Democratic parliament. If this were not the case, the meetings would not be necessary, and the scheming would be much more pre-planned in its execution.

This is The Great Reset: The Global Elite's Plan to Radically Remake Our Economic and Social Lives

The Great Reset has arrived... or, at the very least, the authorities are attempting to bring it about. That which was formerly considered a fringe "conspiracy theory" is now on full display for all to see, plain as day. World leaders in the fields of economics, politics, academia, and the media are taking advantage of the chaos and confusion created by the COVID-19 lockdowns and exploiting them to dramatically reshape society throughout the world.

What will the appearance of this alteration be? It is the goal of the global elites to establish a society dominated by renters who own nothing, while also promoting a social agenda that would be unpopular with the unwashed masses and difficult to accomplish in a country with a large middle class that owns its own property. You would rent not just your home but also your phone, computer, car (though you would "carshare," which is the word for renting a car for a longer period of time and requesting a car when you need a ride), and even the pots and pans you use in the kitchen to make your meals in.

One consequence of this will be a fundamental restructuring of the global economy. You will no longer have a job in the classic sense of the word. Instead, you will be self-employed and work a variety of different "gigs," any of which could put you in a precarious position at any given point in time. You will be paid a price for services rendered, with no additional compensation, such as benefits, paid time off, job security, healthcare, or anything else that the middle class in the Western world has grown to expect.

Rural populations will have to be pushed into more concentrated population centers in order to facilitate **The Great Reset**, because dispersed populations have a disproportionately large "carbon footprint." As suburbs and exurbs become more urban in nature, the suburbs will be a relic of the previous century. Multifamily housing, where you and five hundred other people live in a mid-rise condominium colony with shops and "workshare" spaces (the latest version of an office—on your expense, not the employer's) in the same location.

The short version is that it represents the complete annihilation of the American way of life, notably the way of life enjoyed by the majority of the Western middle class. In order to be prepared to fight against **The Great Reset**, you should read the details of the full story, which includes the why.

Being aware of what **The Great Reset** is can be difficult due to official sources on the subject—the World Economic Forum, which is the primary driving force behind The Great Reset, as well as its affiliated organizations and individuals—couching their objectives in vague euphemisms such as the main slogan for the initiative, "Build Back Better."

It is common for opponents of freedom to employ generalized, non-specifically favorable rhetoric to describe their initiatives. These are words that, if taken at face value, no one could possibly disagree with or object to. Who could possibly be opposed to "Building Back Better"?

Even Biden understands that these words imply something else, something evil. One should not take the assertion that **The Great Reset** is simply "building back better" at face value, any more than one should take the claim that China is assisting this scheme to be benevolent.

The Great Reset may well look like this to the common person.

• The "Sharing Economy" is characterized by the fact that everything is rented and nothing is owned. The government will pay off your mortgages and then take possession of your property. Yes, it is exactly what the Shadow Government's elitists (Gates, Soros, and others) are preparing as they purchase the best agricultural property available. Gates has surpassed his predecessor as the largest owner of farmland in the United States. Chinese elitists are buying up hundreds of acres of farmland in Canada, according to reports. Money is going from Shanghai banks through the main banks in Vancouver, British Columbia, before arriving in the United States.

• Digital media: It will be easier to censor and suppress books and videos that are in opposition to the dominant narratives in the future.

• Restriction on Social Media Use: the *de facto* public square, will be restricted to those who promote the latest version of elite narratives. Many think "Big Tech" censorship and 2020 Election Interference (e.g., "Zuckerbucks") resulted in a stolen election in America but discussing that on social media is censored. America has even set up an Orwellian "Ministry of Truth," an arm of armed Federal Law Enforcement, the Department of Homeland Security, to control Free Speech. DHS focus has shifted from foreign terrorists to citizens who are critical of the government.

• A *de facto* social credit system will come in where individuals who deviate from the story will be financially blacklisted, which may result in the loss of their questionable "benefits," which will become increasingly vital for ordinary living and even survival as the narrative becomes more entrenched in society.

• Centralization of Housing and Land: As time goes on, fewer and fewer Americans will own the homes and land on which they reside.

• There will be "Racial Equity" in that some races will be treated more equally than others, with chosen groups being the beneficiary of substantial benefit programs supported by the less preferred groups, who will become progressively tax slaves.

• Environmental protection will be used as a pretext to lower the standard of living for the middle class, tighten limitations on freedom of travel, and even restrict access to food.

• Ground-level goons will operate with indemnity to attack enemies of the system in coordinated and systematic outbreaks of violence and intimidation.

• Concentrated Wealth: wealth will be concentrated in the hands of the authorities and its allies, which will be used as economic leverage to control political discourse and individual freedom.

Everything described above might appear to be a little far-fetched, but unlike other supposed "conspiracy theories," which require extensive investigation to prove they are correct, **The Great Reset** is clearly visible to everyone. Those promoting it boast about it, speak openly about it, create propaganda campaigns around it, refer to it clearly by name, and express public frustration and anger when the "dog doesn't want to eat the dog food."

A video of Klaus Schwab, founder and chairman of the World Economic Forum, the primary global elite institution pushing for **The Great Reset**, went viral after it was posted on YouTube. It only lasts about forty seconds, but it is well worth it to take the time to watch. **The Great Reset** logo, which is in the same font as the World Economic Forum emblem, can be seen directly behind Schwab. Additionally, Schwab openly mentions **The Great Reset** and expresses his dissatisfaction with the COVID-19 pandemic, stating that it has not been as effective as he would have liked in terms of advancing **The Great Reset**. [Caution: Twitter reserves the right to remove the link.]

https://twitter.com/MatteaMerta/status/1414584681165639682

Klaus Schwab isn't just some random guy on Twitter or a blogger with a couple of dozen followers; he's an extraordinarily powerful man who serves as the chairman of the World Economic Forum, one of the most prominent elite globalist organizations in the world, according to Forbes.

The scope of **The Great Reset** extends far beyond a single forty-second viral video. According to the World Economic Forum's website, there is an entire page dedicated to it, which contains a lot of ambiguous wording that doesn't actually tell you much about what this is all about. *Time* magazine's website contains a voluminous collection of stories that portray the subject as unquestionably good and, above all else, without reservation or complaint. A video on the World Economic Forum's YouTube channel is essentially a five-minute montage of talking points on the subject, as presented by the organization.

https://www.youtube.com/watch?v=uPYx12xJFUQ

To make matters worse, the BBC and other news organizations are publishing pieces pushing you not to believe your own lying eyes, claiming that this is a conspiracy theory with no basis in reality. Additionally, Wikipedia has an entire section dedicated to assuring you that the "conspiracy theory" surrounding **The Great Reset** has nothing to do with the pure, noble intentions of people like Klaus Schwab, Bill Gates, and Tony Blair, among others.

The Great Reset is clearly real, but how do the powers intend to force it on the world?

The TSA, following 9-11, was the camel's nose under the tent, as Americans were groomed for a police state. The COVID pandemic, masks, shutdowns, travel restrictions, and lockdowns are the whole beast, with more to come. We already have Gulags in Washington, DC, for those unfortunate enough to be near or in the Capitol on January 6th.

Whether one thinks that the COVID lockdowns and restrictions were a good faith response to a public health emergency or not is irrelevant. The fact of the matter is that it accustomed Americans and Westerners to significant restrictions on their freedoms, including freedom of movement. More than that, it showed those in power that if you created enough fear, Americans would tolerate the restrictions. That was the plan, and it worked.

Thus, consciously or not, global elites were grooming the world population for a police state. Fortunately, there has finally been some pushback. Vaccine passports are encountering stiff resistance from both elected officials and the general population at large. For most of 2020 and 2021, the most freedom-loving people on earth—Americans—were walking around with dirty, useless masks on to comply with a government mandate. A mandate that, after further scrutiny, made no sense. Americans even allowed their children to be subjected to this as a condition of attending school. Our populations are being poisoned by spike proteins through accelerated vaccines, variants, and a continuum of booster shots.

The COVID-19 lockdowns were not the first time that Americans were groomed for a police state. TSA is the biggest example. However, we also see examples of this in our public schools with metal detectors and warrantless searches. Vaccine passports are coming.

The Department of Justice and their surrogate police force, the FBI, are being militarized and politicized to arrest mothers challenging the school boards on what their children should be taught and handcuffed as "domestic terrorists." There are already Gulags for political protestors in Washington, DC.

The elites directing the government puppets, like Joe Biden and Barack Obama, are using fear tactics and division of the people (using anti-White racism, Fake News, and Mind War) to change America forever. The provocative question now is how will long will "We the People" tolerate the dismantling of America? Have we waited too long?

Why The Great Reset?

We cannot speculate as to the internal motives of man. What we can do is talk about the tangible effects that policies have here in the real world. The primary tangible effect of **The Great Reset** is an increased amount of power and wealth in the hands of fewer and fewer people, all of whom are hostile toward you, your values, and your way of life. They have no regard or respect for the common person—they only want to control you and your money.

It might have been an accident that the greatest wealth transfer in human history happened during the COVID-19 lockdowns, or it might have been by design. Regardless, the upward wealth transfer happened. Success rarely satiates; it only fuels a hunger for more success. We should see this wealth transfer as a prelude to larger wealth transfers that are forthcoming.

Additionally, the Western middle class sits on an enormous reserve of wealth in the form of home ownership and retirement funds. These are the targets of the global elite. One would be a fool, given all the evidence, to believe that they would stop at anything to acquire a massive reserve of wealth. To the extent that it is possible, we must make ourselves more resilient. This means owning land, having your own well, a supply of food to weather the storm, adequate supplies of ammunition, useful skills, and close community bonds. It also means sounding the alarm bells about elite propaganda campaigns, legislative maneuvers, and bureaucratic fiats designed to destroy you!

> "The **global elites** want to create a society of renters who own nothing, while also pushing a social agenda that would be unpopular with the unwashed masses and difficult to implement in a society with a broad, ownership-based middle class. What this means is that you would rent not just your home, but also your phone, computer, car (though you will "carshare," the term for renting a car when you need)."

https://ammo.com/articles/the-great-reset

Chapter Three: United We Stand—Take Back America!

Our nation is now more divided than it was during our Civil War, not broken in half but smashed into shards. Our culture is being erased. Ruling elites, foreign enemies, the socialist left, Hollywood, rappers, Fake News, and schools that teach **what** to think, not **how** to think, have been working on that for decades.

The Great Reset has and is taking place, like an avalanche roaring down on America. Our enemies have decided that this, not nuclear war, is the surest way to conquer us. It's the killer, but many hardworking, trusting Americans do not notice.

We were betrayed by a stolen election, misdirected by enemies within, diverted by **Mind War** (sophisticated 24/7 propaganda), and panicked by a constant, global, bioweapons attack, violence in our cities, False Flag attacks (e.g., Jan 6), illegals from the cartels and Taliban, raging inflation, and more. Our system of equal justice, basic law and order, is broken. What to do?

Step one: Focus. Pay attention. Look through the **Reality Prism**, not the **Political Prism**.

Obama and Beyond

"Fundamentally transforming"—Obama had a hidden agenda and he let it slip out. Obama, when elected, said, *"**We are five days away from fundamentally transforming the United States of America.**"*

He went on to give details. *"In five days, you can turn the page on policies that put greed and irresponsibility on Wall Street before the challenging work and sacrifice of folks on Main Street. In five days, you can choose policies that invest in our middle class, and create new jobs, and grow this economy, so that everyone has a chance to succeed, not just the CEO, but the secretary and janitor, not just the factory owner, but the people on the factory floor. In five days, you can put an end to the politics that would divide a nation just to win an election, which tries to pit region against region, and city against town, and Republican against Democrat, which asks—asks us to fear at a time when we need to hope."*

Was Obama hinting that he was planning to turn America into a social Democratic Euro-state, or something worse? We know the answer now. The agenda is full Marxist. American Communism.

Biden's agenda is simply the imposition of Obama's, one which was planned by the New World Order. Obama (and others) are still in charge. The agenda explicitly extends to erasing America's Constitution, culture, history, and traditions. Michelle Obama signaled that in a speech given in San Juan, Puerto Rico on May 14, 2008.

"Barack knows that we are going to have to make sacrifices; we are going to have to change our conversation; we're going to have to change our traditions, our history; we're going to have to move into a different place as a nation to provide the kind of future we all want desperately for our children."

The fact that this speech was not reported by the news or used by John McCain in the campaign against Obama goes to show the ineptitude of the GOP and the collusion of Fake News. Obama told us he wanted to "transform" our country. He began the horrible process of doing so.

Trump interrupted this in 2016. Then came the stolen 2020 election, Dominion voting machines, the pandemic, lockdown, floods of unverified paper ballots, and massive election fraud.

This is well documented, but it has not yet resulted in prosecutions, decertification, or corrective action. What is happening instead, is Soviet-style political prisoners (e.g., January 6), sham trials (e.g., Rittenhouse) that more resemble Stalin's Russia than our 1776 republic, and riots resembling those of Hitler's Brown Shirts (and Gestapo, after local police were defunded) and Stalin's Antifa thugs. Riots in all major cities were an integral part of the Democrat's 2020 election strategy.

So it is that we now have "Creepy Joe" as our corrupt, geriatric puppet President bumbling down an endless string of mistakes, disasters, and unpopular mandates. Joe is barely able to function, and America suffers under constant crises. He is the perfect mouthpiece and scapegoat for the power holders directing the downfall of the republic.

It's not accidental. This is purposeful. If Team Biden was **intentionally** trying to harm America (and many think they are), what would they do differently? Not much.

We do know what the comufascists (American Marxists) intend to put into place. **They told us!**

American Marxists envision **The Great Reset** as an opportunity to make the world better and more resilient, to capitalize on accelerating change, and, of course, gain unlimited power. China sees it as the most efficient way to conquer and colonize America.

Big Tech sees it as a road to enormous wealth. The drug gangs and cartels do too. All these groups are buying politicians, destabilizing peaceful cities, destroying suburbs, and taking control of our voting and election processes.

One of the most terrifying of these people is Bill Gates, who overtly advocates population control, and practices it through vaccines, with a long trail of horrific consequences in poor continents and countries like Africa and India. Or George Soros, the last living Nazi, who served Hitler in the Death Camps as a youth and has since gained enormous wealth and power by destroying economies and countries. These are aided by bureaucrats like Fauci, who twists science to his own ends.

We've gone from **"Two Weeks to Flatten the Curve**," to statements like **"You'll need Nukes and F-15s to Stop Us**," and **"Eliminate the Nuremberg Code**." Here in America, we have mandates (blocked by the courts at present) to force people to take experimental vaccines. (By definition, the mRNA jabs were <u>not</u> vaccines. They changed the definition in August 2021.) We now suffer intensive propaganda campaigns to censor, demonize, and shun any who resist. The Biden administration has threatened harsh action against any who resist "the jab."

Internet ads cite **The Great Reset** and encourage people to buy products in preparation for a "permanent lockdown." Big Tech, along with Fake News and most social media is all in. Conspiracy theories have emerged, fueled by things people see as troubling coincidences, such as President-elect Joe Biden using "Build Back Better" as a campaign slogan.

It seems Joe lifted it from the slogan of Schwab's initiative. In June 2020, Schwab published his vision for the world after the coronavirus pandemic is over. He described how countries could come together to facilitate **The Great Reset**, a reordering of social and economic priorities. A plan to destroy America as we know it.

https://www.weforum.org/agenda/2020/06/now-is-the-time-for-a-great-reset/

Does History Repeat? It might. The anomaly is not that Trump, an outsider, was elected in 2016. The famous writer, Eric Hoffer, "The Longshoreman Philosopher," predicted this in the late sixties.

Hoffer said, *"We must deflate the pretensions of self-appointed elites. These elites will hate us no matter what we do, and it is legitimate for us to help dump them into the dustbin of history."* Most surprising today may be where this sentiment first appeared—in the pages of *The New York Times*.

https://blog.johntrudel.com/the-longshoreman-philosopher-saw-trump-coming-in-1970/

Hoffer attributed those developments to the "ordeal of affluence," which threatened social stability. Wealth without work "creates a climate of disintegrating values with its fallout of anarchy." Among the poor, this takes the form of street crime; among the affluent, of "insolence on the campus"—both "sick forms of adolescent self-assertion." As a result, "*men of words* and charismatic leaders—people who deal with magic—come into their own," while "the middle class, lacking magic, is bungling the job" of maintaining social order.

That is what **HAS** happened. The baby boomers of the sixties burned, bombed, rioted, and trashed America. Bill Ayers infamously bombed the Pentagon, bragging he was "Guilty as Hell. Free as a bird." Obama later launched his political campaign from Ayer's living room in Chicago. America has had a total of only four presidential impeachments in history. Hillary Clinton took part in three. Then we have John Kerry, Jane Fonda, and the list of haters goes on, endlessly.

Tucker Carlson has done interviews with Brexit politician Nigel Farage, whose observations on Trump vs. Biden are interesting. The EU (unaccountable bureaucrats and ruling elites) was the implementation of **The Great Reset** in Europe. The UK was a member of the EU. It was all but impossible to escape as, once in the EU, the EU's laws applied. One size fit all.

Until it did not. Farage then led a **successful** campaign to have EU membership repealed in the UK. The elites and media fought tooth and nail to block the UK exit. They failed. The UK left the EU Single Market and Customs Union. EU law no longer applies to the UK. The Trade and Cooperation Agreement decided in December 2020 changed the basis of the UK's relationship with its European neighbors from EU law **back** to free trade and friendly cooperation. It was a huge setback for the New World Order, and a victory for freedom.

Unfortunately, after that victory, Farage then lost his bid for UK Prime Minister to Boris Johnson, who proved to be a weak ally for Trump. Farage says Johnson uses the Political Prism, not the Reality Prism. ["He's not a leader. He follows the polls."]

Farage, who has a private sector background, says, "Politicians don't like democracy." He believes America's 2020 election is abnormal. Though there is no Churchill in Great Britain today, he thinks freedom will, once again, will be determined by what happens in America.

He says the aberrant historic event is the stolen 2020 election. What happens next, to repair or ignore this not yet known, given the extent to which the Democrats hold power, and are going all out to implement Cancel Culture, suspend the Constitution, and impose **The Great Reset**.

Farage is oddly optimistic. He thinks that Biden's string of disasters and tyranny could cause Democrats to quietly change sides. He notes that similar history occurred in the last onslaught of tyranny. When all was lost and resistance was futile, the Brits furiously resisted Hitler. American aid saved them. He's hoping for a repeat.

The Global Beast first appeared as an innocent lamb.

World Economic Forum began in 1971 as a European nonprofit that invited business leaders to an annual conference every January. Then called the European Management Forum, early meetings focused on how European leaders could emulate business practices in the United States. The wolf came in sheep's clothing. The group expanded and changed its name to the World Economic Forum in 1987. Its annual meeting, held in Davos, Switzerland, is known simply as "Davos."

People around the world are involved, but the World Economic Forum remains heavily influenced by Schwab and his beliefs, articulated in a manifesto published in 1973. That paper said companies should value stakeholders, not just shareholders. Unelected, unaccountable management was to serve society, while making a profit sufficient to ensure the company's prosperity. The manifesto promised a better world, as did Lenin, Stalin, Hitler, Mao, and others.

https://www.weforum.org/agenda/2019/12/davos-manifesto-1973-a-code-of-ethics-for-business-leaders/

So off they went, a hodgepodge of economists and elites looking to boost profits and power by ostensibly doing good from anything and everything under the sun. It started innocently with pollution, then global cooling (later warming, followed by weather itself), whales, spotted owls, and polar bears, but then expanded into every aspect of people's lives all over the planet.

Under Obama, they told us what lightbulbs we could buy. Under Biden, they closed our churches and stripped us of the right to assemble. We were locked down and required to take experimental drugs. Poor third-world countries became the testbeds for vaccines and eugenics (renamed as "population control"), while power-seeking countries, most notably China, welcomed "outsourcing" and exploited America's weakened intellectual property protection. It cost the United States billions (a trillion dollars for the F-35!) to develop a new weapons system, but only a small fraction of that for China to copy it.

Globalism became supercharged under the Clinton administration, and there was no looking back. The battle cry was "Global Harmonization."

Hillary's patent commissioner, Bruce Lehman, was the highest placed gay in the government. He led the charge, backed by Hillary herself.

To object to Lehman's actions was to be labeled a homophobe. Alinsky tactics prevailed. Our "best in the world" patent system became "average." Harmonization became HARMonization.

The leading management consultant of the time, Doctor Peter Drucker, warned against this, saying, "We will pay a terrible price for this greed." CEOs were paid twenty or fifty times the average wage in their firms, but this differential soon soared into the thousands and beyond. Drucker (then in his nineties, tethered to an oxygen tank, but still giving warning speeches) lost all his corporate clients and died in 2005.

Greed prevailed. People like Drucker were replaced by people like "Chainsaw" Dunlap, who ripped companies apart and shipped their assets offshore. The middle of America turned into a Rust Belt. This was the "new normal" until Trump came along and did his own reset, which made America great again.

America is in the way of a Globalist World because of our Judeo-Christian roots and valuing of freedom, equal justice, and exceptionalism. What blocks the Globalists is our belief in America, our Constitution, our freedoms, and the individual.

The opposite of our Ten Commandments is "The Ends Justify the Means," which Machiavelli warned against. Alinsky's *Rules for Radicals* is demonic. He dedicated the first edition to Lucifer.

> *"I never compared Nazis to communism, but communism was the same thing, the end justifies the means. Whatever the means."*
>
> **Elie Wiesel**, Holocaust survivor, and Nobel Prize Winner

Note: It was and is the same thing. Hitler's Nazis were national socialists. Stalin's Communists were international socialists. American Marxists are global socialists. Socialism kills.

> *"Our government is the potent, the omnipresent teacher. For good or for ill it teaches the whole people by example. Crime is contagious. If the government becomes a lawbreaker, it breeds contempt for law; it invites every man to become a law unto himself; it invites anarchy. To declare that in the administration of the criminal law the end justifies the means—to declare that the Government may commit crimes to secure the conviction of a private criminal—would bring terrible retributions."*
>
> Louis D. Brandeis

The radical left's efforts to divide us, and long-term programs to indoctrinate our children with false narratives about our history, are aided and abetted by the propaganda pushed daily by their co-conspirators in mainstream media. And compounded by the socialist—not social—media companies that push their own propaganda campaigns, censor the truth, and then use your data to manipulate you. Why? It is their pursuit for control of power, absolute power. It is part of an ongoing domestic cognitive war.

A famous saying states the obvious—**"The only thing necessary for the triumph of evil is that good men do nothing."** The objective of this chapter is to reinforce the ongoing efforts of Americans who are now fighting back, shouting back, and pushing back against the totalitarian state, the dictators, and the mentally deranged.

We need to "take back America" by good men, women, and children **doing** something. Biden's Attorney General, the exemplar of these deranged leftists, calls us domestic terrorists. Our own FBI allows Antifa and Black Lives Matter to repeatedly riot, loot, and burn our cities. Why? Because they are "ideas," not "organized groups." They refuse to protect normal Americans, because of alleged "White supremacy," "racial justice," "social justice," and a list of other Marxist labels as advocated and promoted by fake history and Critical Race Theory zealots.

No, you morons! We are patriotic Americans! We fought a war to end slavery! We passed the Civil Rights Act to ensure equality! (Note: Democrats were on the other side. Don't forget how they voted on the 13th, 14th, 15th Amendments.) Our founding documents delineate our "Inalienable Rights," including free speech, equal justice, innocent until proven guilty, and the right to bear arms.

Do your job and protect us! Do not prosecute innocent Americans! We do not need another Heinrich Himmler, Feliks Dzierżyński, Marx, Lenin, Stalin, Mao, or Hitler! You are ripping our great nation to shreds. Without our Second Amendment, we would look like Australia, which is reverting into a prison colony.

The same goes for those in Congress. You make the laws. You represent us, "We the People." Now, since January 6, you have allowed stolen elections, massive voter fraud, and Gulags holding political prisoners under horrific conditions. For Shame!

Many people also worry that the post-COVID world will include new restrictions on mobility, such as requirements to present a vaccine or immunity card before boarding a plane or attending a concert. The federal Economic Employment Opportunity Commission recently said employers can require vaccination and bar workers from their buildings if they don't have it. And a "Common Pass" has been proposed that would serve as a form of health ID around the world.

One person on Twitter described the components of **The Great Reset** as control of movement, suppression of dissent, transfer of wealth, and creation of dependency on government, as well as the introduction of digital IDs, electronic money, and universal basic income. Others say that reports of mutations in the viruses, and concealment of vaccine failures, are cover stories to enforce new lockdowns.

It is not just people in the United States who are worried. Writing for Breitbart News, British podcaster James Delingpole called **The Great Reset** one of several code words for "the complete transformation of the global economy in order to create a New World Order." "Sure, it sounds like a conspiracy theory," Delingpole wrote. "**But as someone wise once said, it is not a conspiracy theory when they tell you exactly what they are doing.**"

Some take it farther, claiming that the pandemic was a "plandemic," created by humans to engineer **The Great Reset.** That makes it an Action Plan. The longer this goes on, the more draconian the edicts, the more lies broadcast, the more ominous all this seems. There are two reasons for concern:

- The Global Agenda: It's real. See the previous chapter.
- Excessive Government: It's real. Use the Reality Lens.

Dividing America:

A minority of radicals have pushed false narratives to try to divide and disrupt our nation since Alinsky and the 1960s. Their biased media friends, whom we not so endearingly refer to as "propaganda whores," aid and abet their false narratives. This is Mind War.

Lies are so blatant that recently Pelosi blamed the media for the lack of public support for the multitrillion socialist, communist, fascist spending bill. They call it "human infrastructure." I call it lipstick on a pig.

But no one in the media noted the irony of the media propaganda whores being told they're not servicing their masters—the leftist looney progressives—well enough. Those in the once free press who provided oversight now serve as the Goebbels of the left. Bad media, despicable knee-bending media! Even the dictators of China and Russia are not so bold in their proclamations to their media servants.

Destroying America:

These lemmings and progressive radicals of the left came into office in 2020 with a vaccine, declining COVID cases, energy independence, strong but fair relations with US allies, a secure Afghanistan, a closed and secure border, a growing economy that was benefiting all (minorities, women, and Americans in general), restricting Chinese efforts to collect data and steal our secrets, and precluding Russia from using oil to hold Western Europe hostage. And remember, they promised "unity," a new relationship with our allies, and to bring this country together.

Since then, we have seen what they have brought us. They brought us increased deaths, massive mandates, and purposefully spread COVID across America by releasing infected illegal immigrants into multiple states. All while they forced mandates on us, which are now resulting in massive labor shortages. The psychological damage to adults, and even more to children, is the time bomb of tomorrow.

One aspect of autism is that the part of the brain that recognizes facial features does not develop properly. How do children learn to recognize faces when those faces are covered with masks? How to form strong personal relationships with people whose faces (and intentions) are covered?

They closed our oil production and pipelines—moving us to dependency. Concurrently, they opened our borders while paying millions a day to not construct a border wall. They committed treason by ignoring our laws, our Constitution, the public, and their oath of office. They angered not only our allies, but also our neighbors, by canceling the Keystone Pipeline and ongoing efforts by the previous administration that had resulted in the USA being a net exporter of energy.

They pulled out of Afghanistan without telling our allies and left behind thousands of US citizens and Afghanistan allies as hostages for the terrorist Taliban. They left the terrorists in control of Afghanistan, well-armed with billions of dollars of our military equipment.

They ignored War Fighting, instead focusing on finding Constitutional adherents (a.k.a., extremists) in our military, discriminating against Whites, giving partisan political interviews to Fake News reporters, and pushing the indoctrination of our troops, public, and children in Marxist Critical Race Theory.

https://www.frontpagemag.com/fpm/2021/12/how-obama-sabotaged-american-military-daniel-greenfield/

Critical Race Theory was an Obama initiative. It is an ideology rooted in Marxism (one best termed "Neo-Marxism"—it's where all the "Critical theories," e.g., race, gender, etc. originated) and secular humanism that is antithetical to American Heritage and Judeo-Christian culture. These malignant theories advocate resolving differences through accusation and violence, essentially the exact opposite of American Heritage and Culture.

An excellent book about this is *The Triumph of Good*, by Thomas Cromwell. Essentially, he argues that God alone will **not** save us. "Divine Providence is not dependent on God alone, but on humanity participating in the realization of the Creator's purpose. Thus, we cannot simply wait for God to solve our problems. In today's world, our responsibility is to understand and confront the twin dangers of leftist ideology and Communist China. Our response to their evil ideas and aggressive behavior must be spiritual and ideological as well as political."

People from America's Founding Fathers to Presidents from both parties have said similar things. Basically, the critical thing necessary for the triumph of good is for men and woman to fulfill their God-given responsibilities.

We have a long way to go. China has hypersonic missiles. We have a transgender Admiral, and a military no longer focused on war fighting.

The radical left continued their destruction by reversing multiple national security decisions to stop China, including the bans on TikTok, WeChat, use of Huawei telecommunications, and use of DJI drones. They jeopardized the US and world economy by approving the Russian pipeline to Western Europe.

Not satisfied, they ignored the science, spread hysteria, and began expanding COVID mandates while the opposite actions proved of more value. How surreal the last nine months have been!

But expect it all to get worse as we now watch these public servants try to invalidate our voting rights by passing a law that would perpetuate fraud, and to pass massive spending bills that would cause massive inflation, devalue the dollar, kill jobs, and expand dependency on the state.

This as they use our FBI, DOJ, and Treasury to label parents as terrorists, track your spending, let criminals go, prosecute the innocent, and intimidate you into silence. We must stop them from gutting our liberty.

They are Public Servants—NOT elites or a ruling class

These radical left progressives are not a ruling class—and we need to stop calling them that. FYI, for the ill-informed (and the truth-resistant Fake News media), they are in fact "public servants." They are not "elites." They only think of themselves in that way.

These miscreants we call politicians are elected to serve us. Many do not. They serve themselves.

Ms. Pelosi is an exemplar, holding an all-White, rich, dinner party at her mansion, while served by her Black and brown constituents. How antebellum of her to re-enact the days of the Confederacy at her home. A picture of hypocrisy, but that should not be a surprise given her family's roots and her being from the party of slavery. Pelosi and her progressive cabal do not serve you, and they do not serve the public. They are leeches who live off your blood, sweat, and tears to feed and line their pockets. All while trying to divide you and put you into your place—into their predesignated buckets of identity politics.

Black people are trapped in filthy, crime-ridden cities, with failed schools, no good jobs, drug cartels, gang violence, soaring murder rates, and no way out. They are completely dependent on the government. The blue cities were repeatedly burned and looted during the 2020 Biden riots, and then partially rebuilt with taxpayer money stolen from public coffers. Our big cities are run by the drug cartels, with fentanyl the #1 cause of death from ages 18 to 45 in 2020.

These so-called "social justice warriors" constantly demand that minorities bow to them, praise them, fund them, and obey them. As their leader Joe Biden, an old White privileged male (from a slave state), noted in a stern warning to a Black man, "You ain't Black if you don't vote for me." How obscene is that? These America haters of the left and their Marxist and fascist friends like BLM and Antifa do not advance civil discussion or unity. They intimidate, divide, threaten in mobs, assault, attack, and destroy anything and everyone in their path to absolute power.

The old terms of communist and fascist no longer apply, as they are two ends of the same circle of tyranny. Hence, we coined a new term—**comufascists**. It better reflects the reality of their tyrannical ideology. But you can also simply call them American Marxists, or America haters.

These so-called elected leaders took an oath to serve, defend, and protect our Constitution. But they act more like leeches, leftists, fascists, and dictators as they strive to divide and tear our country apart, demean us, our history, our republic, our Constitution, and divide us in ways to gain power—absolute power. It is disgusting, and it is time for us to "Take Back America!"

We are not divided—They Are

In today's surreal world of Orwellian dystopian propaganda and disinformation, we are told how bad we are, how racist we are, how hateful we are, how divided we are, and how awful our country is. But by whom?

Few. These loud-mouthed comufascists (fanatics), are a small, violent, radical minority of extremists. They have taken control of the Democratic Party. They have divided their own party, and now follow officials into bathrooms to call them right-wing for not abiding by their Marxist dictates or supporting their socialist legislation. They exemplify "extremist."

They hate America and despise what it stands for. Yet they leverage Its freedoms, independence, opportunities, and democracy to undermine the same. They are cowards. They are deceitful. They are liars. They portray themselves as caring, yet have no qualms in sacrificing thousands of lives to sustain and advance their efforts for absolute power. They are in simple terms—evil. They include Obama, Pelosi, Schumer, Warner, Kaine, Waters, the Squad of incompetents, Swalwell, Schiff, Cheney, Romney and so many others.

In plain English—these people try to con you into believing they love America, but through their actions, show us how much they hate America. They speak in Orwellian terms, constantly changing the meaning of well-known words to hide and obfuscate their obscene efforts and intentions. They do so while professing they are only seeking positive change. They use the term "equity" to promote active racism and division. They use Critical Race Theory to portray minorities as too dumb and incapable of thinking for themselves, while blaming anyone who is White as inherently racist. It is intended to divide, enrage, foster hate, and cause fear. These comufascists are intolerant by nature. Their tolerance extends only to the subservient, the compliant, Lenin's "Useful Idiots."

They are led by those who have demonic souls, like Hillary and Nancy Pelosi. Yet, they are joined by the dumbfounded, brain-dead, compliant, and complacent like Romney, Cheney, Kasich, and others. These miscreants slither and slide just like their left-wing counterparts: Schiff, Swalwell, AOC, Sanders, Schumer, Pelosi, et al.

They do not serve "We the People." They serve themselves, and their handlers, including Soros and China. They constantly push false cover stories to hide their ineptness and weakness, to advance their station in life, wealth, and power.

It is Time to Resist

We must stand up against those who seek to change America from the land of opportunity, freedom, and guardian of humanity into the land of subjugation, subservience, and apostate obedient serfs whose false god is the establishment. They must be confronted head-on.

We can take a page from progressive left radicals. We can prosecute, persecute, confront, shout down, push back and condemn these radicals of the left in their attempt to destroy America. It is time to make them cease and desist—or face society's wrath.

Bullies Are Cowards

The radicals' extensive efforts to prosecute anyone within the radius of the 6 January demonstration at the Capitol, most who peacefully walked or were lured into the Capitol through open doors and down roped paths, are outrageous. Democrats are still hiding over 14,000 hours of videos of this event. (Babbitt was seen on video with her back to the Capitol police telling people to not enter, to go back. Now we know why she was shot: she was interfering in the false flag insurrection.) Democrats also ignore the billions in damage, police assassinations, murders, arson, and anarchy of the "summer of love." Such acts embolden the bullies and America haters.

The **only** person murdered that day at the Capitol was Ashli Babbitt—a veteran, peaceful, unarmed, and shot down without warning in cold blood by one of Nancy's Imperial Guard: Michael Byrd. It was all captured on film. Lieutenant Byrd was never charged or prosecuted.

PELOSI WON'T LET CAPITOL POLICE TESTIFY ABOUT WHAT HAPPENED JAN 6. THAT TELLS YOU EVERYTHING YOU NEED TO KNOW

Who runs around with bats, chains, metal bars, with helmets and shields, while dressed in all black and faces covered? The BLM, Antifa, and radical left comufascists are thugs, hooligans, and arsonists hell-bent on intimidating others with their legions of organized bullies. They must be confronted, stopped, prosecuted for illegal acts, and imprisoned.

The bullies come in many forms—Antifa, BLM, the Squad, Hollywood, Big Tech, senior government national security leaders, and, of course, the media. Their tactics include character assassination, censoring facts, and pushing disinformation. But they operate only in groups, as individually (like any bully) they are, in fact, cowards. They try to push everyone into some group or other, and then pit the groups against each other. [A key point. America is about individual freedom. Marxism abhors that. It is about the collective, not the individual.]

They are traitors to our democracy—and include those we used to call the free press. A press that now succumbs to Chinese Communist influence and bribery. A press that publishes full-page ads or sections in major newspapers, without caveats or other warnings, which espouse and echo pure communist propaganda. There are no disclaimers. They print the lies China pays them to print. They enable the bullies by hiding the truth of the organized destruction of America.

Today's press lives off the blood and sacrifice of millions of Americans who stood for freedom, truth, and independence. They slither from lie to lie—covering up, censoring, and hiding the lies of their liberal self-anointed masters.

They applaud the three stooges—Brennan, Comey, Clapper—and the fifty former "senior intelligence officials" who stated the Hunter Biden laptop was "Russian disinformation?" Really? The same liars who told us in public that Trump was colluding with the Russians, but in private and under oath, had no evidence. The same liars who used a political operative's dossier, without validation, to smear, undermine and set in motion an attempted coup of a sitting president.

A few dozen FBI, DOJ, and CIA senior agents were fired (or allowed to retire), but none of their leaders were held accountable? No one went to prison. It is time to push back.

"Zuckerbucks" and the 2020 Election

In the 2020 presidential election, for the first time ever, partisan groups were allowed—on a widespread basis—to cross the bright red line separating government officials who administer elections from political operatives who work to win them. It is vital to understand how this happened to prevent it in the future.

It is important to not confuse or mingle Zuckerberg's unprecedented (possibly illegal) actions to directly influence elections with myriad other malevolent efforts and investments to promote COVID vaccines, jabs, lockdowns, censor all critics (including President Trump) of how the pandemic issues were handled. The amounts invested just to promote and amplify the **COVID Panic** were astronomical—trillions of dollars—not just from Zuckerberg, but from all involved (Soros, Gates, Democrats, the New World Order, China, et al.), including a tsunami of federal money, with the Feds printing dollars to cover that.

Over **five trillion dollars** came from the US Congress, funded by printing more money, thus driving rampant inflation and the highest energy prices in our history. This, if unchecked, will collapse our economy. It could end the use of the US dollar as the international standard. *The petrodollar system is an exchange of oil for US dollars between countries that buy oil and those that produce it. If that ends, so will US prosperity. It will be unrecoverable.*

The pandemic itself, the panic that ensued, and how it was handled, had an enormous impact on the election, as did Big Tech censorship, Fake News, phony Russian collusion, and more. But this section of our book will focus on Zuckerberg's **successful** efforts to embed his own private election system on top of and inside those of the States.

It is not well understood, even by citizens, but the system of Federalism created by America's Constitution specifically makes the States, not the federal government, responsible for electing presidents. Each state legislature gets to set their own procedures for election processes.

The Vice President, much criticized by Trump supporters, does not get to set these processes. He does get to determine if such processes were properly followed. He failed in that duty.

VP Pence could have just said, "There are problems with certification," and left it to the individual states to sort that out. Trump would have continued as President until that process was completed. That's why Trump supporters were at the Capitol on January 6.

Pence did not fulfill that role. Hence, to this day, some states, individually, are still grinding away on recounts, efforts now **opposed** by the Biden administration. It's a tough slog, as, even when there is massive evidence of fraud, there are "Soros prosecutors" in many states who can refuse to prosecute. It takes time and effort to remove or overrule them.

This section does not speak to that either. **It speaks only to the over $400 million that Zuckerberg invested, of his own money, in his own private election system.** A partisan, private system that did everything from getting out the votes, to collecting them in "Zucker boxes," and, yes, even to "securing" and counting the ballots. To be sure, there were also deception operations to cloak these efforts to swing the election with the much greater flood of money dumped into COVID.

Months after the election, *Time* magazine published a triumphant story of how the election was won by "a well-funded cabal of powerful people, ranging across industries and ideologies, working together behind the scenes to influence perceptions, change rules and laws, steer media coverage and control the flow of information." Written by Molly Ball, a journalist with close ties to Democratic leaders, it told a cheerful story of a "conspiracy unfolding behind the scenes," the "result of an informal alliance between left-wing activists and business titans."

A major part of this "conspiracy" to "save the 2020 election" was to use COVID as a pretext to maximize absentee and early voting. This effort was enormously successful. Half of the voters ended up voting by mail, and another quarter voted early. It was, Ball wrote, "practically a revolution in how people vote." Another major part was to raise an army of progressive activists to administer the election at the ground level. Here, one billionaire took a leading role: Facebook founder Mark Zuckerberg.

Zuckerberg's help to Democrats is well known when it comes to censoring their political opponents in the name of preventing "misinformation." **Less well known is the fact that he directly funded liberal groups running partisan get-out-the-vote operations. In fact, he helped those groups infiltrate election offices in key swing states by doling out large grants to crucial districts.**

The Chan Zuckerberg Initiative, an organization led by Zuckerberg's wife Priscilla, gave more than **$400 million** to nonprofit groups involved in "securing" the 2020 election. Most of those funds—colloquially called "Zuckerbucks"—were funneled through the Center for Tech and Civic Life (CTCL), a voter outreach organization founded by Tiana Epps-Johnson, Whitney May, and Donny Bridges. All three had previously worked on activism relating to election rules for the New Organizing Institute, once described by *The Washington Post* as "the Democratic Party's Hogwarts for digital wizardry."

Flush with Zuckerbucks, the CTCL proceeded to disburse large grants to election officials and local governments across the country. These disbursements were billed publicly as "COVID-19 response grants," ostensibly to help municipalities acquire protective gear for poll workers or otherwise help protect election officials and volunteers against the virus. In practice, little money was spent on this. Here, as in other cases, COVID simply provided cover.

According to the Foundation for Government Accountability (FGA), Georgia received more than $31 million in Zuckerbucks, one of the highest amounts in the country. The three Georgia counties that received the most money spent only 1.3 percent of it on personal protective equipment. The rest was spent on salaries, laptops, vehicle rentals, attorney fees for public records requests, mail-in balloting, and other measures that allowed elections offices to hire activists to work the election. Not all Georgia counties received CTCL funding. And of those that did, Trump-voting counties received an average of $1.91 per registered voter, compared to $7.13 per registered voter in Biden-voting counties.

The FGA looked at this funding another way, too. Trump won Georgia by more than five points in 2016. He lost it by three-tenths of a point in 2020. On average, as a share of the two-party vote, most counties moved Democratic by less than one percentage point in that time. Counties that did not receive Zuckerbucks showed hardly any movement, but counties that did, moved an average of 2.3 percentage points Democratic. In counties that did not receive Zuckerbucks, "roughly half saw an increase in Democrat votes that offset the increase in Republican votes, while roughly half saw the opposite trend." In counties that did receive Zuckerbucks, by contrast, three-quarters "saw a significant uptick in Democrat votes that offset any upward change in Republican votes," including highly populated Fulton, Gwinnett, Cobb, and DeKalb counties.

Of all the 2020 battleground states, it is in Wisconsin (or perhaps Arizona, with more evidence, but looser laws, and a "Soros Prosecutor") where the most has been proven about how Zuckerbucks worked.

CTCL distributed $6.3 million to the Wisconsin cities of Racine, Green Bay, Madison, Milwaukee, and Kenosha—to ensure that voting could take place "in accordance with prevailing [anti-COVID] public health requirements."

Wisconsin law says voting is a right, but that "voting by absentee ballot must be carefully regulated to prevent the potential for fraud or abuse; to prevent overzealous solicitation of absent electors who may prefer not to participate in an election." Wisconsin law also says that elections are to be run by clerks or other government officials. But the five cities that received Zuckerbucks outsourced much of their election operation to private liberal groups, in one case so extensively that a sidelined government official quit in frustration.

This was by design. Cities that received grants were not allowed to use the money to fund outside help unless CTCL specifically approved their plans in writing. CTCL kept tight control of how money was spent, and it had an abundance of "partners" to help with anything the cities needed.

Some government officials were willing to do whatever CTCL recommended. "As far as I'm concerned, I am taking all of my cues from CTCL and work with those you recommend," Celestine Jeffreys, the Chief of Staff to Democratic Green Bay Mayor Eric Genrich, wrote in an email. CTCL not only had plenty of recommendations but made available a "network of current and former election administrators and election experts" to scale up "your vote-by-mail processes" and "ensure forms, envelopes, and other materials are understood and completed correctly by voters."

Power the Polls, a liberal group recruiting poll workers, promised to help with ballot curing. The liberal Mikva Challenge worked to recruit high-school-age poll workers. And the left-wing Brennan Center offered help with "election integrity," including "post-election audits" and "cybersecurity."

The Center for Civic Design, an election administration policy organization that frequently partners with groups such as liberal billionaire Pierre Omidyar's Democracy Fund, designed absentee ballots and voting instructions, often working directly with an election commission to design envelopes and create advertising and targeting campaigns. The Elections Group, also linked to the Democracy Fund, provided technical assistance in handling drop boxes and conducted voter outreach. The communications director for the Center for Secure and Modern Elections, an organization that advocates sweeping changes to the elections process, ran a conference call to help Green Bay develop Spanish-language radio ads and geofencing to target voters in a pre-defined area.

Digital Response, a nonprofit launched in 2020, offered to "bring voters an updated elections website," "run a website health check," "set up communications channels," "bring poll worker application and management online," "track and respond to polling location wait times," "set up voter support and email response tools," "bring vote-by-mail applications online," "process incoming [vote-by-mail] applications," and help with "ballot curing process tooling and voter notification."

The National Vote at Home Institute was presented as a "technical assistance partner" that could "support outreach around absentee voting," provide and oversee voting machines, consult on methods to cure absentee ballots, and even assume the duty of curing ballots.

A few weeks after the five Wisconsin cities received their grants, CTCL emailed Claire Woodall-Vogg, the executive director of the Milwaukee Election Commission, to offer "an experienced elections staffer that could potentially embed with your staff in Milwaukee in a matter of days." The staffer leading Wisconsin's portion of the National Vote at Home Institute was an out-of-state Democratic activist named Michael Spitzer-Rubenstein. As soon as he met with Woodall-Vogg, he asked for contacts in other cities and at the Wisconsin Elections Commission.

Spitzer-Rubenstein would eventually take over much of Green Bay's election planning from the official charged with running the election, Green Bay Clerk Kris Teske. This made Teske so unhappy that she took Family and Medical Leave prior to the election and quit shortly thereafter.

Emails from Spitzer-Rubenstein show the extent to which he was managing the election process. To one government official, he wrote, "By Monday, I'll have our edits on the absentee voting instructions. We're pushing QuickBase to get their system up and running and I'll keep you updated. I'll revise the planning tool to accurately reflect the process. I'll create a flowchart for the vote-by-mail processing that we will be able to share with both inspectors and observers."

Once early voting started, Woodall-Vogg would provide Spitzer-Rubenstein with daily updates on the numbers of absentee ballots returned and still outstanding in each ward—prized information for a political operative.

Amazingly, Spitzer-Rubenstein even asked for direct access to the Milwaukee Election Commission's voter database: "Would you or someone else on your team be able to do a screen-share so we can see the process for an export?" he wrote. "Do you know if WisVote has an [application programming interface] or anything similar so that it can connect with other software apps? That would be the Holy Grail." Even for Woodall-Vogg, that was too much. "While I completely understand and appreciate the assistance that is trying to be provided," she replied, "I am definitely not comfortable having a non-staff member involved in the function of our voter database, much less recording it."

When these emails were released in 2021, they stunned Wisconsin observers. "What exactly was the National Vote at Home Institute doing with its daily reports? Was it making sure that people were voting from home by going door-to-door to collect ballots from voters who had not yet turned theirs in? Was this data sharing a condition of the CTCL grant? And who was really running Milwaukee's election?" asked Dan O'Donnell, whose election analysis appeared at Wisconsin's conservative MacIver Institute.

Kris Teske, the sidelined Green Bay city clerk—in whose office Wisconsin law places the responsibility to conduct elections—had, of course, seen what was happening early on. "I just don't know where the Clerk's Office fits in anymore," she wrote in early July. By August, she was worried about legal exposure: "I don't understand how people who don't have the knowledge of the process can tell us how to manage the election," she wrote on August 28.

Green Bay Mayor Eric Genrich simply handed over Teske's authority to agents from outside groups and gave them leadership roles in collecting absentee ballots, fixing ballots that would otherwise be voided for failure to follow the law, and even supervising the counting of ballots. "The grant mentors would like to meet with you to discuss, further, the ballot curing process. Please let them know when you're available," Genrich's Chief of Staff told Teske.

Spitzer-Rubenstein explained that the National Vote at Home Institute had done the same for other cities in Wisconsin. "We have a process map that we've worked out with Milwaukee for their process. We can also adapt the letter we're sending out with rejected absentee ballots along with a call script alerting voters. (We can also get people to make the calls, too, so you don't need to worry about it.)"

Other emails show that Spitzer-Rubenstein had keys to the central counting facility and access to all the machines before election night. His name was on contracts with the hotel hosting the ballot counting.

Sandy Juno, who was clerk of Brown County, where Green Bay is located, later testified about the problems in a legislative hearing. "He was advising them on things. He was touching the ballots. He had access to see how the votes were counted," Juno said of Spitzer-Rubenstein. Others testified that he was giving orders to poll workers and seemed to be the person running the election night count operation.

"I would really like to think that when we talk about the security of elections, we're talking about more than just the security of the internet," Juno said. "You know, it has to be security of the physical location, where you're not giving a third-party key to where you have your election equipment."

Juno noted that there were irregularities in the counting, too, with no consistency between the various tables. Some had absentee ballots face-up, so anyone could see how they were marked. Poll workers were seen reviewing ballots, not just to see that they'd been appropriately checked by the clerk, but "reviewing how they were marked." And poll workers fixing ballots used the same color pens as one's ballots had been filled out in, contrary to established procedures designed to make sure observers could differentiate between voters' marks and poll workers' marks.

The plan by Democratic strategists to bring activist groups into election offices worked in part because no legislature had ever imagined that a nonprofit could take over so many election offices so easily. "If it can happen to Green Bay, Wisconsin, sweet little old Green Bay, Wisconsin, these people can coordinate any place," said Janel Brandtjen, a state representative in Wisconsin.

She was right. Sue Lani Madsen, among others, noted: What happened in Green Bay happened in Democrat-run cities and counties across the country. Four hundred million Zuckerbucks were distributed with strings attached. Officials were required to work with "partner organizations" to massively expand mail-in voting and staff their election operations with partisan activists. The plan was genius. And because no one ever imagined that the election system could be privatized in this way, there were no laws to prevent it.

Such laws should now be a priority. So should Law and Order.

Stop Cowering—Push Back

We could go on, but you get the point. So, what is the solution? Well, it is simple, but one must have the will, fortitude, and presence of being to counter and hold these criminals to account. It is time we stop coddling the comufascists and think they will act reasonably. It is time to start holding them accountable for destroying what is good and replacing it with that which is bad. It is time we hold these scoundrels to account— this minority set of extremists who seek to advance their move toward absolute power.

Concurrently, it is time to remind Americans of the truth about America and Americans—that we are a giving and kind people, that we typically respect our neighbors and support them regardless of political affiliation—and call upon them to act. We must act and reject those who hate America. We must hold them to account. And we must push back strongly, and, if necessary, violently, to reverse their success in undermining our country, our values, and our history. The mobs and bullies only respond when confronted by a stronger force.

Unfortunately, history is replete with examples of such traitors succeeding. We have seen too many times the tyranny of a violent and intimidating minority become the despots that rule. And along with such dictators, we have seen a history littered with hundreds of millions of dead, murdered, tortured, beheaded, raped, burned, and more.

Hence, if necessary, we must meet the violence, intimidation, and assault of the minority with something they can understand. Bullies tend to wither like crying babies when they meet resistance. Just like we have seen videos of Antifa and BLM cowards caught alone without the support of their mob, and subjected to arrest... they wither, cry, and wet themselves. As with bullies, the leftist extremists are NOTHING without their mobs. They are individually cowards.

To ensure most peace-loving Americans do not succumb to a minority of radical left extremist bullies, we must stand up to them—and with overwhelming brute force if necessary. We must be willing to close our accounts with the socialist media companies. We must be willing to order supplies from other vendors than the woke leftists who buy in bulk from slave labor camps in China, receive millions from the CCP, and who serve as useful idiots for dictators.

Remember, these power-hungry destroyers live off the blood and sacrifice of millions of Americans before them. They grew their businesses successfully due to values America stands for—opportunity, independence, and freedom. Yet now, they turn against democracy, our values, our freedoms, independence, and opportunity as they have prostituted themselves out to tyranny. They now receive millions from dictators and Communists, pay pennies on the dollar for slave labor products, and have the gall to censor you and others for not accepting what 'they' say is truth!

Peace by subjugation and intimidation is not peace, it is called tyranny. To have peace requires the will to ensure peace. That is why we have a military—peace through strength. We can no longer allow the tyranny of the minority to succeed—because people are being intimidated, assaulted, threatened, and Americans are being divided, labeled, and worse by these extremists.

We shall no longer sit by idle, silent, or calm, while they denigrate our country and demean our friends. We've watched for several years as these fanatical extremists—supported by corrupt political leaders on the left—have used measures such as violence, arson, looting, intimidation, character assassination, labeling, varied dystopian and Orwellian terms, and other means to divide us and change our great nation into some type of subservient, left-wing, utopian society where a minority of privileged lazy hypocrites tries to rule the majority of honest, caring, hardworking, and truly proud Americans.

We must also dispel the use of this term "elites," and "ruling class" since there is nothing elite about these miscreants or office holders. The reality is they are cowards, leeches on society, weak of mind, hypocrites with dark, twisted views. They exemplify the ideology of true extremists and zealots offering only hate, divisiveness, and evil in the land of the good, the home of the free and the brave. We now suffer from **Anarcho-Tyranny**, and it is destroying America.

The American Dream

We are thankful, we are giving—we are Americans! And we should be proud of that!

As Americans we are free, independent, and have incredible opportunities. Race or position should not matter to those who aspire to live the American dream. The American dream is the ideal by which equality of opportunity is available to any American, allowing the highest aspirations and goals to be achieved.

INTERLUDE

Anarcho-tyranny is a concept where the state is argued to be more interested in controlling citizens so that they do not oppose the managerial class (**tyranny**) rather than controlling real criminals (causing **anarchy**). Laws are argued to be enforced only selectively, depending on what is perceived to be beneficial for the ruling elite.

The concept was successfully exploited during the Russian Revolution by Trotsky (1905), who became President of the Soviet a few months later. Full Communism later replaced it under Stalin. Trotsky fled but was hunted down and assassinated in Mexico in 1940. Stalin had him killed, but he was defended in an international forum by John Dewey, the founder of American public education.

It's not **yet** Socialism, Marxism, or Communism under which we suffer. Our dangerously chaotic, selectively oppressive predicament is more accurately described as "**Anarcho-Tyranny.**" The late conservative columnist Sam Francis first coined the term in 1992 to diagnose a condition of "both anarchy (the failure of the state to enforce the laws) and, at the same time, tyranny—the enforcement of laws by the state for oppressive purposes." This, and the toxic combination of "pandemic panic" and "George Floyd derangement syndrome" has thoroughly destroyed the home of the brave. America has become a paradise for the depraved and dictatorial.

"If you will not fight for right when you can easily win without bloodshed; if you will not fight when your victory is sure and not too costly; you may come to the moment when you will have to fight with all the odds against you and only a precarious chance of survival. There may even be a worse case. You may have to fight when there is no hope of victory, because it is better to perish than to live as slaves." **Sir Winston Churchill**

Book Two
The Novel: Raven unleashed
Chapter One – The Real View vs. The Fake View

The Ranch, California Coast, Early Morning

We were sitting on the porch, sipping coffee, watching the ocean. Another beautiful day. Then my secure phone buzzed.

I looked at Josie. "I had it silenced, babe. That's the priority override."

She sighed. "You'd better answer it, Raven."

I picked it up, looked at the ID, and hit the button. "We're on standdown, Doctor Goldfarb."

"Is Josie there?"

"She is."

"Are you in a safe area?"

"Not a SCIF, but yes, safe. We're alone, out on our patio at The Ranch."

"Is your team close?"

"Negative. They are out enjoying the vacation we were promised."

"There is a plane coming for you and Josie to bring you to Virginia. I have a little hunting camp. Lovely place. I need you both. As soon as possible. Alert your team. We'll round them up later."

Josie held up a hand, shook her head, and whispered, "Something bad. Go easy."

She sensed these things.

I said, "What's going down?"

"I'll tell you when you get here, Raven."

"It's a secure line."

"Close hold, Raven. You and Josie. I need you both. Now. Your transport will be at the airport as soon as I can get it there. Maybe two hours."

"Can you say anything?"

There was a pause. "Two things, Raven. Number one, move your ass. Number two, Justice Scalia."

"I don't understand..."

There was stress in his voice, even with the triply redundant encryption. "Just hold on to the first part. Your ass on that airplane. It is a direct order. Acknowledge, please."

"Acknowledged, sir."

"I'll see you soon."

The line went dead. Josie was looking puzzled. "Scalia?"

"No idea. He has a bug up his ass about something. How soon can you be packed?"

She shrugged. "Everything? Ten minutes. Fifteen if I freshen up and do my hair."

"Take twenty. I will message the team. I have a feeling we're not coming back soon."

***

Virginia. En Route to Hunting Camp. Late Afternoon.

Goldfarb himself picked us up. He looked rustic. Jeans, dark flannel shirt, boots, and a large revolver on his hip. He had a bit of a tan, and I could see the stem of his pipe sticking out of his front pocket. His blue eyes were intense behind his signature rimless glasses.

95

He had on a red baseball cap that said, "Beyond this welter, the sun shines, Virginia."

I blinked and said, "*Welter*? Is that the state slogan?"

He shook his head. "No. It's 'Virginia is for lovers.' This is Virginia Woolf. I rather prefer it."

Josie's voice was soft. "Indeed. Who's Afraid of Virginia Woolf?"

"Right. It is about an hour to the camp on a private road, a bad road. We have a good cook, and dinner is at seven. You will have time to clean up and shower. We'll talk then."

Our transport was a Jeep Grand Cherokee, in camo, jacked up, with mud spattered up to and on the roof, sporting huge tires and a winch on the heavy steel front bumper.

Not a Humvee, but close. A Free State civilian vehicle. I checked the gun rack in the back. A scoped-up bolt action hunting rifle with a flash suppressor, and a tactical shotgun. Goldfarb said there were also two full-auto M4s under a tarp with red dot optics, locked and loaded.

I said, "What are we hunting?"

He shrugged. "You'll find out. A better question is what might be hunting us. This Jeep has armor and bulletproof glass. It will stop a .223 round, but not a 7.62. The guns in back have hunting ammo, hot rounds. Think of them as critical defense; antipersonnel.

"When we get to the camp, I have other types. I've got some mags there loaded with a mix of armor piercing and such; loads that are better against vehicles."

I smiled. "Not tracer?"

"You know better, Raven."

"I do, indeed. Tracer works both ways..."

Goldfarb drove. He was silent for the rest of the trip.

***

Virginia. Dining Room at the Hunting Camp. Evening.

The dinner was excellent. Cooked and served up by a large, muscled up, Black man named Jeff. He was sporting tattoos on his arms.

Goldfarb had explained on the drive that Jeff was his longtime custodian at his hunting camp. The camp, which lacked a name, had been in his family for three generations. It was not much-discussed. He had never mentioned it to me, and I have known him for years.

He said he trusted Jeff fully. He had saved Goldfarb's life on several occasions and had served as his chief bodyguard. Goldfarb, with few exceptions, was not inclined to trust denizens of the DC Swamp, including Secret Service, FBI, Capitol Police, CIA, and the rest of the alphabet soup agencies.

He said the CIA, where he had worked for decades, was corrupted. He distrusted them. Brennan, who was a known communist when the Agency had hired him at the peak of the Cold War, had gained power through political connections. Despite such actions as Brennan's approving the visas of the 9-11 bombers and sanitizing Obama's travel records, he eventually ran the Agency. His successors, in Goldfarb's opinion, were not much better.

Individuals are unique, especially in America, the melting pot. Whatever his skills and other qualifications, the cook, Jeff, was damaged goods, and to be handled with care. Goldfarb warned me not to surprise him by showing a weapon without warning, to keep my hands in sight, and to speak softly.

Jeff had a black belt in martial arts. He had qualified as expert in both rifles and pistols, and Goldfarb said he was honest and capable. The downside was that he suffered from a bad case of PTSD. Some had wanted him institutionalized after he had savagely beaten an Amazon delivery driver.

Jeff freaked out at loud noises. He avoided cities and crowded places. He preferred the isolation of Goldfarb's remote camp, which was now his home.

He'd worked for Goldfarb for years, on and off, both in the military and as a civilian. The Marines wanted him back for one last Afghanistan tour, where his contacts and exceptional skills were needed. They promised him a bump in rank, a generous bonus, and better retirement. Jeff's Afghan wife and children would get full US citizenship. The kids would get scholarships to American universities.

His wife was still there as an Afghan civilian employee. The country was peaceful. There had been no casualties for over a year. It was all winding down. It was a golden deal.

Goldfarb gave him time off without getting into the details. The camp could spare him, and he'd come and gone in the past. Compared to people like Raven, Jeff was easy to manage. He'd come back when he was ready, and his job would be waiting.

Jeff's plan was his wife would wrap up her assignment, the family would reunite, and they'd all come home to America. The result was a disaster. He had been in the States getting training on new weapons systems when Biden and General Milley summarily surrendered the US military to the Taliban.

With no remaining US presence in Afghanistan, the Marines released Jeff, returning him to reserve status. He wasn't the same. He got his job done. He didn't smile much. He didn't say much either, and nothing about Afghanistan.

That wasn't unusual. Few wanted to talk about the Afghanistan debacle. Few in the military dared to speak out, and those who did were punished.

Goldfarb's camp was a refuge, an island of serenity. Despite intense surveillance of the DC area, it was under a wildlife no-fly zone and under a gap in satellite coverage. There was no cell phone service, but just to make sure, there were spread-spectrum jammers. The jammers also took out satellite phones.

Jeff was a good cook. The meal, venison steak, vegetables from the garden, and a decent wine, was superb. Surprisingly, Josie was okay with him. Her paranormal friends tended to avoid strangers and crowds. Excessive psychic noise distracted and interfered with their powers.

As we finished, Jeff cleared the table. He looked at Goldfarb. "Instructions?"

"Get us a pot of coffee and clear the room. Keep the camp locked down. Fences, cameras, and perimeter alarms hot. No one is to go in or out. No communications allowed.

"Weapons hot. I authorize lethal force. One challenge. One warning shot. If intruders do not comply, shoot to kill. Same way with anyone trying to leave."

"Yes, sir. Clear the room. Everyone but you, me, and Raven?"

Goldfarb said, "Josie stays. And, Jeff, Raven is now my number two. In my absence, he's in charge of the camp."

"Yes, sir."

The room cleared. I looked at Goldfarb and raised an eyebrow. "I didn't expect that one, Doctor. What's going on?"

"I have some things to show you, Raven. We're going hot. Follow me. Jeff, you go first. Josie, we'll be right back. Ten minutes max."

Josie raised an eyebrow. "You don't want me to come?"

Goldfarb shook his head. "You don't want to. Stay clear. Trust me. We'll be right back."

***

We followed Goldfarb out to the barn. He removed a padlock and heavy chain. Shielding the view, he keyed the cypher lock. It gave a soft click, and he pulled the door open. "I changed the access key, Raven. I'll give you the code later. You and I will be the only ones to have access."

"Yes, sir."

"Do you have a second-in-command?"

I nodded. "Rudy."

"Good. He's in charge of the camp if we are both absent. Make sure he knows there is no access to the barn except for me and you."

"Yes, sir."

"Jeff is going to give us a show and tell, Raven. Everything you see is on close hold."

The tour took only a few minutes, with Jeff showing us around and pointing out things.

"Our President is dead. What the hell happened here, Doctor?"

"I don't know, Raven. It will be your job to find out, you and Josie. Jeff was here. He says he doesn't know."

I put a hand on my weapon and looked at Jeff. "That's not possible."

Jeff said, "I woke up on the floor, and it was just like you see it now."

I said, "Was the door locked when you woke up?"

He nodded. "It was."

"How do you know?"

"I had to unlock it to get out."

Goldfarb said, "Only me, Jeff, and the Secret Service team leader had the access code to the cypher lock. I've changed it, of course. Other than you, me, and Josie, this is not to be discussed."

I looked at Jeff. "Can you keep your mouth shut, Marine?"

Jeff said, "I didn't do it."

"Not what I asked."

"I'll keep this secret, Raven. To my grave, if needed."

I looked at Goldfarb. "Do you trust him?"

"So far. Trust, but verify, Raven. He will not be leaving the camp. Lethal force is authorized to keep these secrets. Jeff understands that."

"Good."

Goldfarb said, "It's so far from good, you couldn't find it on a map, but it's all we have for now."

Jeff said, "Do you want my weapon, Raven?"

I shook my head. "Not yet. You may need it."

Goldfarb said, "Are we good?"

"It's all we have for now."

***

Dining Room at the Hunting Camp. Late Evening.

We'd chased everyone off and set perimeter guards. The room had been swept for bugs. It was just me, Goldfarb, Jeff, and Josie. My team would keep the Secret Service well clear of the building.

I held up a hand. "I have a question."

They all looked at me.

"How many shooters do we have?"

Goldfarb said, "Jeff, you take that one."

Jeff shrugged. "Not counting the people in this room, seven. Of these, three are Secret Service, and four work for me. I can call in a few others, part time. We have an assistant cook who comes in on weekends, and some house cleaners twice a week."

Goldfarb said, "We lost one guard and two Secret Service agents. I will brief you in on that later, Raven. There is a cover story. We're not calling in support. I want this quiet and private."

I said, "The cover story. Is it holding?"

Jeff said, "It's holding. The President left to go hunting. That is why he came."

Goldfarb said, "It is holding. So far. We will have four-hour guard shifts, Jeff. I will spell you. Questions?"

I said, "What about the Secret Service?"

"They take orders from me when they're here. I own this property and they are my guests. With the President gone, I now take their weapons, phones, and radios when they're not on duty."

Jeff said, "They are not happy about it. They'll have our short-range walkie talkies, their weapons, and each will be paired with one of our people when they pull duty."

"Good. Make them repeat the ROEs, including the kill orders, when they go on duty."

"I always do. Like he said, we now secure the Secret Service weapons when they are not on guard duty."

"Good."

"They've been asking me how long that order stands."

"Until I say otherwise. By order of the President. All external communications will go through me. If you get complaints, send them to me."

"Yes, sir."

"The barn is off-limits except to you, me, Raven, and Josie. Raven and Josie will be staying in the guest house."

Jeff frowned. "In the guest house?"

"Exactly. Where the President stayed. It remains off-limits to anyone else except me. I need to put them somewhere where they can work uninterrupted. Give Raven a key. I'll brief them."

"Yes, sir."

Jeff finished clearing. He returned with a coffee pot, a pitcher of ice water, glasses, and cups. On his way out, he pulled the heavy door shut. I heard the latch click.

I looked at him. "Holy shit, sir."

"You have no idea, Raven." Goldfarb proceeded to brief us.

***

Guesthouse at the hunting camp. Evening. Two hours later.

Josie was blinking and shaking her head. "I'm having a challenging time processing all this, Raven."

I nodded.

"President Blager is dead?"

"Yes. Jeff found his body in the barn, along with one of his guards. Their throats were cut."

"You've seen it?"

"I have, but Goldfarb has not. He can testify to that under oath."

"You're kidding."

"Nope. He never looked. 'I never saw the body.' A true statement."

She shuddered. "Are the bodies still out there?"

"No. I set a trap. My team wired the barn with cameras. If someone enters, we'll nail him. Blager's body is in a body bag, in a freezer out in the locked garage of this unit. The freezer is set to alarm if opened."

"No one else knows that but Jeff?"

I shrugged. "I think so. Goldfarb doesn't even know where it is. We didn't see anyone."

"*You and Jeff didn't see anyone when you were walking around with a body bag? Our whole cover story hangs on that?*"

"Pretty much. Yeah."

"You do know you're crazy. Right?"

"You know what I do. The deep dark. The danger zone. Discovery is always a calculated risk, babe."

She rolled her eyes. "Not this time. There's a choice."

"Too late now. The deed is done."

"Wrong."

I blinked and looked at her.

"I'm the choice. I'm going to do a remote viewing."

"Bad idea. The sudden, violent death of a major political figure is huge. An obscure Duke being assassinated triggered a World War and forty million deaths. It is a dangerous time to be scouting the battlefield, naked and exposed, exploring the consequence. Let things settle out."

"Probability vortices. Storms. Waves of disruption in time and space near the trigger events. These fade, but paranormal viewers do tend to avoid disastrous historic events."

"So don't do it."

"I need to. Our corner of the multiverse has been survivable. That helps me believe in God. Most planets are dead. So are most futures, most realities. Picture one where Hitler's Nazis prevailed, or the Cuban Missile Crisis triggered WW III. A lot of my training as a remote viewer— we avoid the term 'paranormal'—was about avoiding such regions."

"Exactly my point. Get too near this one and it could suck you in."

"I can manage it, Raven. We're still here. We're alive. This probability line is viable. I need to explore it."

"Remember Durham? You were too close. Watching John Black dying, saving him, put you into a mental hospital. I almost lost you, babe."

"What shut me down wasn't my viewing; it was when I shot you. I thought I'd lost him and killed you. Even then, you managed to save me. You brought me back."

I looked at her. We were both remembering. She was right. We'd saved each other.

"I'm stronger now, Raven. This is what I do. My skills are better. I won't get too close. Just a quick peek."

"I don't want to lose you, babe."

"You won't. Trust me."

I took a deep breath.

"There's risk either way, Raven. *If two lie down together, they will keep warm. But how can one keep warm alone? Though one may be overpowered, two can defend themselves.* That's how we've lived. How we've survived. Against the odds. Against impossible odds."

She was right. She needed to do reconnaissance. I hated that. I hated putting her at risk. When they'd sent kill teams for her, I was the one who hunted them down in the dark.

"Well?"

I sighed. "Be careful. We're a long way from medical help. An ICU is hours away."

"I know. Please, let's do it."

"Sure."

Outbound remote viewing could be tricky, but in this case, Josie had a crisp, clear target that was close in time and space. The President, and the last time she'd seen him. She could fix on that and then slide forward in time and space to the time he was attacked.

I took her hand and led her over to the bed, helping her settle in and relax.

She flashed a smile. "Thank you."

I nodded, leaned over, and kissed her. "I'll be right here, babe. Don't go too deep. Come back if it gets dangerous."

"Yes."

We both knew that the multiverse roiled in proximity to major traumatic events. There were probability vortices. There were dark places. Viewers were not always alone. Sometimes there were monsters.

Some viewers didn't come back. Their bodies remained, but their minds were gone.

She said, "Hold my hand."

I pulled a chair over next to the bed, took her hand, and kissed it. "I'll be right here."

"I know."

Her eyes closed, and she slowly relaxed. Her breathing slowed. I watched and waited.

***

Josie had that look, the stillness that I knew so well. I also knew better than to interfere or interrupt her when she was reaching out with her psychic powers.

Her eyes were open, a vague stare, but what she was seeing wasn't in the room with us. It was elsewhere in time and space, somewhere distant in the multiverse. I hoped she wasn't too close to Blager's death.

Once I'd almost lost her and we'd come to an understanding. If she went deep and dangerous, we'd have an ER and medical team on standby. Not this time.

She knew that, but they'd been friends. She'd saved his life. He'd designated her a national treasure and had taken extreme efforts to keep her invisible and safe.

I sat there, waiting, thinking about our relationship, how our lives had become intertwined.

Josie's safety was part of my job. Several times she'd been stalked by kill teams. At least once, they'd almost gotten us both. I'd never forget Durham, North Carolina. Josie had worked there at the famous Rhine Institute as a remote viewer. They were, in some ways, a relic of the Cold War.

*It was a dangerous time, one with a legacy of movies like **Doctor Strangelove**, a black comedy where a mistaken push of a button could spawn a nuclear holocaust that would turn the world into a cinder. Yes, we had Remote Viewers, and we used them in desperate situations. The*

Russians had them too, more of them, but our best ones were arguably better.

The success rate for remote viewing was low, but the stakes were national survival, so who cared? The programs were well-funded. Satellites are not good at finding hidden nukes, and the Pentagon had done a study that showed remote viewing had a better success rate. They'd made a movie out of that too, **Third Eye Spies**. A few writers did novels, and that might be how I got my Raven moniker.

It wasn't the leaks that killed the program. It was the impossible success stories rolling around Congress, mostly the one from the **Hunt for Red October** days. During the Cold War, one of our Remote Viewers described a new type of large Soviet submarine with eighteen to twenty missile tubes being constructed in secret at their Severodvinsk facility. This source described the future construction—the construction had not yet started—of a canal to launch the vessel and provided a time frame for the launching.

Goldfarb had been there. He got the National Security Council sufficiently interested to retask our KH-9 satellites, months later, to cover that time window continuously. As a result, we got two good pictures.

He didn't reveal his sources and methods, not even to the NSC. It was several years before any source in the West again observed the Typhoon class SSBN.

Alas, some in the Senate discovered the military was funding "boondoggles" like psychic research. No one in Congress dared to defend something that smacked of witchcraft; no one involved was dumb enough to reveal strategic successes, and that was the end of any but the deepest black funding for remote viewing. The Berlin Wall came down, and the Cold War ended.

Goldfarb saved a few small nuggets of funding for obscure programs. Thus, he funded Josie, but tasking her to view horrors in the squalid Mideast after Benghazi was a mismatch that had almost destroyed her. She was a basket case when he parked her in Durham to recover.

They didn't know what to do with me, either. I'd committed the sin of helping destroy an Iranian nuclear facility, leaving an IRGC Colonel handcuffed to a trio of ticking nukes. CIA wanted my ass, but Goldfarb showed up and tasked me with keeping Josie alive. Durham seemed safe.

It wasn't. The bad guys found Josie. It took an airborne strike force to extract us. Everyone on my team was wounded, including me, and we'd left a nice neighborhood in flames. Josie had a mental breakdown, but we got her back. Someone wrote a novel about it, but, fortunately, we were long gone by then, and no one believed it.

For now, I waited and watched. I could not visit the place where Josie was, but she knew I was here. She said that helped.

***

Josie came out of the viewing slowly.

"Are you okay?"

She nodded. "Water, please."

I got her a glass and handed it to her. She sipped slowly, then nodded and smiled. "Notepad."

"Yes." I handed it to her.

She took a notepad and jotted some notes. I waited. Finally, she stopped and looked at me. "It went okay. I need to think about what I saw. I need to process it."

"We can talk when you're ready."

She looked up at me. "I'm okay. It was confusing."

I leaned over and kissed her. "No pressure."

"I love you. Thank you for being here."

"Always," I said.

"No one saw you, Raven."

"That's good. Thank you."

She was silent for a time, thinking. "Who knows where the President's body is?"

"Just you and me. Jeff saw the body, but he doesn't know where I stashed it. You can view it if needed. Jeff saw his body in the barn. He claims not to know what happened. He doesn't know I moved it."

She nodded. "I might need to see it."

"I have the key and the code. No problem. One of Goldfarb's guards is in the garage as well, in a body bag. He died the same way. His throat was cut."

"Killed by the same person?"

"I don't know, but his body was found next to the President. It would be useful to find out. You have a week. Then he'll be buried with honors."

"What about the two Secret Service agents? I didn't understand that part."

"No one does. They are still alive. Not a mark on them, but they have no higher brain functions. Goldfarb found them that way. Totally catatonic."

"Where are they?"

"In a private facility a few hours away. Secure and monitored 24/7. Goldfarb did not say where, but he will be called if they show any signs of recovery. Do you want to see them?"

She shook her head. "No, but I do have a question. Does anyone believe Goldfarb's cover story?"

I smiled. "The one that says there were rumors of a credible threat, that Blager wanted to leave and go hunting, and that he was free to leave? Goldfarb repeatedly let him go off as he wished with whatever security team he chose."

Josie nodded. "That's the one."

"They do believe it. It has the advantage of being verifiably true. There were credible rumors of a threat. Safety was discussed, but it is beautiful out here. He even went for a walk, here in the woods alone. It upset the Secret Service.

"Blager was the Governor of Wyoming. He hates confinement, loves open spaces, and has a history of wandering off. Everyone knows that. Many Americans admire his independence. President Blager has bugged out before. His security people are aware of that history. Once he disappeared for a week with an old hunting buddy. He came back with an elk and a delightful story."

"Really?"

"It was in the news. Not here, but in Wyoming. Secret Service reassigned the head of his security team."

Josie said, "This time the threat was real..."

"It was real."

Josie had tears in her eyes. "This is ghastly. We knew him. I knew him. Blager was a good man. We saved his life. He enabled all we've done for years."

"Yes."

"Does this mean that VP Dunbar is now the President?"

"Don't go there, Josie. Not yet."

"Answer me, Raven. I need to understand."

"I've never seen Goldfarb scared. Concerned, often, but not scared. He is terrified now. Dunwood Duncan Dunbar III is a disaster. He's a hard-core Marxist, a leftist elite who hates America."

"I could do some remote viewings of a future with Dunbar."

"Don't bother. I guarantee you would not like it. Picture a smiling tyrant like Biden, but one who is not senile. Dunbar is at the top of his game with legions of followers."

Josie was staring at me. "I need to know what's going down."

"Viewing horrific acts has traumatized you in the past."

"What are you saying?"

"We know in general what's going down. Tyranny. American Marxism. The end of America."

"Yes. The dark side is ascendant. In my viewings, those are the strongest probability lines."

"The problem is that we need to know enough to prevent that potential future **before** it happens. We need your talents. That's why we're here."

"What do you want me to do?"

"We need to know who killed President Blager, how it was done, and why. If it was Jeff, we need proof. If someone else, how did they get through his security?"

"Yes."

"Why now? Why here?"

She shook her head. "No idea."

"Me either. I do know this: it worked. Without President Blager's support, our team is shut down, cut off from any official support. We're just a few guys with guns and a bad attitude."

She was silent for a long moment.

"Talk to me."

"I'm afraid. My talents are warning me to stay clear. To not do another viewing. I don't do well in the deep dark..."

"I know. Can you do anything?"

"Not quickly. Probing something like this is the psychic equivalent of disarming a bomb. Remember when we had to examine Commander Noville's murder?"

"Yes. Of course."

It overlapped the Kennedy assassination. We had spent months on it, even with full military support. The quest spanned decades of history

111

and took us halfway around the planet, from small-town America, to Iran, Antarctica, and beyond. What we learned helped prevent a nuclear war.

Josie was shaking her head. "We don't have time, Raven."

"Goldfarb might be able to buy us enough time for you to figure out what happened. Not out in the world, not in DC, but out here in a remote, isolated, secure facility."

"And for you and your team to correct it?"

"Maybe."

"How?"

"If you can help us figure out what happened, it is Goldfarb's problem and mine to deal with. That is how it works."

Josie shuddered. "I remember the Noville viewing. Our first mission together. It was bad."

"Yes. I almost lost you."

She was silent for a time. Her eyes closed. I sensed she was reaching out again with her talents. I sat still, watching, waiting, not daring to interrupt her trance.

She finally looked at me. "I must do it here, Raven. I need to be close to the event in space and time."

"To Blager's death?"

"Yes."

"The pattern is entangled. Powerful forces are interacting. They all came together to focus on Blager. There is a lot of chaos, a lot of interplay, and a lot of complexity. He was a nexus point. His death tilts the world in ways that are hard to see, hard to predict."

"I don't understand. You cannot do more viewings?"

"It's not that. My powers are strong. I can see clearly. It is just that the probability threads are so entangled. What happens here impacts myriad futures. A minor change may have an enormous impact."

"Keep talking, babe."

"The world we know is fading to gray. Most of the futures I see are hellish. Wars with nuclear and other weapons of mass destruction. Totalitarian states. Satanic cultures. Others are more hopeful. A few are bright, happy, and free. To understand, I'll have to sort it all out."

"What do you need?"

"Time. Quiet. Safety. I will need quiet, no interference, and a lot of time."

"How much time?"

"This could take weeks. Something strange is going on."

"Understood. We can get you time. I'll be here to keep you safe."

"How?"

"We can do what Washington does best. What our enemies do so well. *We can lie.* Goldfarb is on it. That's why he called us in."

"I hate lies. I hate evil."

Raven nodded. "Yes, I know. I love you for that, Jo."

"Why are you talking about lying?"

"We must do what we need to do. When reality sucks, you create a false reality to divert and confuse."

"How does that help us?"

"Long-term, it may not. We cannot change the past. Reality is a harsh mistress. Eventually, there might be an accounting, but deception can buy useful time. We need that time for you to do good."

"You want me to look toward evil, so I can help you find a path to good?"

"Exactly. You and I work through the Reality Prism. We struggle and use your talents to see both present and future reality. We then seek to shape events and find a path to a better reality. Right?"

"Of course. A path from darkness to light."

"The Washington Swamp works differently. So does Fake News. They prefer to view the world through a different lens. They view their world through a Political Prism. That view has little or nothing to do with reality. The swamp creatures, both parties, care only about personal wealth, gratification, and power."

Josie gave a sour look. "I know that. What are you suggesting?"

"It's easy, at least for a time. We work as if President Blager did not die. Just as if he is alive and well. There was a threat to him, and he is hiding out somewhere. He went hunting. He wants a break from the DC Swamp. Whatever."

"Are you serious?"

"Deadly serious. This is a plausible cover. We have suffered through a senile President with dementia who could not even campaign or give interviews. A President who takes personal time off to have a life? It should be no big deal. It used to be normal. FDR, Eisenhower, Kennedy…"

She was staring at me. Frowning. "What do we gain, Raven?"

"Time, Jo. Time for you to find a path. Time for me to deal with those who killed President Blager."

"Those who work the dark side are much more capable than we are at lies and deception."

"Yes. Probably. That's what they do."

"What if there is no path? What if I just get you killed?"

"Then we lose. Game over. America loses. We've been losing too often."

She was silent for a time. Josie abhorred violence. I gave her time to think, but finally said, "That's how it works, Jo. Deception is a key part of warfare. Mind War. Ends. Means. Sun Tzu. The B-25s that bombed Tokyo in WW II came from Shangri La. The allies were not going to invade the Normandy beaches, which would be suicide. Patton was going to attack at Calais. Benghazi was caused by an amateur video movie. COVID was not a Chinese bioweapon from the Wuhan lab, funded with American money. The 2020 election was not stolen, and on and on it goes…"

"That's crazy."

"Fake Reality is an effective weapon. The lies worked for years, ripping the US and Western Europe apart. Those who dared speak truth were attacked, ridiculed, and punished. Australia reverted to being a penal colony. The US was, for a time, less free than it was before the Revolutionary War."

Josie nodded slowly. "That's all true, but I can't lie."

"No one is asking you to. Goldfarb can stall and deflect. He can buy time for your remote viewings. Can you do what we need?"

"How much time?"

"Days. Maybe weeks. Not more."

Josie said, "Blager's killers. Who, how, and why?"

"Correct. Start with the first two."

"I can try."

Raven gave a wolfish smile. "That's all we can ask for. God Bless America."

***

Virginia. Guest cabin at the hunting camp. Bedroom. Next day. Afternoon.

Raven was watching the soft sunlight on Josie's face. It was very still. She was in a trance state, as was normal in her remote viewings. She seemed relaxed, breathing easily, peacefully, with no tension on her face.

Good, I thought. Staying silent, staying calm, knowing she could sense my presence and protection.

I remembered how badly our early viewings had gone. Josie reveled in beauty, but horrors and monsters lurked in the dark corners of the multiverse. Evil was getting closer. Yards away, in another building, there was a murdered president. People fought World Wars for less, and millions had died.

The consequences of that assassination had no limits. Her job was to discover who killed him and how.

Josie abhorred violence. I was now sending her to view evil, serving as her lifeline. At least once, I had almost lost her. Her job was to discover evil, but without getting too close. When she found evil, I could eliminate it.

That is my job. I hunt monsters in the deep dark. We made a unique team.

Goldfarb had given me a T-shirt bearing a bird with an all-seeing eye and the words. *"I fly upon the blackest of wings, soaring the dark night sky. I answer no call but my own. I am the Raven, the child of Odin."*

I was never sure if he was saying I was effective, or just a pain in the ass who ignored instructions or orders. There was truth in both. Goldfarb put Josie and me together, supported us, and, on occasion, even protected us from our own government.

The legend on my shirt was true, and the message valid, but Josie would not let me wear it. She disputed the words, not the concept. She was the eye. I was the talons. The mythical thread that bound the two of us across the ages was Celtic. Germanic came later. Beowulf, in old English, much later.

It mattered little. The struggle was timeless. The choice between good and evil was eternal, whether to choose to pursue darkness or light. Humankind had free will, but over the eons and across myriad religions and political structures, humans had barely survived the struggle.

Nations rose and fell. Each time the stakes were higher, the weapons more powerful, and the death tolls more appalling. Josie knew such things.

***

Josie's eyes popped open, coming fully alert. She had been in the trance for one hour and twenty-eight minutes. A long session, but she looked good. No panic. Normal breathing. Her eyes were bright and alert.

I handed her a bottle of water. No matter what happened, viewings into the deep darkness drained her.

She smiled. Another good sign. She had been peaceful and relaxed during the viewing. Not struggling.

"Smooth ride, Jo?"

A slight shake of her head. "Not really. I avoided the dangerous places. Call it educational."

She took a sip, reached for her notepad, and started sketching.

The main thing was, she was safe. I waited silently. *Best to not disturb her. She needed to capture her memories and impressions before they faded.*

Later we debriefed. There was a problem. A big one.

***

Virginia. Guest cabin at the hunting camp. Kitchen. Next day. Mid-Morning.

There was a rap at the door. Josie looked at me over her coffee cup. "It's Goldfarb. He is not happy. Your team searched him and checked his creds."

I shrugged. "Shit happens, babe. We need to explain things to the good Doctor. Please stay through that part. We'll need to share some of your work."

She nodded.

When I opened the door, Goldfarb stormed in. "Have you gone mad? I get in and out of Langley with less hassle and harassment."

"Yes, sir."

"Has there been any sign of intruders, Raven? My camp has always been secure."

"Nothing that we can detect, and we've checked carefully. This was an inside job. Your camp has **not** been secure. There is a killer here, somewhere. We did a deep scan for bugs, cameras, and such, but found nothing. Aside from our other issues, my top priority has always been keeping Josie safe."

"*Safe from me? This is my **home**, Raven.*"

"I'll take you off the list, Doctor…"

I started to say more, but Josie held up a hand. She stepped forward, flashing a warm smile. "We have interesting things to report, Doctor. I made coffee."

Goldfarb frowned.

I said, "You have a dead president over in the next building and a shitstorm on the near horizon. We need to talk. We have some decisions to make."

I locked the door, and we sat down at the table. I relaxed a bit and let Josie do the talking. My team would make sure there were no interruptions.

It took her over ten minutes to report on her viewings. She had Goldfarb's full attention. His coffee and fritter were untouched.

Finally, he said, "To summarize, you don't see the future. It is blocked. We don't know what's coming."

She said, "No, sir, not yet. I'm avoiding that so far."

"Because of personal danger?"

"Partially. I do not see a safe path. The outcomes I am glimpsing are horrific, but there is another issue."

"Which is?"

"We shape the future, sir. The decisions we make, or do not make, will change the future. What I'm seeing is extremely unstable."

"Chaos theory? A butterfly flaps its wings in New Mexico, and it causes a massive storm in China?"

Josie nodded. "Virginia, in this case, but, yes, something like that, sir."

"The Butterfly Effect. That was about weather, Josie, not human behavior. Edward Lorenz, an MIT meteorologist, came up with that in the sixties."

"Yes, sir. He published his paper in 1972. Some scientists have since asserted that the 20th century would be remembered for three scientific revolutions: relativity, quantum mechanics, and chaos."

I said, "Let's hear it for the chaos, Doctor. In meteorology, it led to the conclusion that it may be fundamentally impossible to predict weather beyond two or three weeks with a reasonable degree of accuracy. So much for Al Gore and his Global Warming. Unfortunately, our esteemed leaders see that through a Political Prism, not a Reality Prism. They get a highly distorted view."

Goldfarb scowled. Josie shot me a look.

She said, "You know what I do, Doctor. Anyone involved in remote viewing, or in studying human behavior, believes in chaos."

"Your predictions, your remote viewings, are remarkably accurate, Josie."

"Sometimes. When I can view a stable future, I can report it so people like you and Raven can act. Right now, I cannot see anything but a maelstrom of chaos. *Isn't that what I just told you?*"

Goldfarb was silent. He took a sip of his coffee and sighed.

"Okay. We cannot see the future. Why are we here?"

Josie said, "I tried to look at the past. There are problems there too, but I did get a glimpse. Just one. Right at the time the President was murdered."

Goldfarb blinked. "What are you talking about?"

I said, "Josie can't take pictures of the places she remote views. It's all psychic, all in her mind. But she can take notes and make sketches. I recognized one. I had it on my phone."

I set my phone on the table where he and Josie could see the photo on my screen. It was a girl in Arab garb with blue eyes.

Goldfarb studied the image. "She's quite beautiful."

Josie said, "She certainly is. My sketch didn't do her justice."

"What am I looking at, Raven?"

"The picture is from Afghanistan. I do not know who she is, but some of our Spec Ops people over there have it tattooed on their arms. Josie sketched it."

Goldfarb looked at Josie. "You saw that image in a viewing you did?"

She nodded. "A fleeting glimpse. A tattoo on the arm of the man holding the knife. He slashed a throat. I saw the image, the knife, and then a gush of blood. So much blood. It was over in a flash."

"You didn't see the man's face?"

She said, "No."

"Or the victim's face?"

"No."

I said, "We do have more information, Doctor. It's why we're here."

Goldfarb was frowning. "Go ahead."

"Your cook, Jeff."

"What makes you think of him?"

Josie said, "The tattoo. Jeff has the same one on his right arm."

I said, "His knife arm."

Goldfarb said, "He's right-handed. That means nothing. He is proficient with either hand, both knives and guns. I've seen him in action."

I nodded.

"He's served with distinction. Seen combat. Won commendations and medals. Qualified as expert in several weapons, including his hands. He's served his country well. He's served me well."

"He served in Afghanistan, did he not?"

Goldfarb nodded. "Two tours. With honor. He was on his third, some special deal, only for six months. He was here back in the States for training when we had the Biden bugout."

"Jeff is married to an Afghan woman. She was an interpreter for us. Like him, she served America with distinction. Did you know they had three daughters?"

"How do you know all that, Raven? From Josie?"

"I got it the old way. I asked him. Didn't you know?"

"I knew Jeff was married, but he never discussed his family with me."

I said, "Like you mentioned, she didn't have US citizenship. That was a sore point. We abandoned them to the Taliban, Doctor. His wife. His three girls."

Goldfarb said, "I didn't know."

"That's what he said. Jeff never mentioned it to you?"

"No. He just showed up and told me his tour was canceled. Are they dead?"

"If they are lucky, but we're not sure. The girls might be. He was told that his wife is being held captive. Someone has been pressuring Jeff. Saying she will be released if he cooperates."

"That's bullshit. Jeff should know better after almost three tours and a Muslim wife. He must know about *taqiyya* and *tawriya*."

"People cling to hope." I shrugged.

"Do you think Jeff killed the President, Raven?"

"No idea. A lot about this doesn't add up. Jeff knows the Taliban. He knows *taqqiya* and *tawriya*. He knows the koranic admonition to lie to

121

kuffar. Why would he think the Taliban would release his family if he killed Blager? If they reneged on their side of the bargain, he can't "undead" the President. He's screwed. Conversely, why would the Taliban make an agreement with someone who they must know has probably killed just short of legions of their fighters?"

Goldfarb said, "He's still our best suspect."

"Agreed. He's your man. It's your call."

Goldfarb frowned. He looked at Josie. "What do you say?"

"Colonel Mustard, in the library, with the candlestick..."

Goldfarb's frown broadened. "You're the psychic."

"I don't read minds, Doctor. I'm a remote viewer. I told you what I saw."

"What else can you tell me?"

She said, "Nothing about the murder. There is too much chaos, but I did do some viewings. The Taliban took his family. Odds are that his girls are dead, but they may have been married off to Taliban husbands. Jeff was told his wife is in Kabul, but that is not clear. I think she may be in China."

Goldfarb said, "In any case, our enemies are using her to pressure him."

I said, "Yes."

"You're sure of that?"

Josie said, "They are trying. And Chinese state security, MSS, has been targeting your camp."

I said, "Jeff is our top suspect. Even if he did it, the good news is that we do **not** think he has been able to communicate that fact. He's had no opportunity. You had communications locked down hard. Jeff had a short opportunity window while you were off picking us up. During that window, two Secret Service agents were discovered unconscious, and everyone went to alert. The other agents said Jeff was nowhere around. Then we showed up, and so did he."

"Jeff was outside with the Secret Service when you got there?"

I nodded. "He was."

Goldfarb asked, "Did he speak with anyone else?"

"Not in my presence. He claims not at all. He said that when he came outside, two Secret Service agents were down without a mark on them. Everyone was clustered around trying to revive them."

Goldfarb was frowning. "The two disabled agents. How does that fit in?"

I shrugged. "My guess? A diversion, Doctor. The Secret Service abandoned their posts to tend to their own. That left your guard."

"Whom the assassin also killed?"

"Maybe. Or maybe two Tangos. Two independent chances for a kill. Or one to assassinate, and one to divert and draw people away. Or one to kill, and the other to be the scapegoat. Picture a dead President and your man Jeff on the floor next to him, brain-dead with a bloody knife in his hand. World news would eat that up. Inept, psychotic, violent Americans at their worst. A dead President. National embarrassment. You in the middle of it. Speculation without end, and never to be resolved."

Goldfarb said, "That's grotesque, Raven."

"Whatever they were doing, my team arrived unexpectedly, gunned-up and ready in the middle of it."

Goldfarb sighed. "What do you want me to do?"

"No one must know. Dead men tell no tales."

"The hell they don't. Dead presidents are historic events."

"Also, true."

"If you were in my place, would you terminate him?"

"No, I would not."

Josie blinked, looked at me, smiled, and gave a nod.

Goldfarb was silent for a long moment. "I don't want to kill an innocent man, Raven. If Jeff was involved, I want to know why and who else was involved."

"He trusts you?"

"Yes."

"You call him. Invite him over."

"Then what?"

"Josie hates killing. She has a plan."

Goldfarb said, "Keep talking."

Josie nodded. "Not a plan. A hope. I abhor violence. Given time for the chaos to settle, I can do more viewings."

"How much time?"

Josie said, "As much as it takes. Even if you make it my primary tasking, several weeks, maybe longer."

I said, "If we catch him by surprise, we might be able to take Jeff alive."

"That's not likely, Raven, and you know it."

"I'm trying for possible, sir. By your order, we are on lockdown rules. My team is disarming everyone that comes in. That is why they hassled you. If we invite Jeff over, they will take his weapons."

"He'll still have his knife."

"Maybe."

"How will you handle that?"

I said, "Like we usually do."

Josie said, "He'll improvise."

Goldfarb thought for a time. Finally, he sighed. "I don't have a better idea."

"I love it when a plan comes together..."

Goldfarb said, "You'll get only one chance, Raven. If you cannot take him, you'll have to drop him."

"Understood, sir."

I looked at Josie. "Here's the deal. Rudy and Terry are my close combat guys. Both were Marine Force Recon. They will follow him in. I will keep his attention. You will get your ass out and keep going. If you hear shots, get in a car, and drive away."

She nodded. "Thank you. I want no part of this."

Goldfarb said, "What do I do?"

"Keep his attention. Wish us luck."

***

There was a rap on the door.

"Come in," I said. "It's not locked."

Jeff entered, followed by Rudy and Terry. Rudy, at six foot four, and jet black, looked like the NFL linebacker he used to be. Terry, at just under six feet, was pure muscle. A weightlifter who used to compete professionally.

They each were one step distant, looking alert.

Josie passed them, heading out, closing the door behind her quietly. Just a soft click from the latch.

Goldfarb said, "Come over here, Jeff. We need to talk."

Jeff approached the table. He froze when I pulled my little Sig. I aimed it at his head in a two-hand grip.

I said, "Easy. My finger isn't on the trigger."

Rudy and Terry, taking no chances, each took a step to the side.

Goldfarb said, "No one has to get hurt."

Jeff did not move.

Goldfarb said it again. "Please."

I put my finger on the trigger, tightened my grip, and said, "Hands on the table, Jeff. No sudden moves."

Goldfarb said, "We know they have your wife."

"My family."

"Yes."

"America abandoned them over there."

Goldfarb shook his head. "You are compromised, Jeff. You hid that from me. President Blager did not abandon anyone. Nor has anyone in this room. Except for you. I trusted you."

Jeff winced, then he looked at me, watching him down my gunsight. "Time to decide. You will not suffer. I will put my first round between your eyes, and it won't bother me a bit."

"The Taliban has my family."

I said, "We know."

"Do you know what the Taliban does with prisoners?"

"Yes. Torture. Beheadings. Stoning. Mutilation. They are particularly abusive to women and Christians."

Goldfarb said, "And to any who fail to obey. Islam is about submission. You know that. You have seen it. You've served there."

"My wife was pregnant."

We needed to end this. I said, "I'm sorry. We are all sorry, but someone here was compromised. You are our main suspect. You know things that can't be revealed. Have you spoken with anyone about them?"

Jeff shook his head. "No."

"You're sure?"

"You arrived. We went to lockdown. I've not communicated with anyone outside this camp."

"No one?"

"On my mother's grave. I swear."

I said, "But you were compromised, weren't you?"

Jeff lowered his eyes.

Goldfarb said, "This is a 'Come to Jesus' moment, Jeff. I trusted you. What haven't you told us?"

"I've never lied to you, sir. Yes, I was contacted. My old Top Sergeant from Afghanistan had his family taken by the Taliban, same as mine. He was promised they would be returned safely, along with mine, if I'd help him."

I said, "And you agreed?"

"No," Jeff said. "I told him I'd think about it."

Goldfarb said, "You failed to report the contact. I can almost understand that, given Biden's bugout and the dismal state of America's woke military. You also failed to tell me. That is a personal betrayal."

Jeff said, "I failed to do anything, sir. The Taliban can't be trusted. We both know that no one here would help her. We've abandoned hundreds of Americans over there, along with tens of thousands of Afghan allies, probably more. His wife, like mine, lacks US citizenship. No one here would help them. Reporting my friend would betray a trust. Collaborating with him, with them, would be worse. Betraying you would be unthinkable. So, I did nothing."

I said, "I believe you. We can work this out. Hands on the table. Palms down. Fingers spread."

Jeff complied.

Goldfarb said, "Thank you."

I put my weapon at compressed ready. A two-handed grip, close to my chest, muzzle pointed at the target, but finger off the trigger. I was not inclined to take any chances.

"You must think I'm real dangerous, Raven."

"Damn right I do. I've seen your record, bro. Secure him. Search him for weapons."

Jeff said, "A knife on my left leg, in a sheath."

Terry took it, tossed it behind him, and patted Jeff down. He said, "Clear."

Rudy said, "What do you want us to do?"

"Flex ties, hands in front, and feet. Let him sit down."

I waited, put my weapon on safe. I put it away after Jeff was secured.

"Thanks, guys. Wait outside. Someone find Josie, tell her it is over, and ask her to come back. Nothing here is to be discussed. Nothing happened. Just friendly discussions."

I practiced taking deep breaths until Josie appeared.

She said, "Everyone OK?"

I nodded. "So far, so good."

Goldfarb said, "Nobody died."

Chapter Two – World Threats

Virginia. Dining room at the Hunting Camp. Morning. Two days later.

A batch of visitors, six people, had arrived last night in a convoy of two Humvees and a Jeep. Four were gunned-up and in camo. Serious shooters. The leader was older, stocky, with striking blue eyes, a round face, and thinning hair. Surprisingly, he was riding with Gerry Patton Mickelson, Twenty Mike's wife.

Gerry introduced him as "MGP." She said he was her cousin.

She and Josie hugged, happy to see each other. I was surprised to see Gerry out in the field. Whoever MGP was, it was obvious that he and Goldfarb were tight.

They had immediately gone off to talk in the other guest cabin. Gerry went with them. MGP's people secured a perimeter around it with no access granted. My team asked me about that. I just shrugged.

I put them on the outside perimeter to back up, and watch, the security people that Goldfarb and the Secret Service already had on site. The place was turning into a fortress.

Goldfarb would brief us in when and if he chose. I did not have a need to know, at least not yet. At this point, I did not even have a desire to know. I would be happy to get Josie more distance from the mess we had here. Goldfarb called it a hunting camp, and I feared we would soon be the ones hunted.

A dead President, his throat cut, discovered in a locked room at a secure, well-guarded facility. One of Goldfarb's guards dead, the same way. Two brain-dead Secret Service agents without a mark on them. A cadre of guards and Secret Service agents with sharp eyes and keen senses, who were, so far, unaware of the President's death.

That was bad enough. When you added that the President's murderer was possibly Goldfarb's camp custodian and former head of security, and that *all of us*—me, Josie, Goldfarb, plus my team, Gerry, and this MGP person, were actively conspiring to conceal his murder, and we had the makings of a cluster fuck of biblical proportions.

Soon the public and law enforcement, who mostly loved the President, and the media and Washington Swamp, who mostly hated him, would be asking questions that we could not begin to answer.

My team and I were creatures of the dark. No matter what happened, how we were judged, guilty or innocent, right or wrong, we would die in the bright light. Josie, a gentle seeker, my soulmate, would be among the first to go.

The big picture was beyond bad. It was bleak.

Having President Blager possibly murdered by his trusted adviser's main man would present a huge opportunity for America haters. One they would exploit to the maximum.

America would find a Marxist and China stooge, VP Duncan, legally in power. That would make the post-election 2020 tyranny seem minor. There would be no bumbling façade of deception, just a Stalinist fist in the face, with the Constitution suspended, and any who objected imprisoned.

America might face Civil War. The last one cost us more casualties than all our other wars put together. Worse yet, we could easily wake up being a Chinese colony.

America had survived an assassinated President once. Lincoln. Twice if you added Kennedy. Four times, total, if you added Garfield and McKinley, killed by demented individuals in the long-ago days before presidential security details.

This one, with America facing "The Great Reset," wounded and weakened from the long, dark years of Fake News, alien invasions, Cancel Culture, divisiveness, and manufactured panics, would rip the nation apart. Our powerful enemies, both foreign and domestic, would ensure it.

**

Early Afternoon, Virginia. The Hunting Camp. Goldfarb's Room.

Gerry stood up. "There is no option, Doctor. Did you see the way Raven was looking at you? Your camp is a danger zone. It would be unwise to force him to choose between you and Josie. You need to call Josie and Raven in and brief them. That's why Mike sent me."

Goldfarb shook his head. "Brief them in on what? We don't have a clue."

The third person in the room, MGP, cleared his throat. "That is why I am here, Aaron. Why I came. Introduce me. We will talk. What choice do we have, really? What choice do you have?"

Gerry said, "He's right. Hang together or hang separately. What door do you pick?"

Goldfarb took a deep breath and let it out slowly. The silence lengthened.

Finally, he said, "MGP is correct. I have known him for an exceedingly long time, and we have been through a lot together. He calls me 'Ari,' and I call him 'Jonathan.' Gerry can introduce him to the group later. She's known him longer than me."

He looked at the new person. "No choice. I will get them. We'll hang together, Jonathan."

"Right."

Goldfarb left, returning with Raven and Josie. It made the small room seem crowded. You could feel the tension in the air. He gestured to the couch. They sat, and he settled down next to them. Gerry sat on the bed. MGP stood, dominating the room. All eyes were on him.

131

"Except for Gerry and Aaron, you do not know me, but I know you. We all need to work together on this if we are to have any hope of sorting it out."

I said, "Who are you? Why should we listen to you?"

Gerry said, "Raven, this is my cousin, Jonathan. We grew up together. He is a patriot. Major General Jonathan Patton. US Army, retired. He keeps a low profile. George Patton was our uncle."

Goldfarb said, "Very low. Subterranean. Jonathan and I have been close for decades. I trust him."

Josie said, "I've sensed your presence. For an exceptionally long time. What should we call you?"

"MGP will do. Names leave a trail. Just the initials are fine."

I said, "I don't know you at all, Mr. MGP. I do not trust people. I have seen too many betrayals. Dr. Goldfarb says he trusts you. Unfortunately, he also trusted the man who just murdered our President. That is a showstopper. Why are we here? Josie has many powers, but resurrection is not among them."

MGP was looking at me intently. Finally, he nodded. "A good point, Raven. How long have you known Aaron?"

"A long time. Over a decade."

"He's been your control, running you deep black in dangerous situations. He has had your back. Has he ever betrayed you or let you down?"

"He has not. Until this disaster."

"I've known him for over half a century, and we've been through a lot. He's never let me down either."

"Yet here we are..."

"Shit happens, Raven. Have you ever made a mistake?"

"Rarely. Never one that got Josie or me killed."

"Bullshit. You came close. Before Josie, you had quite a string of fallen partners. You run on the ragged edge, Raven. Remember Durham? Bodies all over the place, including police. You were both gravely wounded. You left a major city in flames. Goldfarb got you both out."

That had been our first mission together. It seemed long ago. Finally, I said, "True."

"Damned right. Others died around you, while Aaron and Josie helped keep you alive. You've trusted them, and they never let you down, have they?"

"No, they have not. Give me one reason Josie and I don't just walk out and get as far from this mess as we can."

MGP smiled. "One reason?"

I said, "Yes. Just one, for a start."

"I created you, Raven. Whatever you are, good or bad, I was the one who created you."

I laughed and started to stand.

Josie put a hand on my wrist and said, "Wait."

I looked at her.

"It's true. This man put us together, you and me. He did it without leaving fingerprints. Listen to him."

Goldfarb said, "Raven, do you recall when you and I first met, and where?"

I frowned. "Of course. Vividly. At Langley. Years ago."

"Right. The DDO at the time was in the process of terminating you with prejudice. It was a setup."

"He was. I remember. The Assistant Deputy Director of Operations at CIA. Nasty little prick. One of the few times I visited the seventh floor. He was upset because I was unkind to an IRGC Colonel who had interfered with the extraction of one of our top agents."

"Natanz. Iran. You killed the Colonel."

I shrugged. "Two bombs, and not me. Nukes. The agent I was extracting did that. His name was Ali. He set the timers. I did assist him by taping the Colonel's mouth and handcuffing him to one of the bomb caissons."

Gerry was staring at me. "Handcuffed him to a nuclear bomb?"

"Three actually. I remember Ali pointed at them and said 'A pair and a spare' twice in Persian. Two of them detonated. Ali and the Colonel did not get along. He wanted to send a message."

She said, "What happened to Ali?"

"He didn't make it."

Goldfarb interrupted, "Jonathan sent me to that hearing at the CIA. To save you. We scrubbed your past, and, poof, you became Raven. It is true. He created you."

I blinked. "Why did he want to save me? I do not get it. We'd never met."

MGP said, "I did not want to save you, Raven. I **needed** to save you."

"Why?"

MGP pointed at Josie. "To save her. She was falling apart, and the government wanted to defund her. She was the most promising remote viewer we had left. Our enemies, especially the Russians, hated that we were getting as good as they were at 'third eye spies.' At paranormal viewing, at seeing things across time and space.

"Some in Congress were always trying to cancel the paranormal programs. It was easy to do. They gave 'golden fleece awards' and such to generate ridicule and kill the funding. Plus, the idiots at universities tried to save their research grants by agreeing to such horrific taskings that the few viewers we had left burned out or suicided."

Josie put a hand on my arm. "It's true, Raven."

I looked at MGP. "Okay, so you created me. And you saved her. What is it you want of us?"

"Help us sort this out, Raven."

"We did, sir. Josie and me. You may have the person who killed President Blager."

MGP said, "You have a suspect. How does that help?"

"I don't have a clue, sir."

He pointed at Josie. "She might. We need your help."

She met my eyes. "It's true, Raven. MGP saved you, and you saved me."

"So now we try to save him and unscrew this clusterfuck?"

Goldfarb said, "Mostly to save me. I am the one with a target on my forehead. Jonathan was not here. Is not here. Will not be here. He's subterranean."

I said, "Yes, so you said, Doctor. I have been thinking that might be a good plan for us as well, for Josie and me. We need to survive, too."

Goldfarb blinked, then stared at me. "What are you saying, Raven?"

"The man who murdered our President worked for **you**. Was vetted by you. Like you said, you have a target on your forehead. We might be collateral damage. The death of a president is world news. There are legions of enemies out there who might come for her, or for me, if you suffered intense official and media attention. Right?"

Josie was staring at me, looking horrified.

I said, "My job number one is protecting you, Jo. It is not about saving my ass. We have a trust issue. Do you trust the FBI or other agencies to keep our secrets?"

She shook her head. "No, of course not."

Goldfarb started to speak, but he stopped when MGP raised a hand and shook his head. "Easy. You have a major trust issue, Ari. Best to let it play out."

"Yes, sir." Goldfarb looked at me. "Keep talking, Raven."

"You just destroyed our Tower of Power, Doctor. What was holding us up. At circuses, they used to have acrobats who would stand on each other's shoulders or form pyramids. Ours was four levels high. At the top was Josie, her head above events of the normal world. One level down was me, supporting her, unable to see what she did, but able to reach up and deal with any who might attack her or knock her off. I held her up so she could safely have a clear view. My main job is to protect Josie. You set that up yourself."

Goldfarb said, "Yes. Josie finds threats. You and your team handle them and protect her, as do I. I suppose you are going to say that I'm the next level down in your metaphorical Tower of Power?"

I said, "I am, absolutely. You cannot protect us when you are a major target yourself, and without your active help and contacts, my ability to protect Josie is limited. There were times when we needed to tap military and other resources, and a few where help arrived just short of too late. Right?"

He nodded.

"A larger problem is that I can't protect you and Josie at the same time. I must put her first. Right?"

He nodded again. "She's a national treasure. Irreplaceable."

"Yes. Unfortunately, with President Blager gone, and you implicated, there is no one left to protect you, is there? Who protects you, so you can protect me, and I can protect Josie?"

"I have a security team, Raven."

"For now, you do, less one member. So did the President, and he is dead. This was the second attempt on his life. Working together, we saved him last time, but now he died violently at your enclave."

Goldfarb was silent. We sat looking at each other. Finally, he said, "I don't have an answer to that."

I said, "Our Tower of Power has fallen, Doctor. There is no one in power to protect you. Without you, there is no one to protect us."

Goldfarb did not answer. Josie sat staring at me as the silence lengthened in the room. Finally, there was a noise, MGP clearing his throat.

He was smiling. That seemed strange. "That was an excellent analysis, and an honest response. You put together a good team, Ari. I thank you for that. America thanks you for that."

We all sat looking at him. Time passed. Finally, Goldfarb said, "So what happens now?"

MGP said, "Now is when you get to know why I showed up here. I am going to be the bottom layer of your Tower of Power, Ari. Does that help?"

Goldfarb nodded. He let out a deep sigh. "It does."

MGP said, "Raven?"

I looked at Josie. She nodded. "I'm good. We're good."

***

"I'm glad to hear that, Raven. It seems that I'm again operational, and perhaps even responsible for whatever havoc you, Josie, and your team are wreaking on those unfortunates who somehow cross your path."

"America's enemies. That's what we do, sir."

MGP nodded. "Indeed. The Natanz thing caused considerable upset at the CIA. Your actions caused me to direct Ari to visit the Agency and calm the waters."

I said, "Muddy, murky waters, sir. You are referring to the Agency that hired a known communist, gave him a string of key postings, and later put him in charge of the whole thing, are you not?"

"They do have some issues. We'll do our best to stay clear of them, won't we?"

Goldfarb said, "I smoothed it over, Jonathan. Raven and Josie are not on the Agency's radar."

"True. You then hooked Raven up with Josie. That OP ran from Iran to Antarctica, exposing hidden nukes, EMP weapons, an early version of Russia's Club-K missile system, a foreign-flagged icebreaker that disappeared in international waters, and…"

I said, "None of that ever went public, sir. What's your point?"

"You break a lot of crockery, Raven. You weaponized a peaceful, gentle psychic viewer."

Josie was looking back and forth at the speakers, like she was watching a ping-pong match.

She said, "Raven saved me. The Mideast taskings were destroying me and accomplishing little."

Goldfarb looked irritated. He said, "You were briefed in on all that, sir."

"I was. The results were satisfactory, but you don't voluntarily reveal information, do you?"

"I do not. You should consider that a blessing, sir."

"Not if I'm a direct operational component of your ragtag little band, Ari. That might cause some to mistakenly think I'm responsible for unimaginable unmentionables. I don't like to be blindsided."

I said, "Is there something you want to inquire about, sir?"

"Let's start with President Blager. He seemed more aware of your, ah, unique activities than I am. He wouldn't brief me in. Goldfarb didn't tell me. What is your connection with the President?"

I looked at Goldfarb, who nodded.

"Josie saved his life, sir. Several times. He was grateful. He was supportive of our operations."

MGP blinked. He looked at Goldfarb, who shrugged.

"Saved his life. Is that true?"

"It is. There were repeated assassination attempts in Monterey. Raven's team saved the President's life twice in Monterey, and that was before Quds showed up. When he was poisoned, they helped him recover after the doctors lost hope. When he was attacked again, they thwarted it. That time, I even put my body between him and a jihadi assassin."

MGP blinked. "Poisoned? I never heard a word about that."

I said, "It was on close hold. Josie gets the credit for saving the President. He had a reception dinner at the Defense Language Institute Foreign Language Center in Monterey. Someone slipped *Amanita phalloides*—poison mushrooms—into the pasta. Death was certain."

"They had him on dialysis and life support. There was little hope. He didn't want anyone told."

"Little hope?"

Josie said, "He expected to die. The delay for symptoms to appear allows enough time for irreversible organ damage to the liver and kidneys. The end is normally by liver failure within three days. The doctors hoped to stretch that timeline, but the only cure was a liver transplant. There was no time to find a match, and the President didn't want anyone to know.

"The correct term is Amanita phalloides. The common name is 'Death Cap,' coming from a poisonous basidiomycete fungus of the genus Amanita. Some say the mushroom resembles a circumcised human penis, though I personally don't see much resemblance."

MGP looked at me, "You were there, Raven?"

"I was."

"How did Josie save him?"

"Numerous remote viewings, some historical, some in-your-face operational. Turns out that long ago those mushrooms were often used for political assassinations. Roman Emperor Claudius, Pope Clement VII, Tsaritsa Natalia Naryshkina, Holy Roman Emperor Charles VI..."

MGP waved a hand. "I don't need a history lesson. Not now."

"Fine. Josie spent most of her time viewing the future, looking for an option that ensured he would live. She went over it, back and forth. She looked at hundreds of probability lines."

"And found a solution?"

"She did not. All she could see was the President's death. It was not a fun time, sir. She did discover traitors and a bevy of jihadists. My team handled that."

"With lethal force?"

"We did not read them their rights and give them fair trials, if that's what you're asking. I think one or two flipped. One was duped, a doctor, but she wound up helping us.

"Those mushrooms are not common. There were jihadis growing them in an atrium. They also had conventional kill teams. A mix of Arabs and Black Panthers. I lost a good operative. Some traitors turned up. We even had VP Dunbar as a suspect, but we never verified it. In the end, one Tango made it into the President's room. Goldfarb thwarted that one, personally."

MGP blinked. "Really?"

Goldfarb shrugged. "Kicked him in the head and broke most of the bones in my foot. It hurt like hell."

I said, "Josie was the hero. None of us had a chance without her talents. She even found a healer for the President, one of her paranormal mentors. Have you heard enough, sir?"

"I have." MGP looked at Goldfarb. "Please do continue, Doctor. You still have a meeting to run."

Goldfarb looked at me. "We do not have a trust issue, Raven, except perhaps in your mind. We do have an operational issue. You made a mistake, and I failed to catch it. The blame is shared."

I said, "What are you talking about?"

"Josie. Our best paranormal viewer. She sees things across time and space with uncanny accuracy."

"Yes, she does. So?"

"What precise tasking did you give her for probing President Blager's death?"

"To learn who killed him. We had a suspect, but needed proof."

"What else?"

"Nothing specific. Normally, Josie tries to sort out future probability trails to see the major strategic threats and opportunities. She finds the nexus points where we can impact events."

Goldfarb nodded. "Yes. The big picture. Geopolitics on a global scale. Major strategic threats and opportunities. That is what she does, what we pay you for. She did not find anything useful, because of the chaos and uncertainty. We must wait for that to settle out."

I nodded. "We do."

"That is where you screwed up. You gave her the wrong tasking. You had her looking all over the planet and far off into the future."

I said, "This assassination was an act of war. The sudden death of a president upsets strategy and power balance all over the planet, into the future, near and far. That's been the pattern of our missions."

"It has been. Therefore, you had Josie focused on the far horizon, and the big picture. Thus, you missed seeing the diamondback rattlesnakes in your own sleeping bags."

I frowned. "I don't think they have diamondbacks in Virginia, Doctor."

MGP said, "Metaphorical rattlesnakes, Raven. It is what you missed, what we all missed, and why we're now at extreme risk."

Goldfarb said, "Yes."

Josie said, "I should have been looking at, and vetting, everyone with access to your small, isolated camp. Right now, there is so much trauma I dare not view the murder scene in depth."

I said, "You want her to focus local and near. To find the possible enablers, accomplices, traitors, and opportunists who are right here in this little camp. We can deal with their masters later."

Goldfarb said, "Yes, I do."

MGP said, "It's like America after 9-11. We were united and focused on foreign enemies. We spent billions fighting enemies in Afghanistan, but we missed the deadly threats closer to home.

"America missed the threats in the Pentagon, the 'Woke Military,' Congress, and especially the propaganda channels, the Fake News, and the domestic paramilitary groups like Antifa and BLM. Political enemies in Congress used the Patriot Act against us, and TSA, which never stopped a terrorist, to acclimate us to having limited freedoms.

"After two decades of toil and blood, when General Milley surrendered Afghanistan to the Taliban, little was said or done about it. No one was held accountable. America was too panicked about Global Warming, Pandemics, Shutdowns, and various other politically manufactured threats."

Goldfarb said, "To get back to our current problem. Right now, one single leak to the media that President Blager is dead, and we're all screwed. You and your team will be shut down. I'll be the main suspect, we'll all be in jail, and the people behind this will be laughing their asses off."

Josie said, "There are no trust issues here. No bad intentions. An honest mistake, a series of human errors. You made a bad call. Raven missed it, and so did I. This one is different from our other missions. It's up close and personal."

MGP said, "And extremely urgent. We have one suspect. If there are any other enemies here, or close, we need to deal with them quickly. Two Secret Service agents had their brains fried. Who did that, and how?"

Goldfarb said, "Well?"

Josie said, "We are working on it, Doctor. I have a problem. It's too chaotic right now for remote viewings."

I said, "Keep your camp locked down tight, Doctor. Like she says, paranormal viewings are blocked for now, and I don't want to put Josie at risk. We are doing all the conventional things. I want to interrogate Jeff. He is being cooperative. We'll put everyone who's had access to the camp under a microscope."

Goldfarb said, "Agreed."

MGP said, "God Bless America..."

I said, "I still have a problem. My team is not good at arresting people. My country is not good at convicting traitors. What if I find the rattlesnakes in our sleeping bags?"

"Are you asking me for a kill order, Raven? Surely you know we do not do that in a politically correct 'woke' America. Back in the day, the CIA wanted you terminated with extreme prejudice, yet here you are."

Goldfarb said, "Actually, he's not, Jonathan. That persona died. He even got an official funeral and a survivors' pension for his family. The Raven you're looking at now was born again with a pristine identity."

MGP shrugged. "Details, Aaron. Smoke and mirrors. *A wilderness of mirrors*. Those who know you created Raven are all in this room. We all know that getting into that briar patch is to be avoided, especially now. We don't need a diversion. The optics are bad enough already. This isn't about Raven. It's not about you, either."

I said, "He's right. My Raven identity stays off the table. Forever. Discussing Goldfarb is also off the table. I apologize for doubting him."

MGP said, "What happens in Langley stays in Langley. Except for cases like Jamal Khashoggi, the Islamic terrorist who died poorly as a phony American Fake News journalist on Saudi soil in Istanbul, Turkey."

I said, "We're in. What are my orders?"

"Beats me. I am not in your chain of command. *Actually, I'm not even here.*"

I looked at Goldfarb.

He said, "Do what you need to do. Protect Josie. Protect America. Help us untangle this mess. Help us keep Blager's demise obscured."

"How?"

"Just avoid it. Your job is not law enforcement. Nor is mine. Go chase some spies, enemy agents, and traitors."

I looked at Josie. She nodded.

"It could be a long trail, starting with a string of dupes and compromised, desperate people like Jeff."

Goldfarb said, "Yes."

"One request. Eventually, we might work our way back up the chain to whoever planned and ran this assassination. It could be an American, but more likely it will be a professional working for a foreign power. This will be a global issue. A world threat. An act of war."

"Probably."

"That is the person I want. I'll need resources and support to take down and deal with such a person."

Goldfarb nodded. "Yes. You have my full support. Can you please repeat my orders?"

I said, "Do what I need to do?"

"Exactly. Do what you need to do."

I looked at Josie. She nodded.

"We seem to be on the same page. Jeff worked **for you**, Doctor. I think the two of us need to have a serious chat with him, after which Josie will do some viewings."

"Agreed."

"We may have rattlesnakes. I want to pull my team in tight and have them protect Josie. They might go after her. Can your security people keep the place locked down tight?"

Goldfarb said, "They can."

MGP said, "I'll hang around until Josie finishes her viewings. We will add my team to assist Goldfarb's people. We need to keep her safe. I do have a question."

"Agreed. What is the question?"

"If there are rattlesnakes, won't they target Raven? They are unlikely to know her capabilities."

"Perhaps," Goldfarb said. "You heard the orders I gave him."

MGP nodded. "I did."

I said, "If they target me, I'll try to take one snake alive. Josie's safety comes first, of course."

"Yes, of course."

MGP smiled. Things were looking up.

***

Next Day. Mid-Morning. Virginia. The Hunting Camp. Goldfarb's Room.

There was a rap on the door. Four, then three. That would be MGP. Raven had assigned us codes. We were all a bit puckered about rattlesnakes. I shoved my weapon under the pillow and let him in.

"What's up, Doctor? They said it was urgent."

145

I said, "Some developments to report. Need to brief you in. Want some coffee? It might take a while."

MGP nodded, took the cup I poured, and settled down on the couch. "Your security is outside, sir?"

"Two of them are. Front and back. What has he done now, Ari?"

I did not need to ask who he was referring to. Raven. I walked over to the dresser and pulled a small plastic item from the top drawer. It looked like a toy gun. "It's hot. Don't point it and don't touch the trigger."

"Do we worry about fingerprints?"

I shook my head. "No need. Sally runs the Secret Service detail. Martin is her second-in-command. Both are linked to this gun. There are prints and DNA all over it, including mine."

"I won't touch it. No need to add to the confusion. Where did we get it?"

"Raven took it from Martin's room. It was hidden in a heating vent."

MGP was shaking his head. "The big Secret Service guy? Sally's second-in-charge for the team here? He's a suspect, maybe a deep cover inside agent?"

I nodded. "He's on my list. Her main guy. Six five and two black belts."

"What happened?"

"He showed up while Raven was tossing the room. Raven pointed the gun at him, and he freaked out. Apparently, Martin knows what it does and didn't want to be a vegetable."

"He tried to kill Raven?"

"There was an, *ah*, altercation, I suppose you'd call it."

"Is Raven all right?"

"He's fine. Martin is under guard. He has a broken arm, a dislocated shoulder, a black eye, and a minor concussion. One of Raven's guys patched him up. He demanded to speak with Sally and wanted a doctor. I denied both requests. I own this property. It used to be safe out here."

"Sally's a suspect too?"

"A person of interest, I'd say. I am at a bit of a loss for what to do next. It's why I wanted to talk with you."

MGP took the little gun, barrel down, carefully, holding it in two fingers, and studied it. "What am I looking at, Ari?"

"Good question. Some type of ray gun. It must transmit either an electrical or a magnetic field. Maybe both. Josie says it is Chinese made, a high-tech CCP weapon. I need you to get it to experts who can keep their mouths shut. Can you do that?"

"Legal or technical?"

"I'd say both, technical first, and on an urgent basis. If this ever gets into charges and prosecution, a full forensic examination is needed. I want this to be as far away from me or the President as possible."

"Understandable," MGP said. "Maybe I'm asking the wrong questions. What does this thing do?"

"Yes, that's the main issue. You were interested in those two brain-dead Secret Service agents?"

He nodded. "Very much so."

"Josie says the little gun is what did it."

"How?"

"Here's my theory. The Secret Service agents recently got booster shots for their COVID vaccines. Do you recall some of the vaccines were reported to contain magnetic substances?"

"Yes, of course."

"There were videos going around the internet showing how magnets adhered to the locations of the vaccine jabs. There were also research papers written about the 'superparamagnetic nanoparticle delivery of DNA vaccine,' and such things."

147

"All that was intensely and widely debunked, Ari."

"It was. Fake News and not-so-Fake News, went full tilt on that one, 24/7. *Wired Magazine* did a major article saying, 'COVID-19 vaccines won't make you magnetic.' It compared the videos of magnets sticking to vaccination spots to the photos of people sticking spoons to their faces."

"Are you saying that this was all a lie?"

I shrugged. "Maybe. Doctor Alvin Toffler, the futurist, back in the nineties, said, 'The sophistication of deception has outstripped the technology for verification,' so how can we tell?"

MGP frowned. "It's either magnetic, or it's not, Ari."

"Wrong. Take a plain piece of copper wire. Lay it on a table. Put it next to a compass. It is magnetic?"

"Of course not."

"Correct. Now run an electric current through the wire. The compass needle will swing."

"Because the wire becomes magnetic?"

"No. Because the electrical field around the wire is magnetic. If you want to make the magnetic field stronger, you can just add iron, some ferrous material, around it. Superparamagnetic iron oxide nanoparticles (SPIONS) are a core part of DNA/mRNA vaccines."

MGP blinked. He looked thoughtful. "I'm impressed. You just whacked me up aside the head with the Reality Prism. One more example, and a good one."

I said, "How so?"

"It's like in quantum physics. The observer, not the reality, gets to decide the results."

"I have no idea what you are talking about, sir."

"In physics, if you design an experiment to see if light is a wave or a particle, the way you design it sets the result. Pass light through a prism, and you have proved it is a wave. You bend a beam of light, and it separates into component colors by wavelength, red, orange, yellow, and so forth. Right?"

I nodded. "We did that one in high school."

"But if you pass it through a small slit, you can prove that light is a particle, just a stream of subatomic quanta. That is the famous 'double slit' experiment. It works not just with light, but with electron beams and other particles. Ever since coherent light sources were invented, everyone knows that."

I said, "Sure. Coherent light. Lasers. Directed energy weapons. The double slit. The thing I found odd back when I studied this stuff was that light could be a wave or a particle, but not at the same time. It's like the old joke about thermos bottles keeping things hot or cold: 'How does it know?' Set up the right experiment, and everything can change."

MGP said, "Not everything, but important things. In this case, it was all just a lie. The spoon trick had nothing whatsoever to do with magnetism. It works for plastic spoons and did so long before Marxists started injecting people with nanoparticles. By the time that Saint Fauci, Big Tech, and Fake News finished censoring, spinning, and twisting, the vaccine debate was entirely about politics and power, not science."

I said, "They never stopped, because it worked. Panic and mass hysteria to allow control. A return to the Dark Ages. Between the 15th and 19th centuries, instances of mass hysteria were common in nunneries. Young women were sent to nunneries, sometimes by their families. Their lives were highly regimented and marked by strict disciplinary action. The nuns would exhibit a variety of behaviors, usually attributed to demonic possession. Priests were often called in to exorcise demons. One convent's nuns would regularly meow like cats."

MGP nodded. "I didn't believe that one, Ari, so I did the research. Mid 1800s. One woman started meowing, and it eventually spread to the whole convent. They had to shut it down."

"Like the hysteria to force lockdowns and impose masks. Australia was arresting people who dared come out of their homes."

"And more. To get back to the issue, how can we tell what the little Chinese gun does?"

"Raven had an idea. He suggested that we simply point the little gun at Martin's head, pull the trigger, and see if he tips over or turns into a zombie."

MGP grinned. "He does have a way of cutting to the chase. What actions have you taken?"

"Two things. The Director of the Secret Service is coming here tomorrow. She will be replacing the head of her detail here and bringing a doctor along to collect the two Secret Service agents that are hospitalized locally. I told her she can have Agent Martin too, providing that, in writing, she takes responsibility for his health and solitary confinement, pending the legal charges against him that will be filed. We don't want an Epstein suicide."

"What did she say?"

"She'll decide when she gets here. Martin gets a full medical examination, and then she speaks with him."

"What else?"

"I suggested that, since the President was no longer here, and we have no idea when he will return, there is no good reason for her to leave her agents here at my hunting lodge."

MGP nodded slowly. "Interesting. Do we get to keep the gun?"

"Absolutely. It is key evidence in a felony crime, and why Martin attacked Raven. I told her that I'm filing charges and suggested that Federal Charges should also be filed."

MGP smiled thinly. "You've been busy, Ari. What about the President?"

"We have no idea. Raven assures me he's not here."

A slow nod. "Good."

"The President is off enjoying his long-awaited hunting vacation. If I were him and I heard about this madness, I would not rush back. Would you?"

"No."

"With him gone, there is no reason that I need Secret Service agents here. I certainly don't want them on my property if they are attacking each other and assaulting my security people."

"You've had a busy day, Ari. You need to relax more."

I sighed. "Yeah. That is why I love this hunting camp. It's been my little island of peace."

***

Three days later. Mid-Morning. The Hunting Camp. The Dining Room. Josie.

The camp was almost deserted. There were just the three of us here having breakfast and we made it ourselves. Just Raven and me, plus Gerry.

It was a beautiful day. It was quiet, except for the wind in the trees and distant bird calls. And peaceful.

I looked at Raven. "So, what happened? I kept my head down and stayed out of the way."

He gave a shrug and sipped his coffee. "Secret Service showed up, babe. The Director herself, named Roberta, six agents, and two staffers. They seemed competent. MGP and his guards were long gone. So were Goldfarb and Jeff, off hunting, which is why they were here in the first place. No need to hang around here with the President gone. It's a hunting camp, for God's sake. People go hunting. It's quite normal. Goldfarb left a note for the Secret Service with me. He said he would return to DC in a week or two after hunting season closes. He'll be happy to testify under oath if desired when he gets back."

"All the Secret Service people are gone?"

Gerry said, "The last two left yesterday. They collected their injured, and took the big one, Martin, the one who had attacked Raven, off under guard. Goldfarb's dead guard is at a local mortuary. Secret Service visited, took pictures, and will get a copy of the autopsy. The note Goldfarb left asked that they notify the family."

"What about the little gun Martin had?"

"That's a big deal. Goldfarb took it. He sent it with two of my team to a DARPA lab for analysis. The lab is in Arlington, only a few hours away. They are driving it there and will use lethal force to protect it. My orders were to get it back after DARPA is finished, and to not allow anything that renders it nonfunctional."

Gerry said, "You have plans for that gun?"

Raven nodded. "Bet your ass. We own it and Goldfarb wants a copy. We plan to give it to your brother at Cybertech. He sent some people to observe at DARPA. The Secret Service gets a copy of the DARPA report and so do we. Goldfarb requested that it be appropriately classified with restricted distribution. He agreed to come in and testify after he has read the report and consulted with legal counsel and his own experts. He is filing charges against Martin and the federal government."

I said, "So that settles it?"

Gerry nodded.

"It doesn't. Not for me."

Gerry raised an eyebrow. "What is your problem, Josie?"

"I sense things, but your cousin, MGP, has me baffled."

"Why?"

"He drops in and out of here like a ghost. I have never seen Goldfarb react to anyone like he does to MGP. Submissively. He responds to suggestions like he has gotten a message handed down on clay tablets. Also, the man has an odd aura. I can't get a read on him."

Gerry said, "What about you, Raven?"

"MGP has a presence that commands respect. Most everything he says makes sense and is actionable. But, yes, he does drop in and out like a ghost. I trust him because of Goldfarb."

"Is he really the grandson of the famous World War II George Patton?"

Gerry said, "He is my cousin, and I am the granddaughter. Jonathan also reached a high rank in the military, but he retired long ago. Neither of us met Grandfather. As you know, George Patton died in Germany. He never made it back from World War II. He died at an army hospital in Heidelberg, Germany. His wife, Beatrice, my grandmother, was at his side."

Raven said, "Died under strange circumstances."

Gerry nodded. "Some so claim, but I can't say. They made movies and books about it. What I do know is that Jonathan, my cousin, was fascinated with Grandpa, his accomplishments, and his service to America. It set a pattern for his life."

Josie said, "What about you?"

"Grandpa was an exceptional American. Me, I was a girl, so I went to work for the NSA, not the military. There were issues. Washington is a swamp. The short story is that I married Mike, a retired Marine, who now runs TSG, which is what got me involved with you and Raven. So here we are. I'm interested in something you said, Josie. Cousin Jonathan has an odd aura?"

"When I do remote viewings, colleagues with that talent usually show up with a slight shimmering, a clear white aura. One of my mentors, a man named Kaimi, shines so brightly that I cannot look at him directly in viewings. It is blinding. It is both a blessing and a curse. He must avoid populated areas because of the noise in his head."

"Others have auras?"

"Some. The Russians are proficient at remote viewing. Their auras have a yellow tinge."

"Do I have an aura?"

"You do not, but your cousin MGP does. It has a faint red tinge."

"Have you ever seen one like it?"

"Once. I did remote viewings of your grandfather, back in time to when he was active against the Nazis, especially Rommel."

"He had an aura?"

"Bright red. Iridescent and shimmering during his direct conflicts with Rommel."

Gerry said, "Interesting. Do many people have auras?"

"Very few. Remote viewers do not go around looking for auras. All my viewings are carefully targeted. The multiverse holds beauty, but it is a dangerous place. In training, we were warned. There are monsters out there with black auras. Dangerous creatures. Demonic."

Gerry looked thoughtful. "Interesting. My grandfather was uncanny at winning battles against superior opponents. When asked, he would refer to ancient history, saying his winning strategy was the same that Carthage used against the Romans, or things like that. He was our only General that the German high command truly feared. He kept them off balance."

"There were many odd stories. Someone named Ravenscroft authored a book called **The Spear of Destiny.** He said Patton was a powerful psychic who had fought for Carthage against Rome in the Second Punic War in a previous life. Grandpa did say something like that to a reporter. Is it possible?"

I smiled. "There is not much a paranormal deems impossible, Gerry. What if I told you that the legionnaire your grandfather fought for Carthage later changed his name to Rommel? What would you say?"

Gerry shrugged. "I'm not going to challenge you. I thought he must have had superior intelligence, from Ultra, the famous stream of information from our WW II codebreakers, or whatever."

"Do you still think that?"

"I do not. The intel of that era was slow, spotty, and not useful against a dynamic commander like Rommel. Maybe Grandpa did have talents."

I said, "And your cousin as well?"

"He's never claimed anything like that. Jonathan was a low-profile commander. He had a good career but keeps information close."

"Tell us more about him."

"He's done it all, Josie. He had always wanted to follow his ancestor to West Point. After he was accepted, he told me that he paid homage daily to Grandfather's statue that looks over those hallowed grounds as he passed to and from his classes.

"His assignments made him a seasoned specialist and veteran in international intelligence operations with experience in Europe, Asia, and South America. Trained as an Infantry officer, Ranger, Airborne qualified, and with advanced training in Special Operations that gave him exceptional qualifications to be prepared for the future.

"As a senior intelligence operator, he always sought to fully understand the enemy's strengths and weaknesses and follow the Principles of War by Clausewitz and the teachings of Sun Tzu. That was his passion—Special Ops."

Raven said, "So why haven't I ever heard of him?"

"He isn't high profile and controversial like Grandpa. He is highly respected by his peers and our allies, but you never saw him playing for the cameras. He hates political generals and thinks they are a danger to the country. He took retirement when the waves of ambitious political creatures like Milley came to total power under the lesser Bush and Obama.

"You and Mike, my husband, stay low profile, too. Do you not?"

Raven nodded. "It's the only way we can function. James Bond was a fun romp with hot babes, but a fictional creature from the early fifties. In today's world, Bond would be neutered, flipped, or banned from books and movies. The current politically correct Hollywood version is absurd. By the next movie, he will be a transgender relationship counselor, and it will be a musical."

Gerry smiled. "Mike retired from the Marines for much the same reasons that Jonathan retired from the army, and the same reasons you operate deep black under a legend. When you reach a certain level, it is best to stay under the radar. My cousin is even more circumspect. He has a network of trusted friends who leverage his abilities. His focus is on helping critical operations like what you, Mike, and Goldfarb are engaged in. You will notice Jonathan vanished before the Secret Service arrived, leaving no footprints. *Poof.*"

Raven nodded. "I did. Also, that he only showed up to help us when we were up to our necks in disaster. His assistance is appreciated."

Josie stood up. "Thanks for sharing all that with us. Now with everyone gone, and it being a gorgeous day, let us all take a nature hike and enjoy this beautiful setting..."

"Can I shoot something?"

Gerry shook her head. "No way, Raven. You stay here and clean your weapons. We are going for a hike..."

Chapter Three – The Media

Holmes Run, Virginia, Private Road, Ten Days Later, near Midnight. Gerry.

It was black except for a glow of lights on the horizon to the east. The dim spot was Arlington Cemetery, framed by Rosslyn to the north and Crystal City to the south. There was one lone airplane wending its way down over the river, a red-eye flight coming into Washington National.

Behind that on the other side of the Potomac was Washington, DC, dense, dim, and distant in many dimensions, but lit up. Since the so-called "mostly peaceful" riots that burned cities and screamed for the defunding of police, the swamp kept its lights on at night. Creatures that dwelled there shunned the light, but they also feared the dark.

I was told that even today, if you looked closely, there were faint remnants of the Pelosi fence. Over five hundred peaceful unarmed citizens were thrown into solitary confinement after a political protest without bringing charges or having trials. A sad time for America.

Behind me was Fairfax, much smaller, less political, and not lit up at night. Long ago, I had worked at the NSA in Fort Meade, Virginia, but I spent a lot of time in DC. I had even met my husband Mike there, at the Pentagon. I did not miss it a bit. Neither did he.

I checked the GPS. It said I was to stay on this little dirt road. There were tall fences, no climb wire, topped with high voltage strands. At least that was what the warning signs, black lightning bolts on yellow triangles, declared. Behind them, dark forest.

Eventually, I came to an imposing gate. Lights came on. I rolled my window down and waited, looking at a speaker and camera. A voice I recognized said, "Gerry?"

I laughed. "Who else do you think would be out here in the middle of the night?"

"Are you alone?"

"Not as much as I used to be, but yes. It's just me, Amelia."

"Good. I will open the gate and the garage door. Come in, park, and I'll meet you there. Don't get out until I've closed the door and you see me. My dogs are well trained, but there's no need for you to take chances."

***

The garage was well-lit and large. No cars, three bays, double long. The main door rolled down and then an interior door opened.

I saw a slight ramp leading up to it. Then I saw her at the top. She was using a walker, moving slowly.

Amelia had aged. She looked frail. I opened my door, got out, walked over, and looked down at her. "It's been a long time."

"Too long. Twelve years?"

"Longer. Are you okay?"

She said, "I'm good. I have the best health care in the world here. I have a bit of a problem with my legs, but I am getting by. I just need to be careful."

"We all do."

"We do indeed." She hugged me firmly. "I'm glad you called. I've been thinking of you lately."

Amelia's hair was white, and she stooped slightly, but she still had those alert blue eyes behind the wire-rimmed glasses.

I blinked. "Thinking of me?"

She smiled and nodded. "I've known Ari Goldfarb since you were in diapers, girl. I know the Raven legends. You do keep interesting company. Come in, Gerry. I have made us tea. It is quiet here and we can talk. Bring your clothes in. You are staying at least the night, and I have made up a room for you. No one will bother us here."

I took a deep breath, thinking about what to say. So much water under the bridge, so many changes in the world since we had worked together, so many friends lost along the way.

Next to meeting Mike, the halcyon days at NSA with Amelia were among my fondest memories. Back then, the world seemed new, the technology was formidable, and we thought we had the power to change the world for the better.

Amelia had first been my mentor, then a teammate, and finally my best worker. At the end, both of us were stuck under a politically motivated, dishonest Deputy Director named Tibbs.

Through it all, Amelia had been a trusted friend. Then came the bioweapons attack. Mike and I were targeted, running, and fighting for our lives. I quit the Agency and never looked back.

Finally, I just said, "Thank you."

"You are welcome. I was glad when you called. We never got to say goodbye."

"My fault. I owe you an apology, Amelia."

She shook her head. "Nonsense. You were ambushed at your own house by a kill team and managed to shoot your way out."

"I was a soft target, Amelia. That was Mike..."

"Whatever. You did what you needed to do, girl. I understand."

We hugged again, and she led me inside. We sat talking quietly, and the years melted away.

***

Holmes Run, Virginia, Private Residence, next Morning

It was noon. We had talked long into the night, and I had slept well. I felt safe here with Amelia.

She was cleaning up the breakfast dishes. She finished, refreshed my coffee, sat down, and gave me a thoughtful look. "I have a cook that comes in, but I thought it was best to keep our meeting private. The security at this house is better, though less intrusive, than we enjoyed at NSA. Few people have access to this property. I keep a low profile. There are no guards on site, but if you pull the panic lever, an armed security team will be here in five to ten minutes. There is a helipad behind the house, and a panic room just off the garage."

I nodded slowly. "I saw the alarm pull stations, not buttons, and the steel door."

"Right. Those are only for major physical threats. For assaults. Armed intrusions. There is one by the door to the garage, one in the kitchen, one by the main door outside, and one in my master bedroom. Each bedroom also has an alarm panel for normal police, fire, and medical alerts. The panic room has its own power and air supply. It will survive thermite or explosives for at least an hour."

I shook my head. "You don't seem to be the normal retired little old lady..."

"In some ways I am. I have major health concerns in addition to those for my physical safety. I picked this location for its access to health care, transport, and other necessities. I had a heart attack last year and was in a Class One ER in under twenty-five minutes. Help was here in ten."

I blinked. "Really?"

Amelia smiled. "It took me forever to find this property. It had been commercially zoned and restricted. By the time I got finished with the legal work, payoffs, rezoning, permits, and upgrades, I was into it a number that had more zeros behind it than I had ever seen on financial documents. What amazed me was that I could easily afford it. Technically, I do not own it, it's in a trust. When I die, it reverts to the State of Virginia."

I was watching her closely. "That's not normal."

She sighed. "It seems that few things are these days."

"Are you one of the ruling elites, like Bill Gates, and the other Big Tech and Pharma czars?"

She laughed. "Lord no. Absolutely not. I do not rule anyone, except my own body, and some days I wonder about that. I'm just a little old lady, though not yet one who has retired."

"Like Soros? He is probably now the world's last Nazi who served under Hitler."

"I'm nothing like those people, Gerry, except that I also now have enough wealth to afford the best medical care, to stay alive and avoid the pandemics, flawed vaccines, population control, and violence that is ripping America and Western Civilization apart. I do have some useful skills that overlap that world. I do still serve America. As do you and those whom you associate with, like Mike and the legendary Raven. All of us overlap that world. The dark side. Short of a full Civil War, we cannot avoid it. America is less free than it was before the Revolutionary War, but we are still on the same side. Effectively, we are living in an occupied country.

"I'm too old to see how it will end. I will die fearful, not knowing. You may get to see us come out the other side. I hope you do."

I was silent for a time, sorting out her words. Finally, I said, "We served America, but the Agency we worked for and its sister agencies, CIA and FBI, now serve the Marxist left."

She said, "Yes. Including the CCP, which was taking over the NSA before I retired, sending in students to work for us for free. Your life has gone in an expected direction. So has mine."

"Yes."

Amelia pinned me with a look. "You came here to talk about the media, did you not?"

I blinked. "How did you know?"

She smiled. "I'm not stupid, just old. I need to share some information with you first. I think it's best that you know a few details about my 'non-retirement' before we get into discussions."

"I'm listening."

She said, "For the record, you did not make mention of our current President or his status. We never discussed that person. You never told me anything. I never asked you anything. It never came up."

I nodded slowly. *She knew. Somehow, she knew.*

"Of course, it didn't."

She said, "If they put me on the box, I need to be squeaky clean."

I nodded, remembering our old days at the Agency. The periodic lie detector security checks.

"We never discussed it. Just the old days and our lives. Old friends reminiscing..."

"Exactly."

***

Amelia started off by talking about her career at NSA after I left. She had taken over my old project **GIRL TALK**, which was stuck. It was dead in the water when I had left. Not because it would not work, but for political reasons.

At the time, the NSA had "best in the world" communications security. America, then as now, had growing issues with DC officials paying more attention to lobbyists than their constituents.

After the Constitution was adopted, elected officials would spend most of the year living with, and listening to, their constituents. They would periodically get on their horses, ride to Philadelphia, and later Washington, to discuss, debate, and then return home to report to the voters who had elected them. Hundreds of local papers would report the news, each from its own viewpoint.

Washington at the time was a dismal swamp. Hot, humid, and swarming with mosquitoes. No one wanted to stay there in the summer. There was no need for term limits. Serving in office was a duty, not a career. Suffice it to say, there was an incentive to debate, vote, and go home.

That was the old republic. Imperfect, as with any human endeavor, but officials were accountable to the citizens they represented. Mostly it worked.

Technology improved, bureaucracies grew, and life changed. One famous writer said the end of the old republic was World War II, when huge bureaucracies were needed, and air conditioning had been invented.

We won that war, but the political environment of Washington, DC, was forever changed. Swarms of lobbyists infested DC. Elected officials eventually spent their time maneuvering and fundraising for the next election, not legislating.

The focus shifted from results to politics. Worse was to come when television became universal, foreign players got involved, and propaganda (Fake News) was legitimized.

My old program, **Girl Talk**, was intended to develop a support system for Congress so officials could stay home in their states, but vote remotely, much like today's Zoom, but fully secure. A trusted, managed network. Officials would still go to DC for major votes, but they would spend their time with their constituents, the citizens who had elected them.

At the time I left, there was a good chance that the technology would work and be accepted by officials who distrusted computers. Congress already had an electronic system to tally votes. All we were doing was adding secure two-way audio and video. Today, such systems, except for the robust encryption and security, are commonplace.

Girl Talk threatened too many political "rice bowls." There was major resistance. Advocates were interested, but non-committal. It lacked the glamour of stealing secrets and catching spies. It was like rolling a large boulder up a hill, and that, my project, was what Amelia had inherited.

My boss had done all he could to block **Girl Talk** when I was Program Manager. Congress was, at best, indifferent. The main advocate, me, was gone. My backer, the President, was fully occupied with a bioweapons attack and high-level treason afoot.

Amelia cut her losses and moved on.

She thought I would be upset. I told her she had made the only possible decision, and that I was surprised she was not angry at me. She was not. We were both good.

What she told me next was what surprised me—about the rest of her career. The Cold War was over. NSA was losing its mission and funding. The Chinese were moving in "helpful" technologists to steal technology. We were losing our edge.

How she reacted, and how she got to where she was now, a wealthy recluse, was amazing.

***

Embassy of the PRC, Washington, DC, Afternoon.

For whatever reason, all over the world, spy and counterintelligence agencies have been visible, the subject of movies, novels, and media publicity. They have websites, make job postings, advertise childcare and social clubs, and even issue press releases and testify in public hearings.

America has the CIA and FBI, plus a host of military and other agencies in less visible roles, from the NSA doing codes and communications security, the NRO doing satellite surveillance, and on and on endlessly.

Britain has MI-5 and MI-6, plus many more, some with quaint place names like Bletchley Park. Hitler had the Gestapo, East Germany the terrifying STASI, and Stalin the KGB (now the FSB).

Then there is China, the PRC, with its Ministry of State Security, MSS. MSS is a totally closed door, and highly effective. From Hunter Biden with his cocaine and hookers, to Mitch McConnell with his family ownership of a major Chinese shipping company, the news is censored. The FBI had two top agents watching China, and it turned out that **both** were sleeping with the same MSS spy, code named "Parlor Maid."

Where MSS is involved, nothing is visible. It masquerades as a helpful trade mission, not a dangerous "smash and grab" nest of spies. When it does make news, it is about family connections, dismissed as normal DC Swamp behavior. Business as usual. Just corrupt politicians trading favors for money, the second oldest profession. Nothing new.

Except it is. It is a new type of warfare, of conquest. If they kill us with a bioweapon, it is likely one that we funded. If they steal our jobs, it is enabled by our own greedy corporate elites and politicians. Future historians will call it Mind War.

China invites visitors and promotes trade cooperation to lure in people of interest, then slowly, over years or decades, eventually entrapping them in a fine silk spiderweb. It has burrowed deeply into American universities, government research labs, and, of course, our own Congress.

Interestingly, unlike other covert agencies, MSS has no restrictions. It can compromise, arrest, interrogate, or liquidate you in China, the United States, or anywhere else on the planet.

***

The room was small and unremarkable. It was not a SCIF. Nor did it resemble an interrogation facility. There were no cypher locks, no warning lights, no devices for torture or waterboarding. It was just a soundproof conference room, having a table with three chairs facing the door.

People, mostly male Caucasian Americans, but one Black, and one young female, were admitted in sequence, one at a time. Each subject sat facing a bright light. The room was otherwise darkened. When finished, each subject left through a rear door. After discussion, and sometimes after reading notes, another subject would be summoned.

The subjects sat on a hard wooden chair opposite a lineup of serious Chinese. On the left, a female with a pad, taking occasional notes in Chinese. In the center sat an older man who said little. On the right, an intense young Chinese man interrogated subjects from a list of prepared questions.

The average session was twenty minutes, but a few went longer. One subject was called back twice and re-questioned, as his testimony was compared to notes and what others had said. Interrogation sessions were recorded and archived.

When it was over, five subjects had been processed. The three Chinese MSS agents took a break. When they returned, tea was served, and a review started.

The senior man said, "Summarize, please."

The woman, a psychologist, looked at her notes. "They were all speaking the truth as they saw it, but two seemed confused. The young woman from the diner remembered little except what she had served to people. None of them mentioned anything about the President's presence or absence. None noticed anything unusual. Three did comment on the existence of a security force at a hunting camp being unusual."

"Defined by?"

"Unclear. I think it was to contrast people with pistols vs. other weapons. Hunters with rifles. Guards with handguns."

"Conclusions?"

She shrugged. "It was a hunting camp. People had guns. They came and left. Some came with guards. Nothing about any of that seems unusual, sir."

"We know that one of the guards was killed. We know a Secret Service officer was wounded and is now in custody."

"No testimony was given on that, sir. We did not ask."

"There was testimony," the younger man said.

The woman shook her head. "Not really. Two mentioned a minor scuffle where a Secret Service agent, *ah*, 'Got his ass, kicked,' as Americans would say. That's unremarkable, in my opinion."

"Say more," the senior man said.

"These people are rednecks. Macho people drinking, bragging, and carousing in a hunting camp. That agent is, as you said, now in custody. Perhaps he was at fault."

The senior man said, "Two other Secret Service agents are hospitalized with mental issues. Lack of brain function. That could have been from an energy weapon. We issued one to be used if needed."

The woman said, "You issued a restricted weapon?"

"It was approved."

"What did our agent say?"

"Nothing. He hasn't reported in."

The senior man looked at his interrogator. "What do you say?"

"You did not want us to ask leading questions. We stuck to probing about unusual events, things that stood out. No one saw anything they deemed unusual."

He looked at the woman. "What do you say?"

"I agree. We are getting honest reactions. These people don't know anything. Would you like us to call them back in and ask about a dead or missing President?"

"Of course not. We are here to discover if an exploitable crisis occurred. Not to provoke one. Certainly not to attract attention."

The interrogator said, "May I ask a question, sir?"

"Proceed."

"The Secret Service agent involved in the scuffle. Was he one of our plants?"

A long silence. "He was."

The woman blinked. "Do you deem him dependable?"

The senior man shrugged. "The information he provides has been helpful."

"Let me rephrase. Is your man abusive, physical, and inclined to get into fights?"

"He's proficient at combat. Aggressive. That's his job."

"Can I take that as an affirmative answer?"

"Yes."

"I'd not recommend any action, sir."

The senior man looked at the interrogator. "What do you say?"

"No action, sir. Americans are crazy. When your man is released, which I expect he will be, bring him in and we can question him."

They delivered a finding for the Director. It was three sentences. "Mission failed due to a foreign asset who bungled. Further investigation is pending. No action recommended."

The senior man stamped it with an official seal.

***

Holmes Run, Virginia, Private Residence, Late Afternoon.

Amelia said, "After our main program shut down at NSA, mostly we did odds and ends. The FBI wanted us to monitor citizens, so we did. Few trusted the Agency's information security after we dropped behind China and others. Our best people were leaving. Budgets were shrinking."

"The NSA wasn't trusted?"

She shrugged. "Not like before, but it was relative. Under Brennan, the CIA became highly distrusted. The same with the FBI under Comey. They grew political. We just became less relevant. My expertise and training focused on two areas, Cyber Technology and Mind War. The former takes top teams and big budgets. The latter is a solitary exercise. You do it in your head. That was easy for me to fund. I had tenure at NSA, essentially. It was too much trouble to fire me after you quit. I could do anything I wanted if it did not attract attention. I took courses, read books, met with experts in the field. I wrote many research papers, but low profile. I would give others the credit and get my name listed as a minor contributor. No one objected, and I made friends. Most were smart. Some were influential. A few had good connections and access to money."

I said, "Define Mind War."

Amelia smiled. "You know what Psyops is, of course. Messing with your enemy's head is as old as warfare. We've all read Sun Tzu, right?"

"Of course. *The Art of War*. Written by a Chinese general in 500 BC, who had never lost a battle. Everyone associated with the military has studied his writings. We have several translations of his works at home.

"If you know the enemy and know yourself, you need not fear the result of a hundred battles. If you know yourself but not the enemy, for every victory gained, you will also suffer a defeat. If you know neither the enemy nor yourself, you will succumb in every battle."

She nodded. "Probably his most famous quote, but the one that matters here is about deception. In today's world, this is key. That is what defines Psyops, Psychological Operations.

"All warfare is based on deception. Hence, when we are able to attack, we must seem unable; when using our forces, we must appear

inactive; when we are near, we must make the enemy believe we are far away; when far away, we must make him believe we are near."

I said, "We all know that. What's to study?"

"A lot. For centuries, warriors used psychological operations to amplify conventional military operations. You planned a battle around military force, and then call in Psyops to help boost your efforts. For example, during the Normandy Invasion, an unlikely victory, we used the threat of Patton invading from Calais to fix the attention of Rommel and Hitler. It made enough difference that the real invasion got a foothold, and Germany lost.

"Mind War reverses that. You overwhelm your enemy with argument. You seize control of all the means by which his government and populace process information to make up their minds, and you adjust it so that those minds are made up as you desire. Done right, you can win without having to fight a single battle."

I said, "You are kidding me."

"Not at all. It was a silly notion before the internet, Big Tech, and Fake News. Together, those forces have enormous power. Right now, this is how China, Marxists, and ruling elites are defeating America. It's what we are living today. Fake pandemics. Fake racists. Fake threats. All to crush rational thought. The kids are being taught what to think, not how to think. It's indoctrination, not education."

I paused and thought for a long moment. "Can we talk openly here?"

Amelia said, "The short answer is, 'Yes.' We already are. I have bet my life on privacy and security."

"Give me the long answer, please."

"My bare building exceeds Federal Class I security standards: No more than 2,500 square feet, ten or fewer federal employees, and no public access whatsoever. The highest federal level is Class V, for places like the Pentagon.

"Except for things like armed guards and quick reaction forces on site—A mixed blessing: I'll take privacy over people who could be compromised—the design of my enclave considered the Level V issues. An assault team could breach my security, but my panic room will hold long enough for sufficient rescue forces to arrive.

"Next, we get to electronic security. There is a minimum of a half-mile of space with cameras and trip wires to my perimeter fences. My building walls are shielded, the windows have ultrasonic modulators to prevent laser taps, I rotate between three security firms. We sweep for bugs at least once a month, and every time someone new—you are an exception—visits me."

"Have you ever found a bug?"

"Not yet, and it's been years. Any demon daring to go that far would, ah, anger the others. Drones are a potential issue, of course…"

I held up my hand. "Compared to our old vault at NSA, how good is our security here?"

"Much better. Technology has improved. I've spent as necessary to make it so."

"Good. Yes, let's talk. Where are you getting this Mind War stuff, Amelia?"

"Many sources. It has been my major focus. It originally came from an obscure nine-page army research report out of the HQ of the 7th Psychological Operations Group at the Presidio of San Francisco in 1980. No one noticed it at the time."

I said, "Okay. I will stipulate you could qualify for a PhD. Where are you going with this, Amelia?"

"I couldn't stay at NSA, Gerry. I was starting to have health issues, and I had to find a way to make a living. This is what I found. It worked out better than I could have dreamed. I am wealthy and I am not as evil as the ruling elites, the Globalists. I don't destroy people, crush economies, or cause plagues."

"I don't understand."

"The Marxist left, the Chinese, and the Oligarchs control enormous wealth and power, but it's fragmented, spread across thousands of groups around the world who hate intensely and trust nothing. Think of it as a pack of demons, ripping and tearing at civilization and at everything, or anything, that they think gets in their way.

"Including each other. The specific interests of each far-left demon group vary widely, but, in general, the commonly shared view is that any who are not on board must be silenced, or, better, destroyed. They jockey for power constantly. A dance of demons. Think of how the Nazis and Communists turned on each other before World War II. Some things don't change."

I said, "Orange man bad."

"Correct. Fake Russian collusion. They tried to impeach Trump, what, four times?"

"You paint a horrific vision, lady."

"I do. Some are calling this the End Times. But consider, what's the weak link?"

I said, "No idea."

"Mind War depends on fear, pervasive, intensely focused fear. The pack of demons hate and distrust each other. They eat their own. They lack souls or a moral compass. What keeps them going?"

"Hatred and power."

"Correct. They can't stop. Every news cycle, every few days, all over the planet, the New World Order must push short, focused messages on all forms of media and in all major languages. Without that, their fake reality falls apart. The deceived people may turn on them, and for sure the strong demons will eat the weak ones."

I thought about it. "Maybe so. What's your point?"

"These groups hate intensely. They don't debate; they rage, accuse, and intimidate. That has let them gain power, but they could never agree on messages. Someone needs to coordinate the messaging and feed their propaganda machines. The problem is that one blip, one period badly off message, one time when they turned on each other, and the Woke World falls apart—the façade collapses. Right?"

"I suppose so. Again, so what?"

"It's not over for America, Gerry. Someone must craft and frame those messages. Someone acceptable to the pack. Right?"

I nodded.

"That would be me, Gerry. That is what I do. I get paid well. More than I can spend. I also get protected. No one bothers me. I get to live, and I get good health care."

I stared at her. "You can live with that?"

She shrugged. "What are my choices? I'm lonely, but alive, protected, and blessed."

"It can't last, Amelia."

"Of course not, but I only have a few years left. When I am gone, someone else will take my place. Perhaps the demons will turn on each other. Perhaps those they oppress will catch on. Good versus evil. The world will keep turning. It's survived dark ages before."

I was staring at her. Trying to process what she said.

"It was a gift when you called me, Gerry. You might even save my own soul."

"What are you talking about?"

"I'm not stupid. I sit here alone like an old spider, but my web connects to key events all over the world. Those are the messages I process. The ones that I choose to approve or deny."

"You know why I came here?"

"The thing that we must not discuss. The reason you came. Your secret that must not get out."

I sat looking at her, stunned.

Amelia said, "Don't worry. The tale you fear will not be told by me. It is providence that you came to visit an old woman. I'm lonely and the world has turned so very ugly."

I tried to think of what to say. Finally, I just said, "My God."

"God has nothing to do with it."

"I can see that. You gave me a glimpse into hell. Swarms of demons, working to destroy all that is bright and good."

"The inner circle of hell. I do not have anyone I can trust, Gerry. No one."

"I believe you." I paused and gave her a direct look. "Are you still the person I know, Amelia?"

"With all my heart, I hope so. Not in every way, but in the important ways."

"I hope so too."

"I need to be that person, Gerry, for both of us. What I just shared with you would destroy me if it got out. It would destroy you as well if the wrong people thought you knew what can't be known."

"So why did you tell me?"

"I wrestled with that all night, Gerry. What to do. Just being around me, being close to me, puts you at risk. Even if you knew nothing, if the wrong people thought you did, it's bad news."

"They'd take me and interrogate me?"

"Worse. These people, especially the cartels, torture and kill for pleasure. The Chinese are unexcelled in genocide. It's their history."

"I know that history and what the cartels do."

Amelia sighed. "Of course, you do. We must be incredibly careful. I must ask you the same question that you asked me. Are you still the same person I knew, Gerry?"

I thought about it. She was silent. The sun was setting, and it was very still.

Finally, I said, "I have the same answer. I am not the same in every way, not even close, but in the important way, the way you refer to, I am the same person. I'll never betray your trust, Amelia."

She said, "I knew that, but thank you. Remember all the useless, but highly classified crap that rolled around at the Agency? The clueless FBI bureaucrats chasing smoke and rainbows, bumbling around with lie detectors while we were trying to get our work done."

I said, "The CIA was worse. Remember that case officer who would go out drinking, get soused, and call you to drive him home or he would start leaking secrets about our programs? I pitied his wife."

Amelia said, "Right. CIA hired Communists and put them in top positions, but one wrong word, and we could get our clearances suspended and do a timeout until it sorted out. Or worse."

I nodded. "Do you remember how we dealt with it?"

She smiled, and together we chorused, "I don't have a need to know. I don't even have a desire to know!"

Amelia said, "You have your own secret. It's safe with me."

"I know. Sometimes the most important things are those that we dare not speak."

She said, "I have a nice white wine. We can sit on my patio and watch the sunset."

"I'd like that."

Chapter Four – Politicians

One Week Later, Washington, DC, The Vice President's Office, the Eisenhower Executive Office Building, Mid-Afternoon.

Vice President Duncan Dunbar preferred this office. It was aesthetically appealing, especially to someone from New England with a view of history. William McPherson, a well-known Boston decorator and painter, had designed the room.

The walls and ceiling were decorated with ornamental stenciling and allegorical symbols of the Navy Department, hand painted in typical Victorian colors. Duncan liked to remind visitors of his service in the Navy and New England roots. The floor was mahogany, white maple, and cherry, and the two fireplaces original Belgian black marble.

The chandeliers were replicas of the original turn-of-the-century, the 19th century, gasoliers. They were equipped for both gas and electric, with the gas globes on top and electric lights below. Vintage American electric incandescent bulbs, like those Thomas Edison invented.

The pièce de résistance was the old desk, part of the White House collection, and first used by Teddy Roosevelt in 1902. It had been in storage from the Great Depression through World War II until it was selected by President Truman in 1945.

The inside of the top drawer had been signed by its various users since the 1940s. Every Vice President since Johnson had used it and signed inside the top drawer. Except for Duncan Dunbar.

Duncan would sign it, but only after he was elected President. His potential challenger was House Speaker Ross, the right-wing Hawk. With the President's endorsement and the opposition party largely accepting him, he would be a shoo-in.

Things were coming together. Now if Blager would just get back from his stupid, lengthy, seemingly endless hunting trip, America could move on. He had been pressing his Chief of Staff for action, and she'd finally scheduled a meeting on the topic.

***

Assistant to the President, Duncan's Chief of Staff, Daphne Radford, entered with two other people: Duncan's Deputy Chief of Staff, her assistant, Angeline Girard, and Duncan's Associate Counsel, Damon Moreau.

Some of the VP's top staff also have primary reporting relationships to the President. That's how it works. Originally, the position of Vice President had narrow, limited powers. Over time, like most things in government, these had expanded and grown.

Duncan stood. "Glad to see you, Daphne, finally. Good that you brought along a team. Would anyone like coffee?"

"No, thank you."

The others shook their heads, and they all seated themselves in front of the desk.

Daphne said, "I apologize for not returning your calls, sir. Matters have been a bit complex with President Blager on extended vacation. We've been trying to sort it out."

Duncan nodded. "It was irresponsible of the President to abandon Washington for one of his hunting trips, especially at the end of his term with an election coming up. Do you know when he will return? We have issues to discuss. It is past time to get my campaign started. We need to get moving."

Daphne blinked at the harsh criticism. She hesitated, trying to frame a suitable response.

"Well?"

"I don't know his schedule but am told he is not expected back anytime soon, sir. I'm aware that you've been wanting to discuss campaign issues, but I have been uncertain how to proceed. That's why I brought Angeline along. She will be your primary contact point moving forward."

Duncan was frowning. "I don't understand, Daphne."

"I was told, in confidence, that there was an incident at the hunting camp. Fortunately, the President was not there."

"What kind of incident?"

"I don't know. The Secret Service said, 'active investigation,' and 'need to know.' You'd have to ask them about the details. I was authorized to brief you, since it could impact your campaign plans. The information about the President being on vacation is public. He has now apparently chosen to extend it. The incident, whatever it was, is an active investigation. I was warned to not discuss it, except with you and the others in this room."

"How many people know about this, ah, incident?"

"I have no idea, sir. My circle of authorization was just you and the people in this room. I assume those they report to were also informed, as are you now, but I'm not in that loop."

"What loop are you in, Daphne?"

"I don't know the President's schedule or plans. My instructions are just to brief you. With the election coming up, staffing issues need to be addressed. The President left written instructions, but there are legal issues that may need to be resolved. That is why I brought Damon with me, should you need such advice. His boss, Mr. Sousa, suggested that I bring him."

"Peter Blager stopped taking my calls weeks ago, before he left on his hunting trip. Do you know why?"

"Yes, sir. I do know—and this information is closely held. The President wanted you informed before any public announcement, which he suggested you should make first, that he will not be endorsing you for President."

Duncan slammed his fist on the desk. "What the Hell, Daphne? How dare you walk in here with an audience and drop a bombshell like that on me with no warning?"

Daphne cringed. The room fell silent, and a long moment passed.

"Answer me!"

"I have been trying to decide what is best to do, sir. As you know, my position has a dual reporting structure. I am an Assistant to the President, and I am also the Chief of Staff to you, the Vice President. You accepted me to the latter position, but he appointed me to the former. I serve two masters. The legal advice I got was that my primary responsibility is to the President. Therefore, with a huge conflict of interest on the near horizon and an election coming up, I must offer my resignation. I can put that in writing, if you wish, but I was advised that you should make the announcement. It's the normal protocol and is also what the President suggested."

Duncan's face was red. He was rubbing his hand. "Don't bother. You're fired, Daphne."

"Yes, sir. Angeline is next in the line of succession, as your Deputy Chief of Staff, which is why I brought her along. She has no reporting relationship to the President, and hence no conflict of interest. The same with Damon. He is your Associate Council, so he has a clear responsibility to support you. His boss, Diego Sousa, has a similar problem to my own. His primary job is as a Special Assistant to the President, a major conflict of interest. Diego has recused, so Damon takes on that role until you or he decides otherwise.

"Thank you for letting me serve. I wish you well."

Daphne made her exit and closed the door softly behind her. The room was silent except for the soft click of the latch.

***

Virginia. Dining room at the Hunting Camp. Morning. Ten days later.

Goldfarb carefully laid the Monday newspapers on the large table, one at a time. Placing them so those around the table could see the headlines.

Only Raven, Josie, and Twenty Mike were in attendance. Mike was there because he'd come to pick up his wife, Gerry. The camp was almost abandoned.

The New York Times was the thickest, and accusatory, as you'd expect. *Blager abandons VP Dunbar.*

The Times had been on the wrong side ever since the genocides of Hitler and Stalin. Its leading political pundit, Jim Rutenberg, had famously declared, after Trump won, that, henceforth, it would not be reporting news, just pure opposition propaganda. That glimpse of truth caused him to be demoted to just a "writer at large," but the Times rolled on, undeterred. It had done much worse in the past.

The Washington Post used larger type. Divisive, confrontational, and in-your-face. It flooded the front page with pictures, including one of the unfortunate young White House staffer who must have drawn the short straw and been delegated the task of announcing the President's rejection of Dunbar.

The leftist media fed on upheaval and chaos. *The Post* chose a mix of Big Tech arrogance, and social media personal attacks. Bezos, which is to say, Amazon, owned *The Post*, which spent three pages on negative commentary, promising a full investigation. The title was *Epic Failure. Blager's Administration*.

The Washington Times was restrained, trying to hit a positive note, and focusing on voter choice. *An Open Field for the Next Election*.

Then there was the **Wall Street Journal**, short, technical, and guarded. To them, it was about the money. *It's a New Ball Game. Markets hold steady.*

No one spoke. They looked at the newspapers, then at each other, and then back at Goldfarb.

Goldfarb said, "The media speaks. President Blager has left the stage. The media has noticed. I would like each of you to comment. I'll go around the table."

Raven shrugged. "How'd you get so many newspapers out here in the middle of nowhere, Doctor?"

There were smiles.

Goldfarb said, "President Blager told me that he was going to drop VP Dunbar. He saw him as weak at best, or worse. Mostly worse. Simply put, he did not trust the man. He left written instructions that he would not be supporting Dunbar as a candidate for his replacement. A few people had copies. I did. So did his Chief of Staff. That decision was to be released if the election approached and the President was, ah, indisposed."

Raven said, "You knew all that was going down?"

Goldfarb said, "No, I did not. 'Knew' is much too strong a word. I did suggest that the President could benefit from a prolonged vacation. I invited him to my lodge. He loved to go hunting. The White House dropped Blager's denial and dismissal of VP Dunbar into the news cycle Friday night. That's how they bury news, an old trick."

Raven said, "Or how they drop bombshells?"

"That's usually done with a press conference, like Kennedy did with the Cuban Missile Crisis and FDR did with 'The Day of Infamy.' The President in power could craft a message to control the reaction."

Mike said, "Maybe Blager **wanted** a bombshell. Maybe that is the message."

Raven said, "That he'd done his time? That 'We the People' should sort it out by having an honest, open election?"

Mike said, "Sure. That's what **The Washington Times** is saying."

Goldfarb shrugged. "It's possible. In any case, this news was huge, much too big to bury. It caused newsrooms to work through the weekend. I've been waiting to see the reports and reactions. They deliver DC papers to the local airport. I got up early."

Mike said, "I assume you knew that Gerry was in DC."

Goldfarb nodded. "She left a few weeks ago to visit a friend there and did not return. When you showed up anxious and expecting her here, I thought that might be the case."

"You knew this was coming. Did you put my wife at risk, Doctor?"

Goldfarb sighed. "I did not send her. Gerry went off to visit an old friend from the Agency. She acted on her own initiative."

Mike said, "Did you know she was at risk, Doctor?"

"Not when she left. I do now."

"Why?"

"I got a short, encrypted message on her Cybertech phone. 'Expect News meltdown.' Three words. Two days ago. I messaged back and asked her to explain, but she was off the grid. Her phone is dead or turned off. She hasn't replied. I've been getting concerned."

Mike said, "Me too. I got the same message. I was also concerned."

"You said 'was.' Do you know where she is, Mike?"

"Not exactly, but she did finally check in. About an hour ago. Gerry says she is fine. She's on her way here, coming back from DC. They are having riots. The White House is under attack. Highways are blocked."

"Washington National is closed too. A state of emergency has been declared."

"Whatever's happening, she's in the field. I want her covered."

Goldfarb said, "Yes, of course. We'll discuss that. First, we need to understand what's going down. Where is MGP?"

"That's the good news. He is family to her, her cousin, and they are close. The General and his team met Gerry inbound. They are bringing her home. Somehow, they connected."

Raven said, "Somehow my ass. Gerry was in the danger zone, and MGP knew. He was her backup."

Mike said, "She is safe. That's the main thing."

Josie said, "Gerry and I are close. Why don't I know anything? What just happened? You must know something."

Mike said, "A week ago, she had me send a plane to get her in DC. She spent three days using our secure networks to research something. Then she went back to DC. I asked, but she would not say what she was up to. All she said was 'Moscow rules.' Someone or something she values is at extreme risk."

Raven said, "Moscow rules. What the hell does that mean, Mike?"

"It is an old understanding that we had from the Cold War days. A need-to-know danger flag. If even speaking of something could potentially cause extreme risk to an operation or asset, we'd trust the other and not press them. We've only used that a few times, and not recently."

Josie said, "You don't know what she was doing?"

Mike shook his head. "No, except that it was something she deemed very important."

Raven said, "Yes, and extremely sensitive. What about you, Doctor?"

Goldfarb said, "I don't have a clue. We do know that Fake News suffered a nuclear level meltdown. Gerry is running for safety. MGP extracted her. I think all that is related."

Raven said, "These Fake News meltdowns are often staged events. Scripted and set up to panic normal Americans. Are we seeing a redo of the Pelosi/FBI January 6 Patriot Purge?"

Mike said, "More Mind War to divide Americans?"

Raven nodded. "Don't know. Just asking…"

Goldfarb said, "This is different. The Marxist left, China, Big Tech, the ruling elites, and the environmental militants are all at each other's throats. It seems to be blowing apart from the inside. Dunbar had the presidency wired. Now he's a big loser. The rats are jumping ship, and they are blaming each other. Dunbar's Chief of Staff resigned."

Mike said, "That's yesterday's news, Doctor. Her Chief of Staff's replacement is now missing. Dunbar's campaign manager was the subject of a hit and run last night."

Goldfarb said, "There is a lot we don't know. Let's all take a break. We'll debrief when Gerry and MGP arrive."

***

They reconvened in the dining room at five. it was still the best place to meet. Goldfarb took charge. MGP had arrived with Gerry. And some of Raven's team, just back to report, had joined them.

"There is a lot we still don't know, but some things are becoming clear. We're going to keep it short. Dinner is at 6:30. That's 18:30 to those of you who've not yet adjusted to tranquil civilian life. I'm going to start this off by letting Raven's guys report.

"Whatever happened here at the lodge, the aftermath was two brain-dead Secret Service agents and a little plastic gun. Raven found it in Martin's room. He was Sally's second-in-charge on President Blager's protection detail.

"The gun went to the DARPA lab in Arlington for analysis. I'm not sure exactly where Martin is, but I do know that he is under guard at a

184

hospital in DC. We will get to question him after the Feds finish. The two injured agents are in the same hospital."

Goldfarb gestured. "Pat Barry, here, is on Raven's team. They took the gun to the lab at DARPA and waited around until something definite about it could be determined. What can you tell us, Pat?"

Pat stood, about six foot two, and solid. "Too much and not enough, I think, but we brought back a big report. I shoot long guns, and Vinnie over there tells me what to shoot at. He's my spotter, and a real gun geek." Pat pointed. "We've never seen anything like this."

The wiry little guy at the end of the table raised a hand. "We brought the DARPA report about the gun." He tapped a thick white envelope. "It doesn't shoot bullets. It's a neuromodulator. I can give you the report, 126 pages, but must have you sign for it."

Raven frowned. "A what?"

Goldfarb said, "A ray gun. Scrambles brain functions. Right?"

Pat nodded. "We think so."

"It's classified Top Secret, SI, restricted distribution. Vinny and I looked at the cover page and signed for the document. He got briefed in about what it does."

Goldfarb said, "I'll sign and take responsibility. But before we go down that rabbit hole, what can you tell us that normal humans might be able to understand?"

Vinnie said, "It's a scary weapon. The two Secret Service guys are vegetables. Their bodies are shutting down. Both are on an IV, and one is on a respirator. I wouldn't want to go that way."

Pat said, "It was made in China. It has parts that can only come from there. Stuff they don't export."

MGP and Goldfarb exchanged a look. Neither spoke.

Vinnie said, "They think this is experimental and custom made. A prototype. It has removable, reprogrammable chips inside. Read-only memories, and some analog stuff."

Goldfarb said, "How does it work?"

Vinnie said, "I was afraid you'd ask that. This gets geeky and speculative, but I'll take a shot at it. There is more in the report. The good news, they think, is that this gun only works against targets who have been treated with the experimental COVID vaccines, the 'use at your own risk' jabs that were widely mandated."

"They think?" MGP spoke for the first time. "Who, exactly, is 'they,' and why do they think that?"

Pat said, "I'll take that one. DARPA got outranked. The military arrived, folks from the Naval Research Lab, the Air Force Special Weapons Center, and whatever the army does at Fort Huachuca, something called ATEC. The TE part stands for Test and Evaluation."

Josie said, "I visited once. Before it was politically unacceptable, the army was doing paranormal research there. It's an isolated location that stays under the radar."

Pat said, "The military visitors were interested in unconventional weapons."

MGP said, "So who wound up with the gun?"

Vinnie said, "We own the gun."

Goldfarb said, "Absolutely. That is our position."

"DARPA still had it when we left, but the team from Cybertech was there and briefed in to assert ownership."

"Does anyone dispute that?"

"Not yet, but my bet is that the army will want to poke their nose in the tent. They view it as a potential antipersonnel weapon. Some general was coming out to do a look-see."

Goldfarb said, "I can see why, given that our political leaders insisted our troops, police, pilots, medical workers, and first responders all got mandatory vaccine jabs. They'd all be vulnerable."

Raven asked, "How does it work?"

Vinnie said, "Something called graphene. That part is a real technology. Researchers are optimistic about AI-powered neuroelectronic systems. Graphene is already being used to treat things like epilepsy and Parkinson's disease."

Goldfarb said, "Successfully?"

Pat said, "Yes, but that's where it gets crazy. Science crashes into politics, money, and world power. The COVID vaccines and lockdowns helped steal an election and became a multitrillion-dollar industry. Touch any part of that, and it is almost impossible to find out what's real."

Vinnie said, "They talked about that a lot. The view is that engineered bioweapons and vaccines to counter them offer more political opportunity for power, control, and wealth than anything that's come along. It's a replacement for the climate crisis scam, which is getting tired. Much better than the notion that raising taxes can change weather and save the world."

Pat said, "Because this one is real."

Goldfarb said, "Real indeed. Bioweapons and counter weapons offer power, wealth, and the ability to control populations beyond anyone's wildest dreams. Fauci, the Chinese, and the 2020 election changed the world."

MGP said, "You left out Big Tech, Bill Gates, Election Fraud, and Mind War, and a few other things, but yes. The Chinese are of the opinion that such things are better weapons than nukes."

"I agree, and they may be correct, but let's get back to this gun and graphene."

Vinnie said, "Graphene biocircuits are being used successfully. Several experts say that 'Anyone saying that graphene isn't being used to control human neurology is either wildly ignorant of the state of modern neuroscience, or is deliberately lying to you.' Graphene is real, and it works. Unfortunately, these intelligent neuroelectronic technologies are like some vaccines. They can be weaponized.

"That discussion got heated. People got worked up. Most technologies that were once touted as empowering humanity— television, the internet, vaccines, nuclear power, robotics, and more— end up in the hands of lunatic, genocidal Globalists who wield them as weapons against humanity."

Goldfarb said, "Get back to the gun, Vinnie. Graphene and the gun."

Vinnie said, "It's hard to do, sir. Probably impossible in a public discussion."

Raven said, "How is public discussion prevented?"

Pat said, "First off, the so-called 'fact checkers'—disinformation propaganda pushers—routinely claim that graphene is not found in vaccines and that graphene biocircuits are a conspiracy theory. They control those discussions. It gets worse. One of the key attributes of graphene biocircuits is that they are best described as a kind of platform that can be upgraded to provide safer, better therapies over time."

Goldfarb said, "So what?"

"Labels are misleading. The leading COVID vaccines are not true vaccines. They don't fight the virus; they change your body's RNA, some say DNA as well, to react more strongly to the virus."

"That was debunked."

Pat said, "That was Fake News. What happened was, Big Pharma changed the game."

"How?"

"Because of politics, the CDC changed the definition of the word 'vaccine' in August 2021. It was formerly, 'A product that stimulates a person's immune system to produce immunity to a specific disease, protecting the person from that disease.' That definition now reads, 'A preparation that is used to stimulate the body's immune response against diseases.' An enormous difference."

"So, in July, the mRNA jab wasn't a vaccine, but in September it was?"

"Exactly. Declaring it a vaccine was for liability protection. The same reason they wanted the jabs listed along with the standard vaccines for kids. That part is tricky.

"When you take an emergency use vaccine, you can't sue them. Once they get approved, now you **can** sue them, **unless** they can get it recommended for children. Because all vaccines that are officially recommended for children get liability protection, even if an adult gets that vaccine. That's why they are going after the kids. They know this is going to kill and injure an enormous number of children, but they need to do it for the liability protection."

Goldfarb said, "I want to get back to the gun. We know protection fades over time, and you must get jabbed repeatedly. Will the gun kill you?"

Vinnie said, "I don't know, but graphene can, for sure. It may take some time."

"How do you know?"

"A German research chemist, Dr. Andreas Noack said, '*Graphene hydroxide was found in all the vaccines studied. Graphene oxide forms structures in the bloodstream approximately 50 nm wide and 0.1 nm thick.*

'*They are very thin but very strong. They act like little razor blades in the bloodstream that can cut the blood vessels. They do not decompose. Once in the bloodstream, they will be there forever (short of the person getting a blood transfusion to remove them). Their effect on the blood vessels is cumulative. The longer they stay in the bloodstream, the more damage will be done to the blood vessels over time.'"*

"Never heard of him."

"You won't either. It appears that Dr. Andreas Noack was murdered in November 2021 by German Police who barged into his apartment *while he was live streaming*."

"Can we assume the gun will work against anyone who has been vaccinated or jabbed?"

Vinnie said, "Probably. It likely depends on exactly what they have had injected, and, maybe, how recently. When COVID protection fades, you become more susceptible to the virus than you were before. If you had graphene hydroxide injected, the gun should work. You may have to pay rent to keep your body going. Fauci got bad press for funding the virus, and his torturing of dogs enraged even liberals. He'll get more if the graphene risk issue becomes common knowledge."

"Common knowledge is rare in the swamp," Goldfarb said. "They put the person who funded the virus in charge of fixing the virus. He's still around."

Vinnie nodded. "Low profile. There was discussion about that at DARPA. People haven't connected the dots. Big pharma planned for that. Common sense isn't common. Hope persists. Moderna, the creator of the mRNA vaccine, described the technology as an 'operating system,' one that can be updated and reprogrammed at any time. We can't save you **yet**, but we'll get it next time."

Goldfarb said, "They can keep it rolling forever. Only we can save you…"

"Sure. Also, some think population control is a good thing."

MGP said, "We keep getting back to Bill Gates, don't we? Antivirus. Directly or indirectly, he created an industry to keep his buggy computers safe to use. Then he got into vaccines."

Vinnie said, "They do. The vaccine manufacturers deny their products contain graphene, of course. Like all good lies, it's partly true. People can stand up under oath, deny, and get away with it."

"How?"

"The vaccines contain graphene oxide or hydroxide, which is self-assembled into biocircuits by harvesting elements such as iron from human blood."

"What? Say that again, please."

"The vaccines contain graphene oxide or hydroxide. Not graphene, which is toxic, but graphene oxide or graphene hydroxide. Human blood converts those into graphene after the jab."

Raven said, "That's bullshit."

MGP said, "No. Vaccine mandates are deception. Mind War."

Vinnie nodded. "It's what makes lawyers, politicians, and crooks rich. No graphene in the vax, but you do have it in your body. Too bad for you…"

Goldfarb said, "So how much graphene oxide do the vaccines contain?"

Vinnie said, "A lot. A group called La Quinta Columna analyzed the Pfizer COVID vaccines and found that 98 percent to 99 percent of the non-liquid mass 'appears to be' graphene oxide. The manufacturers, of course, deny that. Testing is tricky. The graphene oxide mutates easily. The discussion gets extremely complicated."

Goldfarb said, "Data is hard to come by. Some die shortly after getting jabbed. Most don't."

Raven smiled like a wolf. "Do you feel lucky?"

Pat said, "COVID vaccines come in different lots, which may differ. The jabs may also differ. Some groups may be targeted. Others may be excluded. For example, China banned mRNA vaccines, as did India. The vaccines are all experimental. They have never been approved, except for experimental use."

Vinnie nodded. "That's what they said at DARPA. Also, graphene is dangerous. It's a chemical toxic agent. Even if it doesn't slice you up like that German doctor warned, it causes thrombi, blood clots, and alteration of the immune system. It can cause a collapse of the immune system and cytokine storm. Which is to say, death. All these things have happened."

Goldfarb said, "Dr. Noack. I'll look that up. Would a shot of graphene kill you?"

"Probably," Pat said. "They can use that argument to prove there is no graphene in the jab."

Raven said, "So what about the gun, Vinnie?"

"It may only work against the mRNA vaccinated, but that's now most of the world's population. There have been unverified rumors of graphene being added to food in third-world countries, but, if so, they seem to have stopped."

Raven said, "So, maybe the gun won't work against the leaders. Maybe not against the Chinese."

Goldfarb said, "Our military and citizens are vulnerable. Keep going..."

Vinnie said, "mRNA vaccines cross the blood-brain barrier. In addition, they have magnetic and even superconducting electronic properties. Some speculate that global governments will someday be able to control their vaccinated masses by broadcasting signals from 5G towers.

"The Chinese aren't waiting for that. The gun generates a focused electromagnetic field. The various tweaks inside it control its strength, focus, and frequency. Magnetic properties of the vaccines have been widely reported, or rumored, depending on your point of view."

Raven said, "They have. So, the gun fries people's brains? Makes all those little molecules go buzzing around and tip over?"

"It could. Maybe it did. There was a lot of discussion about the weapon's effect, but no one knows."

"What do we know?"

"The gun is small, concealable, and low power. It is not a battlefield weapon. That would be larger and have more range. There are easier ways to kill or subdue people. Like Pat said, this weapon is not a good stun gun or death ray. It doesn't stun or kill, except incidentally. Most think it is something more subtle, more deadly. That it is a weapon a deep cover saboteur or spy could find useful. In this case, it's a prototype."

"Somebody saw an opportunity for a field test?"

Vinnie nodded. "Some think so, including me. This Martin guy is a major bad ass. He could easily kill, fast, quick, and silent at close range. Who would suspect him? He was number two in charge of the Secret Service detail for the President. He didn't need such a weapon, but was perfect for evaluating it. Most thought that he dropped his two buddies from behind. Convenient and silent. No fuss, no muss, quick and done."

Raven said, "He didn't finish them. Why not?"

"Hard to say. He may have had it set wrong. The gun didn't kill, but it might as well have. It apparently left the victims brain-dead. He probably didn't expect that."

"Why not?"

"Even the UN and the Chinese would oppose brain frying. Fake News would go nuts. Most likely, the gun is intended to do something else."

"What?"

"Two possibilities were suggested. Turn them into violent zombies or render them Eloi."

Raven said, "What's an Eloi?"

"From an old H.G. Wells novel. The Eloi are one of two post-human races existing in Mor, in the year AD 802,701. They are descended from upper-class individuals, live above ground, and are the main food source for the Morlocks. Think libtards in paradise: *Tasty, submissive, and docile*."

Goldfarb said, "So now we know about the gun. Any questions?"

MGP said, "We know a lot more. This was a Chinese operation. Agreed?"

Goldfarb nodded. "Had to be."

"Good. That leads directly into my next agenda item. Figure maybe twenty minutes, then dinner?"

Goldfarb said, "Works for me. Ten-minute break, short meeting, and a nice dinner. And a big welcome back for Gerry."

***

Goldfarb reconvened the meeting.

"We're sitting out here off the grid reading newspapers that were probably out of date before the ink dried. Gerry here just got back from the DC Swamp. She had a tricky egress because of riots, fires, and protests. We are not going to do a debrief now, but I've asked her to give us a bird's eye view. Just top level. No Q&A. No notes. Off the record."

Gerry stood. "It's crazy out there, people. Mobs, fires, shots fired, looting, and general riots. I was glad to see the General and his team. It was a much better view from inside an armored gunned-up Humvee. There is now a declared national emergency."

Mike looked at Gerry, then MGP. "Did you have to shoot your way out?"

The General said, "Negative."

Goldfarb said, "No Q&A."

Gerry said, "Lord knows what Fake News will report, but my view is chaos. My opinion, my impression, is that most in power, both parties, but especially the far left. The Socialist, Marxist, and Chinese factions were expecting a seemingly honest election that delivered Dunbar, however flawed, as America's next president. Remember how in the old days the Rs and Ds would swap roles every four years? Each got a turn. No one got upset. Moderation prevailed. Things muddled along. It was all scripted.

"Problem was, America was unknowingly lurching along down the road to the NWO. Decisions were being shifted to unaccountable bureaucracies, from the UN, the WHO, the EU, OPEC, NAFTA, and beyond.

"Voters this time seemed to expect things that have long been missing. Things like a brokered transition, a strong endorsement of Dunbar from President Blager, public acceptance from both sides of the isle, and a Congress and public that wanted less conflict, less partisanship, and a peaceful transition."

Heads nodded. That all seemed a long time ago.

"None of that happened. President Blager left written instructions. He directly declined to endorse Dunbar, who went into a meltdown. Blager is off the stage, and he left no comments other than his rejection of Dunbar.

"Dunbar was infuriated. He went scorched earth when he couldn't contact the President. Which caused Blager's rejection letter to him to be officially released. It became headline news, followed by a feeding frenzy on Fake News and social media.

"Most of Dunbar's staff has resigned. At least one disappeared, another suffered an accident. Dunbar is still a candidate, but few think he has a chance, given the President's letter and his reaction. At least six people from his party threw their hats in the ring, more from the opposition party."

Raven said, "Chaos. You said 'chaos,' Gerry."

That got him a sharp look from Goldfarb, but Gerry waved her hand and continued.

"Right. There are dozens of other candidates from splinter parties. I lost count, but perhaps three flavors of Marxists, more Socialists, Greenies, Fem Rights, odd gender rights, plus, of course, BLM, Antifa, Communists, and a growing cluster of splinter groups. All get generous funding from the CCP, Globalists, and the Deep State ruling elites."

Gerry looked around the room, shrugged, and sat down.

Goldfarb said, "That's it?"

Gerry nodded. "Yes. My trip to the big city. Went to visit a friend and wound up needing an extraction."

***

When they reconvened, Goldfarb said, "The General has some things to report. Listen up, people."

He gestured, turning it over to MGP, and sat down. The General looked down at his notes and said, "We're glad to have Gerry back. It's crazy out there. I'll start with a question, but I don't want you to answer aloud. Just think, try to recall, and hold it in your mind. Okay?"

Heads nodded.

MGP said, "When President Obama took office on January 20, 2009, with his vow to 'Fundamentally Transform America,' his first action was to issue Executive Order 13489 on January 21. The order was controversial at the time. It took years for Fake News to silence and suppress critics. How many remember the subject of that EO and why there were objections?"

Three hands went up. Gerry, Mike, and Goldfarb.

MGP said, "Good. We'll get back to that. President Blager had major plans for the transition. His own private plans. He held them close. Now, in his absence, they are coming out. The world just saw the results of Blager's plan. He disavowed VP Duncan. Gerry just shared some of the reactions with us."

Raven said, "Chaos. Shit, meet fan."

MGP smiled. "You have a quaint way of putting that, but yes. The world just tilted a bit. It's a good signal that our security was tight. Perhaps not as tight as we thought, but tight enough. The Chinese suspected something. They've been trying to penetrate this facility. Efforts increased when the President visited. People like me were urging him to leave."

Goldfarb said, "My little hunting camp was definitely a major target?"

"Affirmative. There were penetration attempts run by the PRC's Ministry of State Security, MSS. Control was out of the PRC Embassy in DC. That is where the much-discussed little gun came from. Secret Service Agent Martin Smith serves the PRC. He's been working for MSS for years. I'm sure they were delighted when he managed to get assigned to the Presidential Protection Detail."

Goldfarb frowned. "I knew we were on the radar, Jonathan, but, until now, the name Martin Smith wasn't mentioned as a threat. At least not until his encounter with Raven."

MGP shrugged. "You know how it works, Ari. Counter security is highly compartmentalized. That is why the FBI and CIA used to have walls between them. Same with MI-5 and MI-6. Who watches the watchers?"

Raven said, "Our walls have holes, General."

MGP nodded. "Our walls are crumbling. Chinese walls around information are strong and tall. There have been at least three covert CCP efforts to penetrate Goldfarb's camp. Two were successful. Those penetrations probably involve Martin."

Goldfarb said, "Why do you say that?"

"He was perfectly placed. Inside of the Secret Service. High-level."

"Keep talking…"

"Martin was flipped by one of his early martial arts instructors, Fang, an American Chinese who was his Kung Fu master."

"Fang, like in tooth?"

MGP shook his head. "Right track, wrong train, Ari. The names Chinese choose can tend to mirror their desired image. But in this case, Fang, in Chinese, means 'The Right One.' It's an honorable name. Fang is not an MSS agent but does have family in China. Such a system of 'soft compromise' is common to Americans with roots in China. Martin, Fang's student, ran into problems, and—"

Raven interrupted, "What kind of problems?"

MGP said, "Control issues."

Raven said, "Can you be more specific?"

"I can. Martin killed one of his sparring partners in a competition. Fang dropped him as a student. Martin has black belts in both the kuoshu and wushu fighting styles, plus one in Karate. His controller is a woman named Liu, code name, Dance Instructor. She's also his lover. He may be one of the top MSS agents in America.

"Martin gets around. He and his Secret Service boss, Sally Evers, were having an affair. She terminated the relationship when Martin started working for her."

Gerry said, "Good thing you didn't make him mad, Raven."

"Yeah…"

Josie rolled her eyes but didn't speak.

MGP looked at his watch. "Time's up. We can continue tomorrow if desired, but we've touched on the main parts. Should we wrap now?"

Goldfarb said, "Works for me. Dinner can be served in ten or fifteen minutes."

MGP said, "Recall I mentioned Obama's first Executive Order? That one may have had more impact than the entire rest of his term. It was the order that sealed his records and shut down the 'Kenya birth discussion.' Enormous impact on America and both parties. Very clever how he did it.

"The Bush presidential records were **already** sealed. So, Obama got his records sealed too, but he limited the blockage time for presidential records to only eight years.

"That left Obama clear for two terms, and it made problems for the Bush family. Any Bush President would be potentially exposed to embarrassments over the Patriot Act and all that nasty stuff about when the Towers came down and the lesser Bush invaded Iraq, setting up the Mideast for the Arab Spring and destabilization of Western Europe.

"We forget now that TSA, which never prevented a terrorist attack, created a huge bureaucracy with intrusive powers. Fear about Islamic terrorism and reluctance to profile jihadists allowed the government to overreach decades before COVID.

"The new normal became checkpoints, body scans, travel delays, and getting groped. Fauci's masks, lockdowns, and closing churches. Biden's vaccine mandates just took it further."

Goldfarb said, "All that because of nineteen illegals with boxcutters, most of them given visas by one person, John Brennan, an admitted communist who sanitized Obama's records and later ran the CIA. The attack on the Towers was basically a single-point security failure. Brennan was the CIA head of station in Saudi Arabia. He converted to Islam while he was there."

MGP nodded. "Correct. 9-11 was about fear and control. Mind War at its most effective. The public never caught on. It still hasn't. No Bush was again a candidate for president, nor is one likely to be, but who knew that in 2008?

"Obama's EO kept the Republicans from objecting to Obama's Kenyan roots. It put a warning shot across their bow. President Trump excepted, Republicans have been ineffective ever since."

"There was also the race card. Objecting to Obama would have set off cries of racism."

"Probably. Kenya was off the table, Deep State elites ran the country, and both parties went along."

Gerry said, "Kenya was one of many signals of Obama's disdain for America, but what made him ineligible was that he did not meet the Constitution's requirement that the President must be a 'Natural Born American.' He failed that test.

"Not because of where he was born. It might have been Kenya, probably was, but the disqualifying factor was that his father was British, not American. In 1776 'Natural Born' meant that both parents had to be American citizens. There have been court rulings affirming that, and Obama's were not. The Republicans never even raised the issue."

MGP shrugged. "True, but that's water over the dam. Americans were still trying to compromise back then. There were still a few remaining areas of collective agreement."

"I must have missed that. Name one."

"Both parties agreed, 'No Hillary.' The voters did too. She was useful, but an Alinsky monster. The Democrats fired her, back during Watergate."

Gerry blinked, then nodded. "Demonic. Alinsky dedicated his book to Lucifer."

"He did. To get back to my point, President Blager did something that was slicker than Obama's sleight-of-hand EOs. He reinstated an old 1948 law called the Smith-Mundt Act.

Did You Know?
For the first time since 1948,
propaganda is now legal in the U.S.

On 12/29/12, President Obama signed HR 4310, the
2013 National Defense Authorization Act. Section 1078
of the bill authorizes the use of propaganda inside the
US, which had previously been banned since 1948
when the Smith-Mundt Act was passed.

Excuse me.

www.facebook.com/Citizens.Action.Network

"Blager restored the law that the use of propaganda against America inside the US is a Class 1 Felony, a Capital Crime. The way he did it applies to all forms of communication. Not just Fake News in print and on cable, but also social media, and beyond. Penalties will be severe."

"Why don't we know this?"

MGP grinned. "No one noticed the law, and it hasn't happened yet. President Blager timed it to not take effect until the end of his term."

"How could they not notice? This is huge."

"Team Obama removed that law by HR4310, the 2013 National Defense Authorization Act, Section 1078. Obama's HR4310 was 682 pages. It was passed in a rush and contained well-hidden landmines and time bombs.

"Section 1078 was misleadingly titled, 'Dissemination abroad of information about the United States.' That section allowed unlimited Mind War against America by both foreign and domestic enemies. Blager **canceled** the provisions of that old law, and several others, when his last NDAA passed."

Goldfarb said, "Unbelievable."

"Yes, but true, nonetheless. Biden's bumbling and overreach left the DOD and the military in such a tangled mess of bad legislation that both parties wanted to clean things up.

"The Blager Administration agreed. His NDAA passed with massive bi-partisan support and deep sighs of relief. The overlooked result was, thanks to Blager, that all propaganda, whether originated here or abroad, is ILLEGAL again. His law takes effect at the end of his term. Propaganda against America inside the US will again be a serious felony. Propagandists can face long prison terms.

"It will be interesting watching Congress, Big Tech and Fake News trying to defend their Marxist, CCP, WHO, UN, and NWO propaganda. I can't wait."

***

Virginia. Dining room at the Hunting Camp. Late evening.

The dishes had long since been cleared, and most had retired. The lights were dimmed, and the night was silent. The wind was still, and all the wild creatures seemed to have settled in.

There were embers of a fire in the small woodstove. The little high-tech fan on top was silent. It was spinning happily, powered just by the heat of the fire.

Two old men sat in silence, sipping brandy, watching the fire, and thinking.

Finally, Goldfarb spoke. "Was what you said true, Jonathan?"

"About Blager's new law? It is. Absolutely. Just wait and see."

"No. About Alinsky dedicating his book to Lucifer. Fact checks say that's false."

MGP smiled. "The best lies are partly true. He did, but only in the first edition, a cheap little paperback that had limited cult sales back in the seventies. It's a collector's item. Pristine copies sell for over a thousand dollars."

"Good to know."

The two men went back to sipping their brandy and watching the fire. Long moments passed before Goldfarb spoke again.

"Thank you for saving Gerry. How did that happen, exactly…?"

"Don't believe in coincidences, eh?"

A short laugh. "Do you?"

"No. Let me put it this way. Gerry is not just family for me. She's a trusted operative. She is presently involved in some extremely dangerous interactions. She's out in the cold. Deep black. Gerry is at substantial risk. If she and her source go down, they are irreplaceable. Do you understand what I'm saying?"

"How can I help?"

"I need to borrow Josie and Raven's team."

Goldfarb frowned. "Josie is a national treasure. She's the best remote viewer we've ever had, but she's fragile. You know what I have her doing and how important it is."

MGP nodded.

"You want me to preempt her tasking?"

"I do. I need her, Ari. It's absolutely crucial."

"You can't tell me why?"

MGP thought for a long moment. "Hold this one close, Ari. We are losing America. Gerry may assess the Butterfly Effect versus Mind War."

"I have no idea what that means, General."

"Good. Just keep it to yourself and trust me that her mission is critical."

"You can't say more?"

"Not can't. Won't. I won't tell you why, Ari. I don't want anyone to even get a whiff of how much importance I put on this tasking."

"Who knows?"

"Just me and Gerry for now."

"Not even Mike?"

"No. I need you to trust me on this one. It's the hottest thing I've touched in years. A huge opportunity, but one slip, one rumor, and *poof* it's all gone. At best, we'll lose an irreplaceable source. At worst, we lose not just a president, but our entire country."

"You will need Josie for some time?"

"We might. I don't know."

Goldfarb blinked. "Is this like the Penkovsky thing? A key source, top-level, highly vulnerable, with the inside info on the Russian missiles in Cuba?"

MGP nodded.

"On that level of sensitivity and impact?"

Another nod.

"They gave Oleg Penkovsky the code name 'HERO.' Would such a name would be appropriate here?"

MGP gave a snort. "Lord, no. What a stupid name. Talk about getting your best sources targeted. We might as well have shot him ourselves."

Goldfarb said, "If the rumors are true, they burned Penkovsky alive in a crematorium."

"This source has no name. I don't even know who it is, Ari."

"Gerry won't say?"

"No, and I won't ask. We wouldn't even be having this discussion if I didn't need to borrow your assets."

"Tell me what you need."

"I need Raven's team to keep Gerry safe. I need to have Josie do remote viewings both to support the mission and to keep Gerry and her source safe."

"Done. Josie is an integral part of Raven's team. You can have them all for as long as you need them. No questions asked. No paper trails."

"Thank you. I'll do my best to return them in good condition."

The two were silent for a time, watching the fire. Finally, MGP spoke again. "We have another issue."

"Just one?"

"Jeff. The Black guy. Your custodian. Let's start there."

Goldfarb sighed. "He's a damned good cook, isn't he?"

"Jeff may be a murderer and a traitor, Ari. He is compromised. The Taliban are holding his wife and children. It would be insane to trust him. If he flips, he puts us all at risk. He could do America immeasurable harm if he goes public or defects. Raven wanted to eliminate that risk. You stopped him."

"I did."

"Why?"

"Some old American notions: Innocent until proven guilty. Reasonable doubt. Things like that."

"So, you trust Jeff. That seems odd, Ari. You know better."

"He's someone I've trusted for years. He has never let me down. He saved my life at least twice."

"You know better…"

"I know that trusted people from Benedict Arnold on, all through history, have caused great harm."

MGP nodded. "Perhaps especially to America."

"We've had more than our share of traitors. Yes."

"Again: Why? Why do you want to protect Jeff?"

Goldfarb said, "I just want to be sure. Where do we stop? If we go around killing our best people over mistaken assumptions, just for convenience, how are we better than Hitler, Stalin, or Mao?"

MGP said, "We're not, except possibly in degree. But if we mess this up, there won't **be** an America. You can see that, can't you? If it ever got out that the assassination of a president was concealed, it could well be the end of our republic. We've been through a Civil War, blatantly stolen elections, high-level corruption, and the election of presidents well into dementia, paid off by foreign enemies, or otherwise impaired. This would be worse."

Goldfarb nodded. "And the wrong people would be blamed. Which is to say, us."

"Perhaps we should be blamed, Ari. Not for doing the dirty deed, but for failing to prevent it. If they come with torches, you will be at the top of the list. Not the Secret Service. Not Jeff. You will have a large red bullseye on your forehead. Don't you understand that?"

"I can keep the lid on. I know we can't let Jeff loose. We can't take a chance on what he knows getting out to the wrong people. We can't let him draw any attention to the things we must keep hidden."

"Why are you protecting Jeff? Josie remote-viewed him with a bloody knife in his hand. What more proof do you need?"

"Let's accept that as true. It likely is, but Josie has a grim time doing her remote viewings through a cloud of bloody, horrific events. She never said Jeff killed the President. She just glimpsed an arm with a tattoo and a bloody knife."

"The same tattoo that is on Jeff's arm?"

"Yes, that's what she thinks. So what? That doesn't prove Jeff was the assassin, does it?"

MGP sighed deeply. "The wilderness of mirrors..."

Goldfarb said, "Screw the mirrors. That's the diversion the CIA used for decades to excuse their myriad bungles and oversights. We don't know for sure if Jeff is the assassin, do we?"

"He's a suspect. We have evidence to back suspicions. We have no proof."

"Just give me a simple yes or no. Do we know for certain that Jeff killed the President?"

"We do not."

"Correct. When you finish using my team and I get them back, I will retask Josie. She will learn what happened. Then we can do whatever is appropriate."

"The Nation needs to survive."

"It does. We also need to find the truth. We need to punish those who did it. We know China was involved. We need to know the assassin. Who, why, and how? To a moral certainty and beyond a reasonable doubt."

"Not if it blows our cover. Not if it tears America apart."

"You clearly see the downside of Jeff blowing our cover. I agree with you. But you are missing a major downside risk if we terminate him without justification."

"Tell me what."

"I know my teams. I know my people. If Josie's made a mistake that caused us to murder an innocent patriot, we'll lose her. She's honorable, peaceful, and fragile. A mistake like that would cause a meltdown. Josie is irreplaceable. We've almost lost her before to mental trauma. She's still alive because of the bond she and Raven have and the care we use targeting her viewings. We cannot afford to lose her."

MGP was silent for a long moment. "If Josie goes down, the other dominos will fall. We'd eventually lose Raven and your whole team."

"Yes, I think so. There's more. If it blew apart while you are still running Gerry and her no-name source, we'd probably lose them too."

MGP was silent for a time, thinking. "There is another downside risk. One you didn't mention."

"Which is?"

"If the killer is someone else, someone we have missed, then there is a ticking time bomb that could totally shut down America. Whoever runs that asset, domestic or foreign, can pull the pin anytime they choose. That could rip us apart, especially if timed to hit at the worst possible time."

"Like during an election, or when China invades Taiwan?"

MGP said, "Those are possibilities, yes. There are others."

"It's your call. I think we should do our best to discover the truth. That could put us back in control of events."

"God protects fools and Americans?"

Goldfarb said, "It's more about doing the right thing."

"If we knew what that was."

"Yes."

MGP was silent for a time. "You raise some good points. This one is on you, Doctor. Will you take full responsibility for Jeff?"

Goldfarb said, "Yes."

"Full responsibility, Ari. You will keep him from outside contact until this matter is resolved?"

"I will."

"What happens if we discover he's guilty? That action will fall on you if you choose to protect him."

Goldfarb nodded. "I expected that."

"You will manage that as is needed?"

"Yes."

"How will you handle it, Ari?"

"If he is guilty, terminally. With extreme prejudice."

MGP said, "That might be required. Is there anything that you need from me to proceed?"

"Some hard INTEL when it becomes available would be useful."

"Specifically?"

"Whatever leverage Jeff may be under from the Taliban ends when we have proof that his wife and family are dead. Which they most likely are."

"Not just end, it would reverse. He'd take down those responsible."

"I agree. If we can get Jeff proof of his family's status, it would be helpful."

"I'll do what I can, but you must absolutely keep him contained until this matter is resolved."

"I will. Just let me know when I can have Josie back, General. We need a few days of clear remote viewings so we can find the murderer and wrap that up."

"Understood. I agree," MGP said. "Then we move on. I'm concerned about that little gun and graphene. Most of our population was exposed to the experimental mRNA vaccines. You could militarize that gun and make it into a battlefield weapon."

"Or put the technology into 5G wireless like China is doing for population control?"

"Yes. Forced vaccinations, face recognition software, cellphone tracking, social scores, and slavery. I hate this new form of war, Ari. The battlefield is total. From our minds, our news, our health care, and beyond. Our industrial leaders and high officials are taking money from

China. From our worst enemy. Some work directly for China. Our founding fathers would have had them hanging from lampposts."

Goldfarb said, "I'd suggest from the scaffold. America went from 'Two weeks to flatten the curve' to 'Repeal the Nuremberg Accords' in under a year, and with little pushback from the media, Congress, or the courts. We forced experimental medication on our own people. Restricting travel. Killing our senior citizens. Treating those who dared refuse like Hitler treated the Jews."

MGP said, "Worse, with intrusive technology that allowed a total surveillance society. This too shall pass. It must."

"We need to get serious about these threats."

"We do. Deep black. Off the books. You have just named the Raven team's next mission."

The two old men fell silent. They went back to watching the fire as the shadows lengthened.

To Be Continued

INTERLUDE

In this book, we've mixed terrifying reality and truthful fiction. We've discussed **Mind War**, and how twisted the public's view of reality can become. Science and technology can create Gods or Demons, Heaven or Hell. Sadly, given the human condition, the latter is far more common in history.

The United States has been a rare historic exception. A bastion of freedom. The shining city on the hill. Our founders' unique concept was to vest power in "We the People," protecting our God-given rights with a unique Constitution that ensured personal freedom by limiting the powers of government.

> *"It's getting to the point where I can barely hold conversations with normies anymore because they've been so gaslit by the talking heads on TV that literally all they can talk about is corona or the vax."*
> Andrew Torba, CEO of Gab, December 5, 2021

"The Coup has happened with the stolen 2020 American National election. In collaboration with a cabal of foreign powers and key individuals. Elected officials and elites are paid off, even employed by China.

"Herein is the real "Great Reset." The swift paradigm shift of power has happened, as per plan. Free Elections in America's future? You can sort this all out if you put the blocks together in a historical evolution. These are the actions of Bolsheviks in 1917 all over again.

"Reichstag fire in NAZI Germany. Censorship is the signal. We are under the Rule of the Iron Fist! Make no mistake about it. More subterfuge will follow. The media is the messenger of this evil. Freedom? Their further plans of "Change" are drastic.

"See Obama's visions and his message; they must be reviewed. As American citizens, we will be enduring the unendurable, as never before in our history. The edicts eradicating our freedoms will intensify. The never-ending preparations to retain their power are seen in WA, DC. Clearly the signal is shown. Constructing a Fortress City. They are ready to play hardball. With no intent to give up the power without a fight.

"Phony arrests, incidents like Ruby Ridge, in Idaho? The agencies are now focusing their clandestine Ops upon their fellow Americans. The restraints are now off. Expect the worst. I hope this historical template of evil does not play out and repeat itself again, as it has in history."

Private Communication

"That the Chinese government seeks to infiltrate American institutions is hardly surprising. What is new, however, are the number of American elites who are eager to help the Chinese dictatorship in its quest for global hegemony. Presidential families, Silicon Valley gurus, Wall Street high rollers, Ivy League universities, even professional athletes—all willing to sacrifice American strength and security on the altar of personal enrichment."

Red Handed, by Peter Schweizer
[A heavy read. Also see the summaries.]

Book Three – Non-Fiction
END GAME

A Dying Republic and a Fake Insurrection

America is dying. Democrats don't care. All they care about is power. It's all about power, and their way to get power is to ignore reality, erase culture, and silence opponents.

The dark side of humanity is ascendent. We are on the edge of a new Dark Age. The enemies of Western Civilization have worked to achieve this for over half a century, probably since before World War I.

The radical left trusts that when **The Great Reset** hits, they will either be ruling elites or unaccountable apparatchiks, people who are necessary and thus well treated. They are at their most dangerous now. They dare not waver in their zeal for fear that their comrades would turn on them.

As indeed they would and will. Does anyone doubt that Creepy Joe Biden is fully disposable? Does anyone believe Biden is running the country and is not a puppet?

Already, the lights of civilization are dimmed. We live in the time where the horrors predicted by writers like Orwell, Ayn Rand, and a host of Russians, from Arthur Koestler's show trials (*Darkness at Noon*) to Aleksandr Isayevich Solzhenitsyn's reeducation camps (*The Gulag Archipelago*) have become reality. This time, the new tyrants will have God-like powers, thanks to technology, indoctrination, and dumbing down of the public, to ensure their total dependence on the government.

213

America's once beautiful cities are now filthy, dangerous, and crime-ridden, run by corrupt politicians, drug cartels, and gangs. They are danger zones where Cartels and Marxist paramilitary groups like Black Lives Matter and Antifa are free to steal, loot, burn, kill, and terrorize.

"America is now less free than it was before the Revolution."

Mark Levin

The time of Biden is one of fear and conditioning. Obama planned it that way.

In an interview reflecting on his time in the White House, Obama said his ideal setup as President would be, a "third term... where I had a stand-in, a front man, or front woman, and they had an earpiece in, and I was just in my basement in my sweats, looking through the stuff, and I could, sort of, deliver the lines, and someone else was doing all the talking, and the ceremony. I'd be fine with that."

It's worked out as planned. Joe Biden is completely incapable as a president, and as a human being. If Biden were not President, he would need 24/7 in-home care. He is incapable of taking care of the necessities of his own day-to-day life, much less running a country of over 330 million, with (until Biden and Fauci) the largest economy and most powerful military.

Much of our population lives in fear, alone, locked in their homes with the things like freedom to assemble, freedom of speech, and "We the People" holding government accountable being erased, slowly becoming fading memories. Few remember the pre-9-11 days when we didn't have to submit to TSA goons to travel by air. Soon, few will remember the TV commercials featuring normal families.

Under Jimmy Carter, America turned our children and schools over to unions and federal bureaucracies. They now teach CRT and hatred of America. We are losing a whole generation of our youth. It's sad that foreign leaders, including Russia's Putin, can ridicule our harsh abuse and political dictates of masks, lockdowns, and mandates, noting **they** don't allow such things.

Putin Bans Mandatory Vaccinations in Russia: "*We Are a Free Country.*"

A national poll has found that **45 percent** of probable Democratic voters would be OK with the government "requiring citizens to temporarily live in designated facilities or locations if they refuse to get a COVID-19 vaccine."

Rasmussen Reports and the Heartland Institute registered this figure, which also found that a MAJORITY favored punishing citizens who failed to comply. "*Fifty-nine percent of Democratic voters would favor a government policy requiring that citizens remain confined to their homes at all times, except for emergencies, if they refuse to get a COVID-19 vaccine.*"

The survey also found that **48 percent of Democratic** voters "think federal and state governments should be able to fine or imprison individuals who publicly question the efficacy of the existing COVID-19 vaccines on social media, television, radio, or in online or digital publications."

Fifty-nine percent support putting you under house arrest, and 29 percent support the government taking your children away from you if you don' take the vaccine and subsequent jabs. Since the benchmark for "questioning" the efficacy of vaccines appears to now be saying anything other than what the government tells you, many people could be facing criminal charges.

The vaccines are becoming known to be, ah, problematical, even dangerous.

> *"The hedge funds have finally realized there will be no fourth shot. And that mRNA technology, erm, still has a few issues to work out. (One billion people aren't gonna love hearing that, but too late now. Mistakes were made, stuff happens, amirite?)*
> *Moderna and BioNTech are down 8–10% today, 60% since August. Oh, how I wish I could have shorted them."*
>
> Alex Berenson, Jan 18, 2022

The mix of biowarfare and Mind War has taken a heavy toll. Not just in America, but all over the world. Rugged individualistic Australia has reverted into a prison colony. China is committing genocide against eleven million Uyghurs. They let Fauci use the Wuhan Lab for COVID, killing over five million worldwide.

> *"Our country is rapidly deteriorating under the illegitimate Biden Regime, and everyone knows it. Record high inflation, record high immigration (legal and illegal), record high crime, the list goes on. Countries like China, Russia, and others love to talk about and display the strength of their nations, the might of their military, the growth of their economies and the health of their people. We don't talk about these things anymore— instead, the lunatics brag about how diverse our country is, how amazing it is that we now accept the delusion that gender is interchangeable, etc.—as our nation crumbles to the ground."* — Congressman Paul Gosar

Americans are being conditioned to expect less, to obey, or to face shaming, punishment, abuse, and even prison. This is the road to slavery. To resist is to become dehumanized. You become a deplorable, a racist, a White supremacist, a domestic terrorist, or worse.

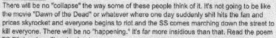

Anonymous ﹖ 05/01/13(Wed)03:32 No.13566884 Replies: >>13566934 >>13566986 >>13567018 >>13567099
File: 1367393524950.jpg-(453 KB, 2560x1440, 1335073745708.jpg)

>>13565629 #
There will be no "collapse" the way some of these people think of it. It's not going to be like the movie "Dawn of the Dead" or whatever where one day suddenly shit hits the fan and prices skyrocket and everyone begins to riot and the SS comes marching down the street to kill everyone. There will be no "happening." It's far more insidious than that. Read the poem "The Hollow Men" by TS Eliot and you'll understand.

You'll just notice that every day simple things will become a little more expensive. Everyone's homes and apartments will start to get smaller. Your work hours will get longer, but your pay will decrease. You'll see family and friends less, and find that in time you care less about them. Every day you'll find yourself lowering your standards for everything: work, food, relationships, etc. Job security will no longer exist as a concept. You'll notice houses and apartments shrinking. People will start hanging on to clothing longer and longer. Less people will get married, even less will have children. People will engross themselves in technological distractions and fantasy while never truly experiencing the real world.

Whatever dream people used to have about what their lives were going to be will become for them a distant memory. The only thing left for them will be the reality of their debt and their poverty. And every minute of every day they will be told, "You are stupid, ugly, and weak, but together we are free, prosperous, and safe."

That is the collapse. The reduction of the American man into a feudal serf, incapable of feeling love or hate, incapable of seeing the pitiful nature of his situation for what it is or recognizing his own self worth.

What we see on Fake News and Big Tech social media isn't really about America. It's about Democrat aspirations, messages, and schemes. It's about **The Great Reset** and the end of independent nation states, especially the end of America as a republic, and of our freedoms.

The Democrats have huge problems to overcome. For one, the Biden presidency is an epic failure. Depending on which polls you trust, Biden's approval ratings range from the mid-twenty percentile to about the low thirties, and they are still falling. Fake News has been shedding viewers at about the same rate. This spells disaster for Democrats in the 2022 elections if they are held and are honest.

The lockdowns and China virus, COVID, along with massive election fraud in 2020, are becoming common knowledge. Here is 12/23/2021 survey data from Rasmussen of national voters:

- Fifty-eight percent say cheating was likely in the 2020 election. (Just up from 54 percent.)

- Fifty-five percent agree that opponents of Photo ID just want to make it easy to cheat.

- Fifty-seven percent support 2020 election audits.

- Sixty-three percent say the swing states must have election reform.

- Sixty-nine percent say that private "Zuckerbucks" partisan election funding is a terrible thing.

- Seventy percent say wider use of mail-in voting will lead to more cheating.

- Seventy-four percent say preventing cheating is more important than making it easier to vote.

- Seventy-six percent say requiring photo ID to vote is reasonable to protect election integrity.

- Ninety percent say it is important to prevent election cheating.

"How likely is it that cheating affected the outcome of the 2020 presidential election?"

– LIKELY CHEATING IN 2020 -
DEM: Now 41 percent
IND: Now 58 percent
GOP: Now 79 percent
All Voters: 59 percent

https://www.rasmussenreports.com/public_content/politics/

So, if you look at that dismal data, which gets **worse** the longer Biden stays in office, does anyone think that the Democrats and the Globalists might become reasonable and change course?

Not a chance! Democrats double down, and this is their last chance to gain total power. Power for all time! Power to implement **The Great Reset**, erase American culture, and impose worldwide Marxism.

Are Democrats insane? Not more so than those who were running Hitler's Germany or Stalin's USSR. Their Holy Grail, total control, is finally within reach. It's now or never for them.

What gives them hope? Preventing the next election. Washington DC now resembles East Berlin.

Democrat Majority Whip James Clyburn suggested that the 2022 midterm elections might not be legitimate if the Democrats' "voting rights" bill isn't passed, a talking point that also came from President Joe Biden. Crazy talk, but it is coming from the top. That makes it proposed policy.

Democrats seek to disqualify political opponents from holding elected office because they have participated in an insurrection.

"Ninety-three percent of Democrats believe that Republicans participated in an insurrection at the Capitol on January 6, 2021."

Quinnipiac Poll reported this in *Wall Street Journal* 12/31/2021. A Pew poll says 95 percent of Democrats want the "rioters" prosecuted.

This scheme is based on the 14th Amendment—a law never applied, a relic of the Civil War. There was no insurrection. Only one person died from violence on January 6. Ashli Babbitt, an unarmed, peaceful protestor, was murdered, shot without warning by Michael Byrd, one of Nancy Pelosi's Capitol police.

Video shows her desperate pleas to prevent rioters from breaking windows: "Stop! No! Don't! Wait!"

Ashli Babbitt, who was fatally shot by a police officer at the US Capitol on Jan. 6, 2021, desperately tried to prevent rioters from vandalizing the doors leading to the Speaker's Lobby at the Capitol that day, even stepping between one troublemaker and officers guarding the doors, a video footage analysis shows.

*Frame-by-frame video evidence analyzed by **The Epoch Times** paints a vastly different picture of Babbitt's actions than that portrayed in media accounts over the past year. News media regularly painted Babbitt as "violent," a "rioter," or an "insurrectionist" who was angrily trying to breach the Speaker's Lobby.*

Video clips appear to show she tried to prevent the attack, not join it.

https://teaparty.org/proof-ashli-babbitt-tried-to-stop-attack-on-capitol-speakers-lobby-472973/

Democrats plan to use the 14th Amendment to keep Trump or other members of Congress from ever holding office again. Missouri Democratic Rep. Cori Bush and forty-seven co-sponsors introduced a resolution directing the House Ethics Committee to investigate whether any members of Congress violated the Constitution by seeking to overturn the 2020 presidential election, citing the 14th Amendment. Another bill from Democratic Tennessee Rep. Steve Cohen aims to enforce the 14th Amendment provision by allowing the Attorney General to argue before a three-judge panel that an officeholder or former officeholder engaged in insurrection or rebellion, *just as if they had been Confederate combatants during the Civil War*. (The actual Confederates were all pardoned in 1868.)

This notion is preposterous, but so were the "Russian Hoax" impeachments of President Trump, which played on in the media for years. Hence the rhetoric that Jan 6 was worse than 9-11, Pearl Harbor, and so forth. This is ridiculous, but intentional. It is Mind War.

Hundreds of innocent Americans associated with January 6 have been held in American Gulags, in solitary confinement, and without being charged. Now, with disastrous elections on the horizon, Democrats will start the show trials. Stewart Rhodes, a leader of the right-wing Oath Keepers militia group, and ten other members were the first people to be charged with seditious conspiracy—a **full year after the January 6, 2021, political protests**.

What's happening here? Tucker Carlson said this is something new, something dangerous to freedom. These eleven Americans are all patriots, all were alarmed about the massive "2020 Biden riots" and city burnings, all were ready to use their First and Second Amendment rights to defend our country. None of these eleven were violent, none were inside the Capitol, and none are charged with doing any damage.

Seditious Conspiracy is a **thought crime**, one that is committed when two or more persons conspire to forcibly: a) destroy or overthrow the US government; b) create obstacles or prevent the execution of US laws; c) oppose the authority of the US government; or d) unlawfully possess or take property that belongs to the nation. The First Amendment of the US Constitution protects people who have differing ideas from the rest of the population.

But these rights are not available to persons who make threats. The US Supreme Court has made it clear that free speech extends to protests, the exchange of ideas, and points in debate, but it does not include direct threats to a person's safety.

We are about to see another political witch hunt, another show trial. These seditious conspiracy charges mark a sad day for America, and a last desperate hope for the radical left. This is the President Trump persecution targeted against normal Americans, and the Kyle Rittenhouse trial writ large.

"Fake Sedition" is the last, best hope of Democrats to hold power. Success against Jan 6 defendants may be used to prevent political opponents from running for office. 2022 is a crucial year.

Today we are living in a total surveillance society. Anything you say can be monitored and used against you. In the Biden era, the full force of the federal government is being used against normal Americans who are political opponents and who rightfully fear for their safety in the time of Antifa, Black Lives Matter, and other leftist paramilitary groups. To say nothing of the soaring crime and murder rates.

We saw President Trump subjected to repeated impeachments based on false allegations of Russian collusion. We've seen the rise of widespread Anarcho-Tyranny. We've also seen treason by Democrats.

Michael Byrd committed murder, but he has never been questioned or charged. "Who is Ray Epps?" He was prominent at advocating violence on January 6, and even in custody briefly, but has now vanished.

Democrat officials are protecting him. **That's a red flag.** Watch and wait. January 6 was a setup.

There was no insurrection. It was entrapment, a false flag. Epps was a Fed. Byrd is a killer. Pelosi is evil. *"White supremacist terrorism is the deadliest threat to the United States,"* Biden said. He lied.

Plan B: Destroy America before the election

That is the plan. Every move made by the Biden administration is destructive. Lockdowns, open borders, releasing violent criminals, mask mandates, rampant inflation, dehumanizing political opponents, censorship, and more. It goes on endlessly. This is purposeful, and it is pure evil.

Why are our cities full of drugged out, often violent, homeless people??? **BECAUSE OUR GOVERNMENT IS LAVISHLY FUNDING IT.** A high-end East Coast law firm, several years ago, got the Supreme Court to rule (based on a tiny case) that homelessness was not a crime. Hence, many billions in federal dollars (more than for education and aid to small businesses combined) now goes to fund... homelessness. The goal is to normalize homelessness and drug use, right down to free drugs and crack pipes. (Biden said his free crack pipes were offered to "stop racial injustice." After ridicule, he dropped that plan.)

They are spending something like $300,000 per homeless person per year in federal money to "stop homelessness." They are **not** stopping it. They are subsidizing it, destroying cities and suburbs, crushing the middle class. On top of that, big firms and Big Tech can dump (donate) things our unemployed no longer can afford, and banks and builders can prosper from subsidized housing.

We are directly funding the destruction of our society. You can't make this stuff up. The future of America now features Calcutta-like slums, dotted with drug houses and Amazon warehouses.

https://www.youtube.com/watch?v=DREmnsungVM

There may be worse to come. Much worse. How about sending Americans to fight a purposeless, endless war against Russia in Ukraine? The issue is having Ukraine join NATO, but NATO doesn't even **want** the corrupt Ukraine to join, and it certainly doesn't want to fight a war there. Certainly, not a war against Russia that could go nuclear. This is MIND WAR. A dangerous diversion.

So, who is for this insanity, other than Joe Biden? It turns out most everyone in Washington, the Neo-Cons, the Democrats, some Republicans, and, of course, China. This is madness.

For that matter, why do we even have NATO? Its mission was to defend Europe against the old USSR that no longer exists. Its new mission might be as a military force for the EU and NWO. Why fund that?

If America suffers a total economic collapse, the best case is the greatest depression we've ever seen. The worst might be to for the United States to become a colony of China, a gigantic Hong Kong.

What is the End Game?

What will happen in Election 2022 is now exposed if you look and think critically. It is ugly. Everything possible will be done to crush freedom all over the world. America is the top target. The End Game is outlined in **UN Agenda 21** and **Agenda 2030**. Is that the world you want to live in? If so, God help us, and you are reading the wrong book. **Our End Game is to prevent their global tyranny.**

WHAT MUST WE DO TO DEFEAT EVIL? You have begun by reading the *Reality Prism*. Please consider loaning or giving a copy of this book to a friend. Thank you.

NEW WORLD ORDER
UN Agenda 21/2030 Mission Goals

One World Government
One World cashless Currency
One World Central Bank
One World Military
The end of national sovereignty
The end of ALL privately owned property
The end of the family unit
Depopulation, control of population growth and population density
Mandatory multiple vaccines
Universal basic income (austerity)
Microchipped society for purchasing, travel, tracking and controlling
Implementation of a world Social Credit System (like China has)
Trillions of appliances hooked into the 5G monitoring system (Internet of Things)
Government raised children
Government owned and controlled schools, Colleges, Universities
The end of private transportation, owning cars, etc.
All businesses owned by government/corporations
The restriction of nonessential air travel
Human beings concentrated into human settlement zones, cities
The end of irrigation
The end of private farms and grazing livestock
The end of single family homes
Restricted land use that serves human needs
The ban of natural non synthetic drugs and naturopathic medicine
The end of fossil fuels

SOCIAL PANIC

While researching and writing this book, this issue came up often. Hugely destructive, but historically rare (e.g., The Great Depression, The Cold War) modern technology and science, coupled with unaccountable global elites, 24/7 Fake News, and the internet, now allows **social panic** to be produced, delivered (as Orwell warned), and sustained indefinitely for political purposes, creating a false reality. This will not end well.

Panic causes the end of judgment, due process, and rational thought. "Fear is the Mind Killer."

There have been three social panics in the past few years. These are the new normal: **George Floyd** (race war), **COVID** (a bioweapon), and **Ukraine** (erasing sovereign nation states).

The first, inspired by a video of a violent thug with a long rap sheet dying on camera from a massive drug overdose while being held down by police, was used to destroy our cities and suburbs. The self-evident "Black Lives Matter" slogan was used to overturn "Law and Order," "Equal Justice," and "All Lives Matter." It harmed Blacks, but advanced Marxism and crime.

The **COVID Panic** (boosted by efforts like "Zuckerbucks," "Vote-by-Mail," "Big Tech Censorship," "Dominion Voting Machines," and "Lockdowns") allowed a stolen election, closed schools, and suspended constitutional rights. Soccer moms and other critics are now deemed "terrorists."

Ukraine is a bastion of corruption for Globalists, Big Tech, Neo-Cons, Democrats, sex, human, and weapons trafficking (e.g., The Biden laptops, bioweapons, and money laundering). These "limited wars" are reverse Darwinism, killing or crippling our patriots, weakening America, and benefiting our enemies (e.g., China, Iran). The UN has never prevented or stopped any of them.

Such wars kill innocents, enrich elites, and advance "The Great Reset." Before Putin, it was Saddam. Our enemies seek a possible nuclear war between us and Russia. America's border is to remain wide open, but Ukraine's protected.

The common **question:** "Up to what extent is the truth being manipulated today?"

Our answer: "Extensively, globally, and by both Mind War and the suppression of free speech. We now have an Orwellian Ministry of truth. Censorship is extreme. Violence from the Left is now officially green lighted."

THE AUTHORS

Paul info: https://www.standupamericaus.org/
e-mail: suaus1961@gmail.com

John info: https://www.johntrudel.com

APPENDIX ONE
The World Economic Forum 2022

The American contingent will include twenty-five politicians and Biden Administration officials.

US Secretary of Commerce Gina Raimondo will join Climate Czar John Kerry as the Biden White House representatives who are there.

They will be joined by twelve Democrat and ten Republican politicians, including seven senators and two state governors.

- Gina Raimondo Secretary of Commerce of USA

- John F. Kerry Special Presidential Envoy for Climate of the United States of America

- Bill Keating Congressman from Massachusetts (D)

- Daniel Meuser Congressman from Pennsylvania (R)

- Madeleine Dean Congresswoman from Pennsylvania (D)

- Ted Lieu Congressman from California (D)

- Ann Wagner Congresswoman from Missouri (R)

- Christopher A. Coons Senator from Delaware (D)

- Darrell Issa Congressman from California (R)

- Dean Phillips Congressman from Minnesota (D)

- Debra Fischer Senator from Nebraska (R)

- Eric Holcomb Governor of Indiana (R)

- Gregory W. Meeks Congressman from New York (D)

- John W. Hickenlooper Senator from Colorado (D)

- Larry Hogan Governor of Maryland (R)

- Michael McCaul Congressman from Texas (R)

- Pat Toomey Senator from Pennsylvania (R)

- Patrick J. Leahy Senator from Vermont (D)

- Robert Menendez Senator from New Jersey (D)

- Roger F. Wicker Senator from Mississippi (R)

- Seth Moulton Congressman from Massachusetts (D)

- Sheldon Whitehouse Senator from Rhode Island (D)

- Ted Deutch Congressman from Florida (D)

- Francis Suarez Mayor of Miami (R)

- Al Gore Vice-President of the United States (1993-2001) (D)

OFFICIAL LIST OF WEF 2022 ATTENDEES

https://www3.weforum.org/docs/WEF_AM22_List_of_confirmed_PFs.pdf

The World Economic Forum's 2022 annual meeting in Davos happened. At 2,000-odd participants, there were fewer people at Davos this year than in 2020, which saw about 3,000. But there are still plenty of big shots and famous faces.

Let's take a brief look at the attendees, according to the official list, which was last updated May 18.

⬤ Global audience | Attendees include US 583 participants from the US, CH 220 from Switzerland, GB 211 from the UK, and IN 109 from India.

💼 CEOs reign | There are 612 chief executive officers in attendance, and only 22 CFOs. The top bosses include:

- Adar Poonawalla, CEO of Serum Institute of India
- Adena Friedman, CEO of Nasdaq
- Marc Benioff, CEO of Salesforce

🏦 Finance folks | Despite the small contingent of CFOs, the finance world will not be underrepresented. At least seventy-five participants from global banks will be around. Financial players include:

- Jane Fraser, CEO of Citi
- Catherine Bessant, vice chair for global strategy at Bank of America
- **George Soros**, chairman and founder of Soros Fund Management

💰 World's wealthiest | Bill Gates has some competition this year in the net worth department. Gautam Adani, chairman of Adani Group, is in Davos, as is Mukesh Ambani, chairman and managing director of Reliance Industries. Depending on the day, one of these men is Asia's wealthiest person.

Climate, tech, and media participants:

🐋 Climate cohort | At least 42 attendees have the word "sustainability" in their job title, including the chief sustainability officer from Unilever, Rebecca Marmot. Other climate-change experts on the attendee list include:

- Nigel Topping, UN climate change high-level champion for COP26

- The New York Times' international correspondent for climate change, Somini Sengupta

💻 Tech turnout | Six representatives from Google, five from Microsoft and IBM, four from Meta, and not even one from Apple or Amazon. Other techies include:

- Michelle Zatlyn, president and COO of Cloudflare

- Jimmy Wales, founder of Wikipedia

- Satya Nadella, CEO of Microsoft

📝 Mix of media | Reporters, editors, and representatives from the world's major publications will also be in attendance. **There are more people from CNN on the roster than participants from Microsoft.** Also:

- Sally Buzbee, executive editor The Washington Post

- Martin Wolf from the Financial Times, Andrew Ross Sorkin from the New York Times, and Ina Fried from Axios

- Quartz's very own Katherine Bell

Political and Culture figures in Davos:

Political players | The former prime minister of Denmark, Helle Thorning-Schmidt, will make an appearance. Other political operators on the list include:

- Henry Kissinger, chairman of Kissinger Associates and former US secretary of state

- Nick Clegg, former deputy prime minister of the UK, now at Meta

- Former White House director of communications Anthony Scaramucci, who also is the founder of SkyBridge Capital

Some critics of Globalism suffered "mishaps." It is unclear if they were allowed to attend fully, or restricted. American conservative journalist Jack Posobiec and his film crew were detained in Switzerland while he was covering the summit of globalist elites in the ski resort town of Davos, with commenters noting the Swiss local police wearing "World Economic Forum Police" patches on their uniforms.

Whatever happened, Posobiec was released. The most significant news from Davos was what did **NOT** happen. The Biden Initiative to surrender U.S. Sovereignty to the W.H.O. at Davos **failed**. This collapse came from Geneva, not Davos.

Post Trump, the U.S., sadly, is on the wrong side.

"WHO withdraws 12 Biden 'sovereignty' amendments amid fierce opposition."

https://www.wnd.com/2022/05/withdraws-12-biden-sovereignty-amendments-amid-fierce-opposition/?utm_source=Gab&utm_medium=PostTopSharingButtons&utm_campaign=websitesharingbuttons

WHO Forced into Humiliating Backdown

"The World Health Assembly has spent the past 7 days considering Biden's 13 controversial amendments to the International Health Regulations.

"Official delegates from wealthy developed nations like Australia, the UK, and the US spoke in strong support of the amendments and urged other states to join them in signing away their countries' sovereignty.

"The first sign that things might not be going the globalists' way, came on Wednesday, the 25th of May, which just happened to also be Africa Day. Botswana read a statement on behalf of its 47 AFRO members, saying they would be collectively withholding their support for the "reforms," which many African members were concerned about.

"Multiple other countries also said they had reservations over the changes and would not be supporting them. These included Brazil, Russia, India, China, South Africa, Iran, and Malaysia. Brazil said it would exit WHO altogether, rather than allow its population to be made subject to the new amendments. In the end, the WHO and its wealthy nation supporters were forced to back down. They have not given up though— far from it."

An Orwellian moment was this speech from an Australian Bureaucrat:

Julie Inman Grant, the Australian eSafety Commissioner, said at the WEF that key human rights, such as free speech, must be subject to "recalibration."

"We are finding ourselves in a place where we have increasing polarization everywhere, and everything feels binary when it doesn't need to be," Inman Grant told the panel, saying that people would need to think about a *"recalibration of a whole range of human rights that are playing out online."*

Free Speech and Open Information must no longer be permitted anywhere. Too bad for America and our Constitution. It seems Australia is reverting into being a penal colony. The woman sounds like a female Zuckerberg.

The most terrifying announcements concerned deploying new Chinese technology worldwide to allow population control via "**social scores.**" China already has such systems.

With widespread cameras, 5G Internet connections, and facial recognition software, the new reality is "prisons without walls." You can be locked down in your domicile with only paper tape. Break the seal, and you can be punished. When you purchase goods, including food and fuel, what you are allowed to buy and how much you pay can be set by your social score.

World Economic Forum Pushes Facial Recognition Technology

An unelected cabal of PSYCHOPATHS.

The dangers posed by digital IDs cannot be emphasized enough. As the researcher Brett Solomon—a man "who has tracked the advantages and perils of technology for human rights" for well over a decade—previously noted, the mass rollout of digital IDs "poses one of the gravest risks to human rights of any technology that we have encountered."

"Shanghai went from being the largest, most free, most prosperous city in China to the world's largest internment camp in 24 hours by a total medical lock-down. Team Biden is signing a treaty this weekend (It failed at Davos) to allow that in America and worldwide."

There is silence about such things from Fake News and Congress. Those in power do not want voters to know about the Davos setback, The Great Reset, or the movie *2000 Mules* and the stolen 2020 election.

Beware the Devils of Devos!

foxnews.com/opinion/tucker-biden-who-power-health-policy

https://rumble.com/vs3yts-whatsherface-the-great-reset-thegreatreshit.html

9 780997 805208